What readers say about Harlequin Romances

"I can't imagine my reading life without Harlequin."

J.L.,* Sioux Falls, South Dakota

"I just read my first three Harlequins. It is Sunday today, otherwise I would go back to the bookstore to get some more."

E.S., Kingston, Ontario

"I'm really hooked and I love it."

M.S., Richmond, Virginia

"Harlequins help me to escape from housework into a world of romance, adventure and travel."

J.R., Glastonbury, Connecticut

*Names available on request

OTHER
Harlequin Romances
by WYNNE MAY

Tamboti Moon

by

WYNNE MAY

Harlequin Books

TORONTO • LONDON • NEW YORK • AMSTERDAM
SYDNEY • HAMBURG • PARIS

Original hardcover edition published in 1969
by Mills & Boon Limited

ISBN 0-373-01343-4

Harlequin edition published October 1969

Second printing January 1970
Third printing June 1975
Fourth printing September 1977
Fifth printing March 1979

Printed in U.S.A.

CHAPTER ONE

THE smell of bikinis and towels, drying in the sun, formed the background to Julia Munro's lazy thoughts and she was conscious of a curiously relaxed feeling at the back of her exhaustion.

It was a relief, after all the tension, to feel things begin to ease up inside her.

Twenty years old, slim, glamorous, in a golden kind of way, Julia was the daughter of a Natal Game Park Superintendent and this was her last day at the Azalea Park Finishing School for Young Ladies.

Until today, life had been a hectic whirl of winding-up parties, when the girls had been at the mercy of newspaper reporters, prominent visitors and parents. Now, most of the girls had already left, although one or two, like herself, were waiting to be collected and taken home.

Home now, to Julia, was going to be a thatched-roof bungalow in the Umkambo Game Reserve, with her father, and every time she thought about it, it was with a tinge of excitement. This was due to the fact that, from the time she was seven years old, home had been an exclusive boarding-school, University and then, finally, the Azalea Park Finishing School. However, for the next year, until Stan Munro, her father, retired from his work at the Reserve she was to live in a bungalow, which she had never seen.

With a sigh, she stirred herself and opened her eyes which were green and long and wide apart, slitting them a little against the angled rays of the morning sun.

Vivid tangerine-and-blue cushions, on the poolside furniture, matched the sun umbrellas, which had dazzling white fringing around them, and the colours seemed to tremble in the gathering heat of the day.

A colonnaded loggia surrounded the blue-tiled swimming-pool, which was of an exciting size and shape and which mirrored the sky so that the water appeared a deep, sparkling turquoise.

Dragging her eyes away from the pool, Julia murmured, 'What's the time, Samantha?' and, in the lounging-chair beside her, Samantha yawned. 'Darling,' she drawled, in an accent which the Finishing School had improved although there had been absolutely no reason to do so in the very first place, 'my watch is over there – on top of my raffia bag, near your feet. What time is your father coming for you, you poor thing?' She did not open her eyes.

As she reached for the watch Julia said, 'He should be here by ten o'clock. That's my reason for wanting to check up on the time. It must be getting on that way now.' Her voice, low and exciting, matched Samantha's, so far as accent was concerned. 'Samantha, your watch is absolutely *baking*, did you know that? Why didn't you put it *inside* your bag, to protect it from the sun?'

'Darling, why worry? There are plenty more watches where that one came from.' Samantha allowed the small cups of her bikini bra to slip down just that little bit farther. She meant what she said. Her father was a mining magnate.

Julia looked at the tiny strips of pale skin that had suddenly been exposed to the sun. 'You'll burn,' she said. 'Surely you don't have to tan that far.'

'When I get home I'll tan in the nude,' Samantha answered smothering another yawn. 'That's how far I'll tan. On one of the roof gardens. I'll have to do something to keep me from going crazy. Do you realize how bored I'm going to be, Julia?'

'And do you realize the *time*?' In one swift movement Julia had put Samantha's jewel-studded watch inside the raffia bag and stood up. 'I'll have to positively fly to get dressed. I haven't had a shower and I still have to finish packing.'

'What are you planning to wear – to your Game Reserve?' Samantha still made no attempt to open her eyes which were almost black. 'Darling, you'll have to be prepared, won't you? Just in case, you know. . .'

'Just in case – what?' Julia stood, with her bright scarlet towel draped over one slender tanned arm, looking down at Samantha.

'Darling, just in case there happens to be a couple of good-looking Rangers around the place. In a way, I almost envy you – another whole year of loafing around in the sun – for that is what it will amount to – only this time you won't be surrounded by a lot of females you'll be surrounded by dashing young men in exciting khaki uniforms and slouch hats and things. Think of me, in the very thick of society, with Mother doing her level best to marry me off to the most eligible bachelor in Johannesburg – no matter how old he happens to be. Do you know, I think she'd die if I made a bad marriage? Sometimes I think I'll marry the first poor man who happens to come my way – just to spite her.' The thick black lashes fluttered and then Samantha opened her eyes and stared into space.

'In a way,' Julia said, still looking down at the beautiful, darkly-tanned girl, 'you don't know what it's been like for *me*. I've never known a home – at least not for years – not since I was seven, actually. To give me some kind of home my father has spent a fortune on my education – a terribly expensive boarding-school, University and then on here. I should have found a job ages and ages ago but,' she shrugged, 'well, you know how it is. I'm all he's got – although he didn't want me around. I suppose he felt that, by having me so well educated, he was tying me up and that he was protecting me.'

'Protecting you – against what?' Samantha leaned over the side of her lounging chair and lazily scratched one tanned calf with long, pearl-tinted finger nails.

'Oh . . .' Julia thought for a moment, and then grinned, 'against the odds, I suppose.'

'Anyway,' Samantha stopped scratching and settled back comfortably, 'why didn't he want to have you around? He sounds just about as selfish as my mother.'

'No, he's not selfish. Honestly, it seems fantastic to say it – you'd never believe that men could go on and on like that,' Julia replied, 'but it was because I reminded him of my mother, I believe, and he didn't want to be reminded about her.' She sighed. 'Maybe he's got over it now – I don't know. Anyway, he wants me now.'

'I still think that it's an act of selfishness, on his part. He wants you to look after him in his old age. Why don't you face up to facts? You should have refused.'

'He's not that old, Samantha.' Julia bit her lip and gazed into sun-drenched space. 'Actually, my cousin Gillian is married to a man who is about my father's age and Gillian is only in her twenties. By marrying him, she landed herself with a stepdaughter, about my own age. A girl named

7

Kathy Feldwood – but you met Kathy, didn't you? That time in Pietermaritzburg when Leon took us there.'

'Oh, Kathy Feldwood.' Samantha made a face. 'She was a cat. I thought she was awful. About how old is your father?'

'About fifty-ish, I suppose. Handsome too. Mind you, I haven't seen him for a whole year. He might have aged, but I don't think so. He's not the type to sag.'

'He must have had to stint and save to send you to Floria's Azalea Park. Being a Game Park Superintendent, he can't be all *that* well off and Floria Lanfield is making sure that she gets her pound of flesh, I'll bet, otherwise my dear mother wouldn't have sent *me* here.'

'But I told you, Samantha . . . my father is really quite well-off, you know. He had the sugar estate and after he sold it the money found its way into the bank and he left for the wide open spaces. The only thing he ever spends money on is me. Poor Dad . . . anyway, my pet, I'm off. I can't stand here talking another minute. In case I don't get time to say this again – you will write, won't you?'

'I'll try,' Samantha languidly waved a limp hand. 'But you know me.'

'Oh, darling,' Julia replied, half in anger and half in jest, 'you're priceless, really you are!

'Thats what my mother thinks. She's set a big price for my head. I only hope she gets it." Samantha rolled over on to her stomach and it was obvious that she was going to sleep that way.

The paving stones round the edge of the swimming-pool felt hot against Julia's bare feet as she ran towards the velvet-smooth lawn which stretched between the pool and the girls' quarters. It came as almost a shock to her to find the large lounge, with its white terrazzo floor acting as a perfect foil to the vivid rugs which were scattered upon it, deserted and, for a moment, she stood still as she allowed the knowledge that the School had broken up to wash over her.

A lot of the time it had been fun, she thought, as her thoughts roved back to the time when she had arrived at Azalea Park. There had been all the excitement of re-decorating the living-rooms and bedrooms. This was undertaken, year after year, as new students arrived and they were taught how to shop for inexpensive fabrics and how to turn them into expensive-looking slip-covers and curtains. This had come under 'Decorating on a Shoestring' just in case, Julia supposed, some of the girls did not make the grade and married poor men!

Where there was no glass, for the room was practically all glass, plain wooden walls and ceiling were set off by bright divan-cushions and vivid rugs. Sparse furnishings added to the feeling of spaciousness while all that glass about the place scooped up views of the garden and swimming-pool with its colonnaded loggia and colourful pool-side furniture. The pictures on the walls, framed in white, had been painted by the girls and were sited to cause an element of instant surprise.

Julia paused a moment to look at Samantha who was still sprawled on her stomach – elegantly, if carelessly – amongst the cushions on her lounging-chair in the sun, her limbs and back like old timber, so tanned were they by hours spent in the sun.

Most of the bedrooms had a forlorn, impersonal appearance about them due to the fact that their previous owners had left the School. One or two, however, with doors open, looked as though they had been washed in by the tide, so littered were they with the semi-packed cases and scattered garments.

Julia's own room was decorated in pale yellow and white. She stripped quickly and ran into the bathroom, which she shared with Samantha, grabbing her plastic hair cap on the way. Stepping beneath the shower, she turned on the taps before she had even donned the cap and then, with her face turned towards the water which splintered down, she began to lather herself with an outsize tablet of bath soap. Her body was still warm from the sun and she caught her breath as the water needled it. Like Samantha, she was gloriously tanned, except for the tiny marks where her bikini had protected her.

With the sound of splintering water all about her she wondered again and again what life was going to offer at the Umkambo Game Reserve. The last time she had visited her father had been when he was Superintendent at a Reserve further north – the Renoster Reserve.

Samantha's rich voice startled her from her thoughts as

9

it never failed to startle her. She was so small, this dark Samantha, and yet she had a voice on her like a busty soul singer. 'Leon's here to see you,' she called out. 'He's over at the Residence having tea with Floria and I told him you wouldn't be long – so don't let me down, will you, darling?'

The pupils of the Azalea Park Finishing School always referred to the stately home belonging to the Principal, Floria Lanfield, and her husband Mark, as the Residence. When they were speaking amongst themselves they always referred to Mrs. Lanfield as simply – Floria.

'What has *he* turned up again for?' Julia called back, above the water noises, before she switched off the shower faucets. She spared a hand to pull off the plastic cap which allowed her tawny hair to fall to her shoulders. 'I said goodbye to Leon last night – at the Ball. Samantha, be a darling and hand me my bath-robe before you go to your room, will you? I forgot it. It's on the bed, or on the floor, or somewhere.'

A few moments later the yellow towelling robe came unceremoniously flying through the open door of the bathroom and Julia dropped the towel she was holding to catch it before it fell on to the water-running mosaic floor. 'Thank you,' she shouted, 'I know you were just trying to be kind when you did that, Samantha darling.'

Back in her room her movements became quick as she dressed and then added more finishing touches to her packing. All at once this room, with its elaborately draped and curtained windows (her own work) looked strangely abandoned. Impatiently, Julia shrugged her shoulders. She was becoming emotional, she told herself, and it was no use becoming emotional.

As she snapped shut the locks of one of the white cases she wondered what Floria Lanfield did with all the discarded slip-covers, cushion covers, curtains, and so on, as the School was once again stripped down to allow the new pupils to start from scratch on 'How to Decorate on a Shoe-string.' Sold them, probably, to cover some of the expenses although, to judge by the Residence, the Lanfields seemed to be doing all right. Of course, there had been the other side to everything at Azalea Park – how *not* to decorate on a shoe-string by knowing how to choose a Persian carpet, how to make ceramic vases, how to recognize genuine antiques and paintings, how to arrange flowers ... in fact, Floria seemed to have covered just about everything from short-hand and typewriting to horse-riding.

Last to be scooped clear was Julia's Dolly Varden dressing-table with its creams, lotions, perfumes and the brush and comb set which her father had given her for Christmas. All these things were bundled into the soft leather case she used for this purpose and, as she turned to see if there was anything she had missed, she paused to gaze at her reflection in the mirror. There was nothing there to show the confusion she felt at having to leave what had been home to her for one year. It was still the same face with its green eyes and bronzed skin. Because of her tawny looks many of the girls had nicknamed her Tawny, but to Samantha, and Leon, she had always been Julia.

It had been through the Finishing School that the girls had met Leon Ladenza, because of his Gallery which was filled with the beautiful things about which they had to learn. Such things as handwoven rugs, in astonishingly divergent patterns and colours, camel-hide pouffes, camel stools, beaten brass trays on elaborate fretwork legs, Russian samovars, Spanish tandirs, pottery, original paintings and even rare antiques.

Julia wondered what the Game Rangers would think of having a girl in the Reserve – an unmarried girl, that was, because, of course, some of the Rangers would probably have wives. According to her father's letters, however, there were not many Rangers in the tourist section of the Reserve but, vaguely, she supposed that Rangers would come and go, all the time, as they dove in from remote outposts in their Land Rovers.

Leon Ladenza was having tea with Floria and Mark Lanfield in what was virtually a treasure house of choice antiques and, at first glance, through the heavy plate-glass doors which divided the hall from Floria's drawing-room, the immediate impression was one of green floor-length curtains, comfortable floral sofas and chairs and a tremendous white fireplace. The fireplace was flanked by white shelves which carried an assortment of books, pottery, copper, pewter and brass. Tall stinkwood Gueridons, which originally came from the Knysna forests, bore great masses of flowers from the extensive garden. It was only as you sat down that you became conscious of the fact that you were in a treasure house of antiques, thought Julia.

'Just in time for tea,' Floria said, looking up as Julia entered the room in her tangerine slack suit dressed up with chunky, honey-brown wooden beads. 'Where's Samantha? I asked her to join us. The other girls are still out, of course. They don't leave until tomorrow.'

'Samantha asked me to tell you not to wait for her.' Julia smiled her slow smile at Leon and Mark Lanfield, who had both risen.

'Well, do sit down,' Mark said.

'Thank you.' Julia sat down and, in the moments to come, did her best to contribute something towards the kind of sophisticated conversation which always took place between people like the Lanfields and Leon Ladenza who were madly interested in antiques. At one stage, while she listened to them, she found herself vaguely wondering whether Floria would ever take her antiques along with her to the moon, one day – when people started moving in on the moon.

When tea was over she felt rather thankful and then she and Leon went outside to the long, white terrazzo-tiled verandah where they sat on white wicker chairs with fuchsia-coloured cushions and where they could watch the azalea-flanked drive for Stan Munro's car.

'Darling, I'm going to miss you like the very devil,' Leon said. 'You know that, don't you?' He had a sullen, hand-some face and his eyes, behind the dark glasses which he always wore, gave nothing away.

'I'm going to miss you too,' Julia answered carefully, although this was, in fact, perfectly true. For all his mannerisms, which were always larger than life, Leon was really rather sweet – once you got to know him, and she had got to know him very well. 'Anyway,' she added, 'don't forget to come and visit us and, by the way, I might keep you to your word about that offer of a job in your Pietermaritzburg Gallery one day. My father has definitely made up his mind to retire there. After all, his sister-in-law is in Pietermaritzburg.'

'Frankly, darling, nothing would give me more pleasure,' Leon answered. 'If you only knew the trouble I have in getting suitable girls to work for me. At the moment, though, it is all right. I have started this creature Nicolette, in 'Maritzburg, and she suits me very well – but how long will it last? I'm positively rushed off my feet dashing from gallery to gallery.' Leon had three galleries. 'You know, darling,' he took her fingers and brushed them across his mouth, 'you are going to be utterly wasted in the Game Reserve. For goodness' sake, whatever you do, darling, don't let yourself get stagnant, will you? Redecorate, or something. I think it's damned unfair of your old man, to say the least of it, dragging you off to live amongst a lot of wild beasts like that. You won't go and get yourself gored by a rhino, will you?'

'He hasn't – he *isn't* actually dragging me off, Leon dear. I'm looking forward to it. No, *honestly*.' She laughed at his look of shocked disbelief. 'For one thing, I'm going to have a good rest. You'll never know how exacting this past year has been. Strict hours, slaving away as we had to learn about the craziest things – landscape gardening, building patios, paved walks and hours of sewing. There's been the pool, of course, and horse-riding, and then there was that crazy spell when Floria even had us *gliding*.' She burst out laughing. 'Darling, do you remember that? Wasn't it too priceless for words? Anyway, it was all very exhausting in a way.'

'Floria has made you girls slave like the very devil,' Leon replied. 'Don't I know it? She has just about finished some of you off. Look at poor Tregurtha Reinados. Darling, where on earth do they raise these names from?'

'I don't know, but, darling, look at Ladenza!' Julia laughed flightily and then kissed Leon on the cheek, smothering the desire to ask him to take off his glasses.

The sound of an engine interrupted their gay little scene. 'Oh, here's my father. ' Julia stood up quickly. 'In a Land Rover, for pity's sake. Well, what do you know about that? I wonder why he didn't use his car?'

'How positively ghastly for you, darling,' Leon's voice showed his horror. Julia watched, with amusement, as he ran lightly down the shallow terrazzo steps on his silent white shoes where he stood at the foot of them, melancholy and elegant, and held out his hand to her. Slipping her fingers into his, she allowed him to guide her down the rest of the steps. It was all very spectacular and it was a game with them because, apart from owning three galleries, Leon was a ballet dancer.

The Land Rover had drawn up now, just short of the steps with their curved balustrades and the white urns trailing pink and green foliage.

Julia drew a surprised breath. 'But it's not my father! It's one of the Rangers, by the looks of things.'

A sun-tanned young man was getting out of the Land Rover. He was wearing khaki gaberdine slacks and a khaki shirt with a tie. His gaberdine jacket was balanced carelessly over one shoulder.

'Good morning,' he said, coming towards Julia and Leon. 'I'm looking for one of your pupils – Julia Munro.'

'You've found her. ' Julia succeeded in looking very cool and very polished. 'I *am* Julia Munro. This is Leon Ladenza – a friend.' She felt a sudden chill of apprehension. 'Is – anything wrong?' she asked, after a slight flummoxed pause. 'Is – it something to do with my father? He's not – ill, is he?'

'There's nothing wrong with your father, Miss Munro. I happened to be making a trip to Pietermaritzburg and your father asked me to call here on my way back to Umkambo. After all, it is on my way.'

Julia's green eyes flew to the Land Rover. 'To take me back with you, you mean?'

The Game Ranger's blue eyes travelled disparagingly over her fashionable tangerine slack suit, dressed up with its chunky wooden beads, and she could feel his summing up of her like a tangible force. She could feel that he didn't like her. To cover up her nervousness she gave him a smile which he did not acknowledge. 'Yes.' His blue eyes had followed her own to the Land Rover. 'To take you back with me.'

'I see – and your name?' The relief she felt in regard to her father was carefully disguised, because she didn't want to appear childish about this thing. She gave him another smile, more uncertain this time, because she was diconcerted that his dislike was so apparent. He might have tried to disguise it, she thought.

'Grant Tyler.'

'I see,' she said again. 'Well, I'm quite ready, Mr. Tyler.

Everything is packed. Just those last-minute cases to snap shut – you know how it is, but that shouldn't take long.' She took hold of Leon's fingers and was annoyed to see Grant Tyler looking at Leon with what only could be described as vague distaste. For this reason, she said, carefully getting his name wrong, in an effort to humiliate him, 'Will you come this way – er – Mr. Grant, is it?'

He gave her a long look. 'Tyler,' he said coldly.

Julia began to lead the way towards the Residence where Grant Tyler could meet Floria and Mark Lanfield and where he could sit with them, in the drawing-room, while she attended to her things.

Beside the Game Ranger Leon looked sullen and eccentric in his black turtle-necked shirt and narrow white trousers and, judging by the look on Grant Tyler's handsome face, he had lost no time in reaching this conclusion himself.

She turned to look at Grant Tyler. 'Before we go to introduce you to Floria Lanfield, the Principal, do let me show you a little of the actual Finishing School itself – where we were put through our paces. It's quite fantastic really.'

'What's so fantastic about it?' he asked.

A small frown betrayed her annoyance. 'Well, I thought it might interest you.' She had thought to show him some of the work which had been done by the pupils themselves – the patios, for instance, and the pergolas with trailing plants, the paved walks. . .

'Most of the girls have left, of course,' she spoke lightly, in an effort to disguise her annoyance. 'At least three of the girls, still here, have gone into town and the fourth, my friend Samantha, takes tonight's Boeing to Johannesburg.' She pretended not to notice Grant Tyler's impatient glance at his wrist-watch. They were next to the exciting cobalt swimming-pool and Julia stopped walking to say, 'This is where we used to spend a lot of our time. I have to use the past tense now, which staggers me. Isn't it perfectly *tragic*?'

'Darling,' Leon replied seriously, 'it's perfectly *tragic*.'

'It goes without saying,' Julia went on and trying to get the better of Grant Tyler by not talking too quickly, now that he had shown his impatience to leave, 'that Samantha and I have only just got out of the pool. I'm going to miss this pool very, very much.'

She linked an arm casually through Leon's. 'My poor sweet,' he murmured, he stooped slightly and brushed her forehead with his lips. 'You aren't going to be able to swim where you are going, are you? What with wicked crocodiles and all that sort of thing.'

Laughing carelessly, and pushing back her hair Julia said, flippantly, 'Let's not be *too* sensitive about it, darling.' However, she was feeling slightly embarrassed with Leon about the ease with which he always said everything that was on his mind.

'Anyway, I'll show you the main part of the girls' quarters.' She began to lead the way again, towards the flagged paving in the direction of the lounges and diningroom. The only time the girls had eaten at the Residence was when there had been a banquet, or when terribly important guests were dining at Azalea Park.

Suddenly it struck her that there were an awful lot of forecourts and plants used to decorate plain walls, pergolas with trailing creepers, sun-awnings to protect glass walls and garden furniture about and she knew that, to Grant Tyler, this must look like something out of a Hollywood setting. Frowning a little, she was tempted to tell him a little of the hard work on the part of the pupils which had gone into it and that practically one pergola was erected every year because of this reason. She found herself wishing that he could have seen the girls at work, dressed in their tight faded jeans and shirts, canvas shoes and thick gloves. He seemed so bored, however, that she gave up the idea.

He seemed quite unimpressed by the main lounge with its white floor, brilliant rugs and glass-to-glass corners of the room which framed the pool and which were sheltered from the sun by yellow sun-awnings.

The three of them stood together near a wide expanse of plate-glass that served the purpose of one wall.

'Over there,' said Julia, 'is the Residence, which is our name for it and which, by the way, is virtually a treasure-house of choice antiques.' She turned to Leon, smiling carelessly. 'Leon here is an expert on antiques and things, as a matter of fact. Aren't you, darling?' She fell easily into their kind of jargon. 'Leon has given us all sorts of brilliant lectures.'

Leon bowed his sleek dark head in mock humility. 'Put like that, darling,' he answered, 'it sounds very sweet and very flattering. Thank you.' The effect was elegant and careful.

'Anyway, Mr. Tyler, I can see that you are obviously bored,' Julia's smile was frankly artificial and she intended that it should be this way, 'so let me take you over to the Residence where you can wait for me and meet Floria.'

The mask of indifference which Leon always seemed to wear lifted a moment. 'Sweetie, I can hardly bear the thought that you are going. Postpone this mad visit to live with a lot of heat-stricken animals. Stay with me, Julia.'

'I can't,' she answered, giving him an impish grin and understanding him perfectly. 'You'll get over it, darling – besides, it's only for a year. Don't look like that ... you know I can't possibly stay, darling.' She brushed his cheek with her fingers. 'Smile ...!'

'You realize, of course, that your going is going to leave me with what almost could be described as a built-in suicide desire. It will be with me day and night.' Leon took her fingers in his own and kissed them.

As he did this Julia became suddenly extraordinarily aware of the Game Ranger standing beside them and she quickly freed her fingers. 'I'll think of you every single day,' she said, 'and I'll write you masses and masses of letters. How's that?'

'Ghastly. Absolutely ghastly!' A nerve flickered in Leon's cheek.

They walked towards Floria's mansion and went up the curved white steps where one of Floria's magnificent Siamese cats washed its face in the sun, completely oblivious of a green lizard which was curled up at the base of one of the urns like a jewel. Julia made the introductions and was relieved to find that Grant Tyler could be amiable, when it suited him. This made the prospect of travelling to the Umkambo Game Reserve with him seem much less awesome. She left him talking to Floria and Mark Lanfield but making a big issue about ignoring Leon.

Samantha, small, dark and intense and wearing a coffee-coloured caftan, embroidered with gold thread, was on her way to the Residence, and Julia met her on one of the paved walks. 'I see that your dear father has arrived?' Samantha thrust an angled chin in the direction of the parked Land Rover. 'Darling, how inconsiderate of the old boy. You're going to be awfully raw in places after your trip in that thing, aren't you? Just fancy, in no time at all now you'll be listening to all the wild animals' noises.' Her lips curled in one of her bitter little smiles. 'Still, cheer up. It's only for a year, after all, and you never know your luck, darling, you might well end up by having the most thrilling affair with one of those tough Rangers.'

'No, I won't,' Julia's voice held a hint of amusement in it, 'not if they're anything like the Ranger back there with Floria and Mark. Samantha darling, do you know what my father has gone and done? He's arranged for the most uncivil individual I've ever met in my life to pick me up and take me to the Reserve. How I'm going to stand mile after mile with him in – *that thing* – I just don't know.' She broke off, immediately ashamed of herself as she asked herself what it was that the Finishing School had done to her.

'Was this intentional, on the part of your father, I mean? Or was it unavoidable? In other words,' Samantha sounded vaguely concerned, 'is your father ill?'

'No. According to this Grant Tyler type my father is not ill. This just happened to be a convenient arrangement. Apparently Game Ranger Tyler has been on a trip to Pietermaritzburg, for some reason or other, and would have had to pass this way, anyway – or within a mile or so of it – on his way back to Umkambo. Anyway, I must dash off.'

'And I must see this,' Samantha drawled. 'I wouldn't want to miss it, Julia. But tell me, do you need any help with that last-minute packing? Don't say yes, darling. I couldn't stand it.'

'No, thank you. Everything is ready – just to fling into the one case. All I have to do after that is to ring for somebody to come along to my room and carry my luggage out to the car – I mean that Land Rover thing. Tell me, Samantha, what on earth am I going to talk about on the journey? I guess Floria didn't cover the kind of conversation I'm going to need right now, did she?'

'The weather is always a safe bet,' Samantha sighed loudly, 'and then, after you've exhausted the weather, get started on *him*. Ask him about himself and about his exciting work – make it sound exciting, darling, even if it is a bore, and then, while he goes on and on – men usually do – you can just sit back and look *madly* interested. That shouldn't be too hard with your big green eyes. Sometimes, when you listen to people – I've watched this – they seem to grow wide with concentration. Fascinating, really. If I wasn't always so damned bored *I'd* try it.'

'I'll see you later,' Julia said, already on her way. She looked over her shoulder. 'Let me know what you think of our Game Ranger friend, will you?'

After she had finished with her luggage she rang for somebody to come along and take it to where the Land Rover was parked and went back to the Residence. She gave Grant Tyler a smile with her eyes beneath their carefully brushed eyebrows. 'Well,' she said, 'Mr. Tyler, I'm ready. My luggage is already on its way to your Land Rover.' She was afraid to look at Samantha. Instead she laughed flightily and said, 'I hope you're going to be able to fit it all in.'

'We can get going, then?' Grant Tyler glanced at his watch. 'Good. I couldn't be more pleased.' His voice was abrupt.

'I'm sure you couldn't. It's a long way and you won't be able to go very fast in that thing, will you? The Land Rover, I mean.' She knew that she was choosing her words badly and her green eyes flew to Floria, who was shaking her head and smiling reproachfully.

Grant Tyler gave her a sarcastic little smile. 'Won't I?' It sounded very much like a challenge and Julia could have kicked herself.

After thanking Floria for the coffee which she had ordered for him, Grant Tyler looked enquiringly at Julia and they all went back down the white steps. Floria's Siamese cat still washed itself and had its back to the lizard now. To make things really pally now that Julia was going, Floria kept an arm around Julia's waist. 'I'm going to miss my girls,' she said. 'The next lot just won't be the same. I know it.'

'She says that every year,' Leon's voice was dry.

Floria gave him a smile. 'Yes, I *know* I do, but this year will be different. I've had a marvellous crowd of girls and I've adored them and so has Mark, haven't you, Mark?'

'Indeed, yes, I have.'

'We were a lousy bunch, and you know it.' Samantha's face was a mask of indifference.

'That's certainly not true.' Floria went on smiling, but she looked betrayed by Samantha's blunt remark.

At the Land Rover they stood around awkwardly while Grant Tyler took it upon himself to stack Julia's matched white luggage. Julia found herself thinking that it was hardly Game Reserve luggage, and the look on Grant Tyler's face only served to confirm this thought.

'Well,' he turned to look at her. 'Ready?' He did not smile. Nearby, Leon's long cream car shimmered expensively in the sun.

'Yes.' Julia turned away from him and extended a hand to Floria, who drew her closer. She kissed Julia very lightly on the cheek. 'Keep in touch, Julia, will you? I always like to keep in touch with my girls. I never forget them.'

'And Floria means that,' Mark was saying. 'She really means that.'

'I will.' Suddenly Julia tasted the salt of tears that were waiting to spill over. After all, the Lanfields had been good to her – even if her father had paid them well to do it. 'You've both been so kind to me,' she murmured. 'Thank you for everything.'

'Poor Julia,' Samantha said, in her husky soul-singer's voice. 'My heart aches for you, and I'll be thinking of you in the thick of the wild animals. You certainly deserve better than that, darling.' She kissed Julia lightly on the lips. 'Anyway, the best of jolly good Game Reserve luck to you. Do you realize that I'm going to have Leon to myself until the great take-off tonight? Don't look so stricken, Julia!' Samantha said this as though she had a private source of information concerning Julia's relationship with Leon. 'Anyway,' she went on, 'think of me, Julia, dancing in the arms of some rich old beast to please my mother – and one more thing, don't forget to invite me to the wedding! I could go for him in a big way myself, so let me know if you don't want him, darling, will you?' Samantha's black eyes slid round to Grant Tyler, and this saddened Julia. Fortunately, however, he had turned away from them, and was saying goodbye to the Lanfields.

When it was Leon's turn to say goodbye he said, 'And as Samantha just said, darling, the very best of jolly good Game Reserve luck to you. I'll be in touch – constantly.' He placed his arms around Julia and kissed her and she accepted his kiss happily. When he had kissed her he rubbed his lips against her ear and whispered, 'Either he's sore about something, darling, or else he doesn't like women. Cheer up!' Frantically, Julia wondered whether Grant Tyler had overheard this remark.

When she looked at him he gave her a cold look. 'How long is this going to go on?' he asked, 'not that it isn't very touching,' and she knew that Grant Tyler was having trouble hanging on to his temper.

CHAPTER TWO

SUDDENLY, as she left them behind, they all seemed rather insufferable, somehow, but she turned to wave as the Land Rover approached the wide ornamental gates, which had been opened for them by one of the gardeners.

Morning shadows were beginning to give up a display of light and shadow in the centre of the road and the day was on the way to losing its freshness.

There seemed to be absolutely nothing to say now that she was alone with Grant Tyler, and even if there had been, he was obviously not going to be the one to say it.

Eventually the silence forced Julia to speak. 'By the way, how is my father?'

'Well, he doesn't spend his days lounging next to a swimming-pool in bikini bathing trunks, if that's what you mean.'

'Presumably you have a reason for saying that,' she replied, after an offended little pause, 'but that's not what I meant.'

The sun was high now and heat rose from the tarmac in humid waves.

'I've never ridden in a Rand Rover – I mean *Land* Rover before,' she said, laughing a little as she became tongue-tied over the words. This was true because, although she had visited her father at the Renoster Game Reserve, he had not taken her out in one. She found herself beginning to enjoy the situation and smiled at Grant Tyler.

'Well, let's hope you don't find it too much of a strain.' It was a declaration of war, and Julia turned her head to look at the sarcastic Game Ranger beside her. Having her most trivial remarks taken up so seriously made her nervous.

'I didn't imply that, Mr. Tyler,' she kept her voice pleasant, although how she managed it she didn't quite know. 'Did I?'

'Not in so many words, no,' he replied, while she sat and seethed.

After a while she tried again. 'We really worked very

hard at the Finishing School, you know. Floria really put us through our paces – to make something of us.'

When he answered Grant Tyler spoke with deliberate slowness. 'It's a pity she failed so dismally, then, isn't it? After all that hard work.'

Julia assumed an astonished air. 'I never believed that people actually *said* things like that. Did I really ask for it?' She put the question to him on a note of genuine interest. The smile she gave him was slow and puzzled.

'What do you care?' he asked. 'Not that it matters.'

Somehow, Julia went on smiling. 'You'll have to put me to the test, won't you?'

'It's not all that important,' he told her, presenting a clean-shaven cheek. 'You seem to forget that there's no longer a part for you to play.'

'Thank you,' she replied, both amused and hurt at the same time.

There was a little pause and then she said, 'We don't seem to get along very well, do we?'

'No, we don't, do we? But I don't see that it matters.'

'I agree, of course.' She was frankly inspecting his face and then she turned away.

They drove in a sort of cold-war silence until Grant Tyler surprised her by saying, 'What are you thinking about? I take it you *do* think?'

Julia felt her pulse rate begin to climb dangerously. 'I *do* think, as a matter of fact. I was wondering whether it's too much to believe that peace might break out.'

A few miles on he said, 'We'll stop for lunch when we get to Hlageni. Will that suit you?'

'Of course. Why shouldn't it suit me?' She was still half angry inside. 'Unless you weren't *going* to stop? I hope it's not merely because I happen to be with you . . . ?' She broke off, confused. Looking sideways at him again, she felt a great splurge of anger and resentment. 'You don't deserve to be so handsome,' she thought.

'I want to stop for petrol,' he told her, 'for one thing and, for another, I want to buy a few things.' The sarcastic tone of his voice aggravated her even more.

'Well, in that case, we'll stop.' She matched the tone of her voice alongside his.

From where they were now they could see the Indian

Ocean in the distance and the clouds which straggled between it and the horizon.

On the outskirts of Hlageni Julia delved into her honey-coloured raffia bag and brought out a mirror and looked at her face. As the day became hotter the air almost steamed with moisture. She bit her lip and turned her face this way and that.

'You'll do.' Grant Tyler's voice was curt. 'Nobody is going to look at you where you're going to. You seem to have overlooked the fact that you're going to live amongst a lot of heat-stricken animals.'

She expelled an angry little breath. 'It's the heat,' she told him. 'I was just wondering whether it – *my face* – will ever come right again. I feel positively shrivelled up.' She turned her green eyes in his direction, appealing to him to be friendly. 'Would you mind if I applied fresh lipstick? I should hate to do anything to offend your sense of values because I realize they must be different after all.'

'Go right ahead,' he answered coldly, 'if you feel it's going to help your face.'

'Thank you.' She opened her bag again, and by the time she had finished applying lipstick and combing her hair, the Land Rover was filled with the scent of her perfume. 'That feels marvellous.' She snapped closed the clasp of her handbag. 'I feel much more like my lunch now.'

'Good,' he said. 'I expect they can stretch to a salad and skim-milk for you.'

'A salad and skim-milk?' She was frankly puzzled.

'You'll be thinking of that pool-side figure, won't you?' Julia made no attempt to defend herself and turned away to seethe again.

For lunch, she ordered a grilled steak, two eggs, chips and a salad, rolls and butter and coffee. Then she had the pleasure of insulting Grant Tyler by offering to pay for it.

And then, because one thing leads to another, and she did not want to quarrel with him, she tried being pleasant. Samantha had come up with the suggestion that she should talk about the weather. Well, she had – and with disastrous results. She'd try talking about his work.

'Tell me what it's like – your kind of life,' she ventured. 'I'd love to learn a little about your work at the Reserve. Did you play any part in Operation Rhino, for instance?'

'What do you know about Operation Rhino?' She knew that he was having trouble concealing his disappointment that she knew something of what went on in a Game Reserve.

'Well, I read about it of course. There've been numerous articles on the subject. Apart from that I saw films about it.'

'Are you really interested?' She saw the warning signals in his blue eyes.

'I'm very interested.' She placed her knife and fork on the side of her plate and sat back and looked at him. 'Why? Does that surprise you?'

'It surprises me very much.' His khaki-clad shoulders lifted in the slightest of contemptuous shrugs as he began to tell her a little about how Operation Rhino had started – how the rhinos were drugged by using a certain type of gun – a gas-operated device, with a range of twenty yards. Sometimes, he explained, a rhinoceros would be darted from a Land Rover or on foot.

'Oh, on foot must have been terribly dangerous,' she said, her mind busy visualizing Grant creeping, hand-over-hand, to within close range of a rhinoceros. 'What would have happened had the rhino charged?' Incredibly, she was in a good mood again.

'There were always a couple of men on horseback ready to make a pick-up.'

'Did the occasion ever arise?' she asked, with a woman's love of danger where a man is concerned.

'No.' He sat back and looked as though he was enjoying her disappointed expression.

'As I say, I've read about it and seen pictures in the newspapers and in magazines, of course, not to mention the screen. It looked terribly dangerous and exciting. The Land Rovers seemed to be bouncing all over the place over all sorts of unseen obstacles which were hidden in the long grass. The Rangers looked perfectly in command and – always so handsome. How they didn't fall over, on these occasions, as they aimed to fire the dart into the – into the – I mean at the . . .'

'The word you're searching for is rump,' he told her, and she knew that this was not said in an effort to help her out but to show her up again. 'You don't have to remember your Finishing School manners with me. Simply say the *rump* of the rhino. By the way, it's spelt r-u-m-p.'

She was determined to carry on – ignore his sarcasm.

'Did the dart work in every case?'

'Not always.'

'What happened, then?' She was beginning to sound impatient. Why couldn't he just be civil and talk to her?

'On occasions the drug-injecting mechanism in the aluminium dart failed to work properly and, because of this, the rhino only got a proportion of the drug.'

'What happened then?' Her green eyes were excited.

'Tell me,' he gave her a long look, 'are you really interested – or are you just wasting my time?'

'That's not very flattering.' Julia was hurt and showed it. 'I'd hardly be asking all these questions if I wasn't. Anyway,' she felt anger beginning to rise up, also bewilderment, 'you don't have to answer, if you don't want to.'

'Look,' he sighed, 'when this drug-injecting mechanism in the dart (it's only a small thing, after all) failed to work properly the rhino would crash about through the bush and then, after about a half an hour of this kind of thing, the chaps usually split up. One horseman would keep on the tail of the partially drugged rhino, while the other chap galloped back to the rendezvous to guide the darting team in for another shot at the animal.'

'Haven't I read somewhere that things are more up-to-date now?' she asked.

'I don't know. You tell me.' For a moment he looked amused and devilish. 'Anyway,' he went on, without waiting for her reply – perhaps he didn't want to give her a chance to snap back at him – 'that's quite another story, but yes, the present drug, a powerful morphine derivative, is so effective that one-and-a-half milligrams is sufficient to lay low a rhino bull of over four thousand pounds in a matter of seven to ten minutes. Small walkie-talkie radios have also been introduced.'

'How small? Do you mean you can carry them about with you?' Her voice was coming alive again.

'Yes, and since they're little bigger than a cigarette case they're easily kept in a pocket of the canvas jackets which are worn for thorn protection.'

'It's marvellous, the way it's all been thought out,' she

26

said, resting her elbows on the table. 'And all these animals are captured and transported to new homes?'

She watched his blue eyes drop to her elbows. 'I have some business to attend to,' he told her. 'What do you intend doing – sitting it out here?' and Julia almost hated him at this moment. She took her elbows off the table. 'I have no intention of sitting it out here. You could have told me you were waiting.'

'I'm telling you now.' As he spoke she stared back at him, his tanned and virile appearance a constant annoyance to her. He glanced at her plate. 'Are you quite sure you've had enough to eat?'

The way he said it made her long to be able to reduce him to nothing, but the only thing she could think of was to say, 'Thank you, I've had quite enough.'

He held her chair for her and she tried to rise above the sense of foolishness she felt because he seemed to be turning the small act of courtesy into some absurd gesture. He then followed her from the hotel dining-room into the sunshine where they stood on the pavement. The street was shabby and hot, but it looked extraordinarily beautiful to Julia because she was on her way home.

'I am sure you must have things you want to do,' Grant Tyler said, 'so I'll meet you here in, say – about three-quarters of an hour. How's that?'

'Couldn't I come along with you?' She looked at him with a green cat-like sobriety.

'Well,' he sounded frankly put out, 'you can come, if you want to, but I thought you'd want to buy some books or something. You're going to have an awful lot of time to kill in the Reserve and I can't see you doing it without a little help.' As she looked at him something told Julia that Grant Tyler was going to make things very difficult for her at Umkambo – but then she'd known it as he'd stepped out of the Land Rover at Azalea Park.

She took his advice about buying books and she even bought a cake and some dried fruit, in case her father didn't like sweets, and some sweets for herself. By the time Grant Tyler had finished his own shoppng and she had made her purchases the Land Rover had been checked over at the garage and the sun was beginning to lose its intensity.

They drove out of Hlageni and, for a while, there

seemed to be a strange harmony between them. The macadamized road ended and the Land Rover sounded noisy on the dust road and then Julia felt a twinge of excitement as the wooden barrier swung up and they drove into the Umkambo Game Reserve. Grant saluted the African Game Scout on duty ... and the wooden barrier came down again.

'You'll find domestic arrangements at Umkambo rather frugal, I expect,' he said, when they were on the way once more, 'after what you've been used to.' The remark put her immediately on the defensive.

'If they are – it won't worry me in the least.'

'I'm sure it won't.' He sounded as though he frankly disbelieved her, and because he seemed to be waiting for her to answer, she deliberately chose not to.

At the top of a long hill they were able to look down into the year-round green trees and bush which sprang up from the valley below. Its brooding beauty screened the kind of violence which could go on there, from day to day, in the form of a furious battle between great rhino bulls to a deadly battle between two snakes.

Julia turned to look at four rhinos which grazed quietly and almost absent-mindedly a short distance away from the road. 'They look so tame,' she remarked, 'don't they?'

'Well, tame as it appears, the white rhino is not to be taken for granted,' Grant told her. 'When circumstances demand action and it presses a charge, it's every bit as frightening as a black rhino charge, believe me.'

'I don't know the difference between a black and a white rhino. They all look alike to me,' Julia told him. 'I know it has something to do with their lips, though. The white rhinoceros is sometimes called the square-lipped rhinoceros, isn't it?'

'You're coming on,' he replied, coolly mocking her, but she thought she detected a flicker, certainly no more than that, of interest in his expression.

Although she felt flattered at the change in him she had to remind herself that she couldn't take this change of mood too seriously because Grant Tyler had made up his mind, in advance, about her.

'What about the black rhinoceros?' she asked, a moment later.

'Well, what about it?'

Half in anger and half in jest she said, 'Well, I thought perhaps you'd explain a little about it to me.'

'Okay, if that's the way you want it. The black rhino is the most dangerous animal in the Reserve. He's the fellow who is renowned for his murderous temper. He'll charge on sight – so you'd better learn those lips off by heart.' He turned to grin at her, and it was a nice grin – all tanned face, blue eyes and white teeth – and she liked him very much at this moment. 'What's more,' Grant went on, 'he refuses to quit until he has destroyed his enemy.'

Her eyes went wide. 'It must be a terrible sight to see him charge. Is he fast?'

'Once you've seen it you'll never forget it. Believe me when I say it's pure hate. First of all, he charges with incredible speed. He does this by holding his head high and swinging it from side to side. At the end of his run it looks almost as though he has put on invisible brakes, and then he veers his legs round and comes back at you and you get a glimpse, before you run – that is if you can still pull yourself together sufficiently to run – of his small, spiteful eyes, filled with hate and fury. Then there's his horn to take into consideration. That nasty horn protruding between those hate-filled eyes of his.'

'You sound as though you speak from personal experience.' Although Julia was laughing she was inwardly thrilled.

'Actually, I do speak from personal experience.' He turned to smile at her again and for a brief instant they looked straight into each other's eyes.

They were just outside the camp now and he said, 'I'll drive you right to your father's door – Umkambo style.'

'Thank you,' she replied. 'I'd like to thank you.'

'Not at all.'

They were passing the picturesque hut accommodation for tourists now and then what was quite obviously the office on the opposite side of the huts and which Julia knew must have a glorious view of the valley and distant mountains. This would be where her father worked. As though in answer to her unspoken question Grant said, 'Your father won't be at the office now. He'll be at the bungalow.'

29

Stan Munro must have been listening for the Land Rover because he had come out to the verandah and was already stepping directly on to the lawn in front of it. 'Well,' he said, coming forward to meet his daughter, 'and how are you, Julia? By jove, I've been looking forward to this. Good to see you, my dear. Welcome to Umkambo.' He bent his head and kissed Julia lightly on the cheek and then, awkwardly, he took her hand and patted it. He raised green eyes to Grant Tyler. 'So you found her all right, eh?'

'Found her, fed her and delivered her – all in one piece.' While Grant was speaking Julia stood looking at her father, allowing her hand to rest in his and thinking all the time that she and her father were practically strangers and that a new relationship would have to be built up between them. She found that she didn't even know what to call him. Their letters had not managed to keep them all that close to each other. She could see that now and felt a stab of dismay. Then, feeling the strain of everything that had happened to her, she glanced helplessly at Grant Tyler and a strange shock went through her as he looked back at her. For an instant it seemed as though he had been wondering how she would react to seeing the bungalow and then he gave her a sarcastic little smile. When the sarcastic half-smile became a whole one she could almost read his mind.

'Let me help you inside with the cases,' he said, picking two up from the lawn and beginning to make for the verandah.

Stan Munro picked up the other two and called after him, 'What about a drink before you go along to your own place? It must have been a hot trip.'

Grant put the cases on the verandah right next to the glass doors which led into the living-room. 'What I'm longing for most is a shower, Stan.' His smile was full of polite dismissal.

Some birds flew over the bungalow, in a formation of clumsy wing movements, looking like pieces of ragged black cloth. They were making a raucous but mournful cry that seemed to carry far over the Reserve.

'Oh,' Julia exclaimed. 'We had the same birds passing over Azalea Park almost every day.'

'The Ah-de-dah Ibis – the call of Africa itself,' Stan

replied, looking up. 'One gets so used to them that one hardly gives them a second thought.' He turned to Julia. 'I hope you're going to like it here – after the Finishing School?'

'I'm going to love it. I've been longing for the time to arrive for me to leave Azalea Park.' As she spoke she gave Grant Tyler a level look.

'Good,' Stan answered. 'I'm glad to hear that, Julia.' She noticed how the remark seemed to have pleased her father. 'I hope you won't be lonely, however, that's all – but we'll do our best, eh, Grant?'

'Sure,' Grant replied easily. 'That's the very least we can do, Stan. I'm the very first to agree with you.'

Grant made another move to take the cases into the bungalow and Julia followed him. The surge of excitement she felt at going into her father's bungalow gave way to panic as she looked at the nondescript furniture and curtains. Vaguely, she could remember their home on the north coast, a white-pillared building with a cool, tastefully decorated interior. While she had certainly not expected her father to live in a show-place she nevertheless felt a shaft of disappointment that he should allow himself to slip like this. As she turned away from her quick scrutiny of the room the disappointment she had experienced must have shown itself on her face and she realized that Grant Tyler had been given the satisfaction of watching it.

'Well,' their eyes, green and blue, met again, 'I don't want to keep you from settling in.' She noticed that his blue eyes were softened very slightly by mockery and she turned away. 'Thank you,' she murmured, 'for everything.'

After he had climbed back into the Land Rover and driven off, in the direction of the office, Julia said, 'Where does he stay – your Grant Tyler?'

'One up,' Stan Munro told her. 'Nice chap.'

'With – his wife?'

'Grant Tyler happens to be a bachelor. Carl Bramley, next door, is married, though. Girl named Roberta. Nice enough couple. First baby on the way.'

'I see. There are just the three bungalows, then?'

'Three up here, and you probably didn't notice another

at the entrance to the tourist section down the way. Chap by the name of Findlay Kruger and his wife. Both work at the office – but she's away at the moment. Gone on a cruise round the coast. Findlay and the Bramleys will be along later, no doubt, to welcome you. By the way, I can't help but admire your tan. You put all of us here in the shade. Lots of swimming, eh?'

'Yes. We swam a lot and did quite a good deal of horse-riding and gardening. It all went towards getting an even tan.' The look she gave him was frightened. 'I'm – I'm glad to be here. I – I want very much to be happy here and to – make *you* happy. I'd like you to know that. I've been looking forward to this moment, but now that it's here,' she shrugged, 'I know that I'm handling it badly.'

'Not at all.' Her father sounded embarrassed and shy, and Julia was unprepared for the tears which came to her eyes; she brushed them away and smiled through them.

'That's all I want,' her father was apparently raking up enough courage to go on, 'believe me.' He gave a small confused cough. 'What kind of trip did you have here? Hot enough for you? That reminds me, I must see about a drink for you. An iced lime juice. How does that appeal to you? You weren't used to anything stronger at the Finishing School, I take it except, perhaps, a little table wine, eh?'

Smiling at him, Julia realized now that he'd got her with him he didn't quite know how to handle her, and she was a little touched. 'A lime juice will be marvellous. I'm looking forward to that. We had an enormous lunch, by the way.' At the memory of her steak, eggs, chips, salad and rolls she laughed lightly.

Grant Tyler drove past on his way to his own bungalow and Stan Munro looked up. 'There's a sort of mystery attached to that young fellow,' he explained.

'Oh?' Immediately, Julia's voice tightened. From where she was standing she could see Grant on his way across his lawn which had an African sandalwood tree growing in the centre of it.

'Something to do with a girl – girl in the background, somewhere. Jilted Tyler, I'm led to believe. Didn't want to end up a Game Ranger's wife, apparently. Anyway, Julia, let's go through, shall we? I'll show you all there is to be seen. Make any changes you like, my dear. The place is all yours now. Hardly ever in it myself, and when I am I usually have my head buried in a file or a good book.'

As she followed him from the living-room she said very cautiously, 'It's an attractive bungalow. I adore all this grained wood about the place and the white walls and stonework.' Her eyes dropped to the highly-polished black slate tiles on the floors and she could visualize some of Leon's brilliantly handwoven rugs upon them.

'I'd love to accept your invitation about making a few changes for the simple reason that we learned quite a bit about that sort of thing at the Finishing School. You wouldn't be hurt, though, would you? I don't want to hurt you by doing anything I . . .'

'Nothing would give me more pleasure than to see you occupying yourself with something that will make you happy.' Her father seemed absolutely genuine about this as he stood next to her, his legs slightly apart and the collar of his khaki shirt open to reveal his tanned skin. At fifty-odd he was graceful and compact with the same sort of strength about him that she had noticed in Grant Tyler.

'How does one go about shopping here?' she asked.

Stan laughed. 'That's something you'll have to get used to here. Actually, we have a lorry call here on certain days for our order books and post. They, of course, deliver post in return and deliver the stuff we order. Very simple, really. However, you'll gradually get used to going out by yourself in the car. It's a matter of forty-odd miles to Hlageni, as you probably noticed on your way here. There's no reason why you can't make the trip yourself, eventually. In the meantime, until you get used to conditions here I expect that Carl Bramley or Grant will always be prepared to give you a lift – when they happen to be going into town. Roberta Bramley used to make the trip herself, at one time, before the baby was on its way. She's not well, at the moment, I believe. Heat, most probably. Anyway, come along . . .'

As he led her from room to room Julia's spirits rose as she visualized just how much could be done around the bungalow at very little cost. She did not intend asking her father for money as she had saved quite a bit herself. However, when he had finished showing her over the place he said, 'Don't spare the expense when you start to do up the bungalow. What we buy we can take with us to Pieter-maritzburg at the end of the year. Just let me know how much you require, will you?'

'I wasn't going to bother you – about money,' she said.

'Nonsense. I want to do this. I'm looking forward to it.' He looked at the shabby old brown lounge suite. 'Picked that up, second-hand, for a song at Hlageni when I came here. Should be thrown out.'

'I'll have it traded in,' she told him. 'Cane would look very attractive in this setting – with lots of colour.'

'I'll leave it to you. Now you know where everything is you can begin to settle in. By the way, you don't have to do much. Attend to your personal laundry, that's all. Otherwise, Samson sees to the cleaning up and the house-hold laundry and my own, of course. He also sees to most of the cooking. Sometimes, however, I boil myself an egg, although I'm not supposed to eat the confounded things. Samson is an amiable fellow. Come along and meet him. Do you speak Zulu? But of course, you wouldn't have had occasion to use Zulu, would you?'

'I know a smattering of Zulu,' she said. 'I intend to study it. It's very necessary, I think.'

'You might also like to meet Samson's wife. Come to think of it, she'd probably appreciate making a bit of extra money by attending to your personal laundry for you. You might like to prepare the menus for Samson. He's a good enough cook, but he's in a bit of a groove just at present, but I suppose I'm responsible for that. There's lots of fruit and plenty of meat in the refrigerator – I always know that, although I'm not supposed to eat that either – a little grilled steak, chicken . . .'

Julia brooded over these remarks, in some bewilderment, and then she said, 'Why aren't you supposed to eat all these things?'

'Diet I happen to be on. Nothing to worry about. Fat-free diet, to put it in a nutshell.'

'I see,' she replied, but she didn't see at all and studied his face carefully. 'What *are* you supposed to eat, then? Does Samson know?'

'Most things, really. Fish, chicken, fruit, vegetables. It's nothing to worry about – just thought I'd mention it.'

'I'd like to know more about it.' She smiled at him. 'I also happen to like cooking. I'd like to cook and I'd like to know what to cook for you.'

'So you can cook, eh?' He returned the smile. 'Didn't think you'd like that sort of thing, as a matter of fact.'

'Oh no . . . !' she wailed, half amused, half angry. 'Not you too! But of course I can cook. Not only plain cooking but exotic dishes into the bargain. I'm – far from useless, believe me.'

After she had met Samson and his wife, Tina, she went through to her room, which didn't look half so bad now that she knew she was going to change it soon. For a moment she stood staring out of the steel-framed window. It had been quite a day, she thought. She'd seen game – warthog, impala, rhinoceros, giraffe and, last but not least, she'd been reunited with her father in her new home. Hearing her father's suede shoes on the slate-tiled floor, she turned round.

'By the way,' he said, coming into the room, 'I didn't quite know what to do about this room. I thought I'd leave it to you. One thing in its favour, however, is that everything is spotlessly clean. Samson sees to that.' There was a small pause and then he said helplessly, 'I suppose I should have seen to it that there were at least some flowers – but you'll have to forgive me, Julia. I've grown very out of touch, you know. Still, it will give you an interest – having something to do . . .'

'I'm very glad you left it,' she told him. 'It doesn't need much,' she tried desperately to be kind, 'just – well – new curtains, maybe, and a colourful bedspread – one of those cottage woven things.' She went to stand next to him. Both were slimly built, with long bones and the kind of skin that automatically goes with tanning. Julia kissed him on his cheek. 'Don't worry,' she said, thinking that his skin smelled of the sun, 'I'm thrilled about everything.' And suddenly it was true.

'After you've settled in, perhaps you'd join me for a drink on the verandah? In the meantime, I want to put in a show at the office before it closes. Findlay Kruger is there at the moment. I'll be back in a matter of minutes.'

'Good, I'll be looking forward to that. May I have a bath?'

'By all means, my dear. Towels and things in the cupboard in the passage and there's plenty of soap and – oh, we'll need a key for the bathroom now, won't we? Better check up there. Never lock the place myself – can't even remember seeing the key for a long time. I'll check up on that, don't worry.' With another smile he was gone and Julia stood looking after him and her own smile was a sad, tender thing.

Somewhere outside the bathroom window a male African voice sang a song while she took her bath. It was obviously a song of his own invention and it consisted of six urgent little notes – Julia counted them – which went on and on with an exciting kind of urgency. Idly, while she soaped herself, Julia wondered where Samantha was now – winging her way over the Drakensberg Mountains, no doubt, on her way to Johannesburg, where she would be expected to "dance with some rich old beast" to please her mother. Julia did not envy Samantha and she wondered what the dark, beautiful girl would have to say about the bungalow and the black iron bed, which was in her room and which Stan Munro had probably "bought for a song" at a shabby little shop in Hlageni. She'd paint it, of course – white – and she'd top the cinnamon-coloured blankets, which had been neatly tucked in by Samson, with a brightly woven bedspread with white fringing and with cushions, picking up the colours in the bedspread. Everything was going to be all right – if she avoided Grant Tyler as much as possible.

She stood up in the bath and as the water trickled down the tanned length of her body she reached for one of her father's towels, which really came as a surprise, after everything else. They were thick and expensive, and if her father went in for luxuries at all, this seemed to be one of them; it gave her a sharp kind of pleasure.

By the time Stan Munro arrived back she had finished dressing and her yellow caftan-style frock left her tanned knees bare. She slipped her feet into gold sandals which she preferred to silver.

When she joined her father on the verandah she immediately stiffened to find Grant Tyler there with him. Smiling, she was determined not to lose her self-confidence again.

36

'I talked Grant into coming over for a drink,' Stan said. 'After all, this occasion calls for some sort of celebration, doesn't it? The Bramleys will be over shortly.'

'Well, that's nice,' Julia said, noticing the cubes of cheese and the pickles and the peanuts which Samson had apparently placed in small wooden bowls. She cast a look in Grant's direction and the sight of him looking so cool, aloof and handsome in a fresh change of khaki clothing was maddening, and she chose the chair farthest away from him.

'By the way,' her father looked at Grant, 'you won't know the old bungalow soon. Julia's going to redecorate. Can't say I blame her. Anyway, the point is that she'd like to cadge a lift with you the next time you go into Hlageni. She'll want to make her own choice as to material, furniture and so on. That be all right with you?'

In the fading light Julia's eyes met Grant Tyler's and she knew what he was thinking. 'So?' There was a mocking edge to his voice. 'Things didn't quite come up to expectations?'

'My expectations have nothing to do with it,' she couldn't keep the feeling out of her voice. 'I just happen to want to make my father comfortable. It's a long time since anybody fussed over him.'

'Better late than never, I suppose.' Grant's tone was lightly bantering, for her father's benefit, Julia knew, but his blue eyes were hard – and this was for her benefit.

At this moment Carl and Roberta Bramley came across the lawn and Stan Munro made the necessary introductions. Roberta Bramley looked pale, even in the fading light which had just about gone now, and whenever she had a chance, she complained bitterly about the heat.

When they were alone in Julia's room, Roberta said, 'Oh, I feel so hideous and uncomfortable, Julia. You just have no idea.' Her eyes flickered over Julia's slim figure. 'I can't wait for this baby to be born. Carl wants me to go home to my mother for a week or so, until the heat eases off a bit. Mother is thrilled at the very thought, of course, but it seems so unfair to Carl. However,' she shrugged a hopeless kind of shrug, 'I'll probably take the easy way out in the end and go. It can't be all that pleasant for Carl, having me around, the way I am – always sick and always moaning. Do you think you're going to like it here? It won't be much fun, after the kind of life you've led, will it?'

'I'm going to love it, Roberta. It's funny, I have to keep on saying that – everybody seems to think that I won't be able to settle down here. This is my first real home since I was just a small girl and I'm longing to do all sorts of things – help Samson with the cooking, for one thing – redecorate for another.' She cast her green eyes about the room. 'I'll leave this room to last and start on the living-room and dining-room first.'

Roberta laughed. 'It sounds funny to hear you say redecorate. It makes one think you're about to re-vamp a country mansion instead of a thatched-roof bungalow in a Game Reserve.'

'Well, to me, it's just as exciting as re-vamping a country mansion. I know I'm going to hate having to leave here at the end of the year.'

After a short pause Roberta said, 'What do you think of Grant Tyler?'

Julia's expression changed. 'What am I supposed to think?' She hoped her voice sounded light. 'I haven't thought about him at all, to be perfectly honest.' That was a lie, she told herself. She'd thought about nothing else. She felt the dull ache of disappointment that Grant Tyler should be here to spoil things for her.

'Well, that's just as well, Julia, because Grant happens to be a genuine woman-hater. It's not just an act with him. He's all right to me, of course, because I'm married and I'm pregnant and I don't fit into the scheming female category. To be quite honest, Grant thinks more about his juvenile crocodiles than he could ever think of any girl.'

Julia's eyes widened. 'Juvenile crocodiles? Does he keep crocodiles – as pets?'

Laughing, Roberta said, 'No, not as pets. Game Rangers are always making notes on this and that and working on personal experiments of some kind or other. This study of crocodiles is nothing new, of course, but I suppose Grant thinks he can go one better and find out something *really* unique about the little horrors. At the moment, his juvenile crocodiles are his main interest. I wonder if there are any females amongst them? I forgot to ask. Actually, at the moment, he's watching several clutches of eggs. Still, I shouldn't talk – Carl is just as bad. Although your father is in the office he is also interested in experiments being carried out.'

'Frankly, Roberta, I couldn't care less about Grant Tyler.'

'I just thought I'd warn you,' Roberta went on, 'because, after all, he is quite a heart-throb, isn't he? But you won't let on, will you? I should hate it to get back to his ears that I'd let slip that he was practically jilted at the altar. The girl changed her mind about being the wife of a humble Game Ranger. Pity about her, that's all I can say . . .'

'Perhaps she just changed her mind about the man. About Grant Tyler. After all, good looks aren't everything. I can't say I blame this poor girl. She'd probably had enough of Grant's sarcasm. Anyway, I suppose we'd better be getting back to the verandah.'

On the way to the verandah Roberta said, 'Honestly, I envy you, Julia. You're utterly gorgeous – not like poor me.' She glanced down at her wash-faded, sun-bleached maternity frock. 'I feel a perfect freak. My maternity frocks are just about worn out – but I don't want to go to the expense of buying new ones at this stage. It's not long to go, but with you around now, looking the way you do, I think I'd better begin to do something about myself!'

'This may surprise you, Roberta, but I'd been thinking how attractive you look.' Julia felt slightly irritated. 'I envy you. You and Carl are obviously so much in love. You have this baby coming and you have your home. I'd love to have all these things. Apart from that, you certainly don't look like a freak. There's a quiet beauty about you at the moment. I think all women waiting for babies to be born have this particular look about them.'

'Beautiful?' Roberta made a face, but the remark seemed to have pleased her. 'Come off it, Julia! When your turn comes to have an infant you won't think that, believe me.'

They had reached the verandah now and the three men who had been joined by Findlay Kruger were discussing drought conditions.

'What are you two girls gossiping about?' Carl asked.

'Julia says there's something beautiful about a woman who's about to have an infant,' Roberta told him, sitting down. 'So I said, "Wait until it happens to you. You won't say that then, Julia." Which is true. What you men must think of me walking round, looking like an army tank, next to this exciting Finishing School beauty, I shudder to think. Looking at Julia makes me dislike myself so much.'

'Stop talking like a petulant child, Roberta,' Grant made an impatient gesture. 'You seem to have lost sight of the fact that you're doing a job of work at the moment.'

Listening to them, Julia felt a sort of sick, sad feeling and her nails, she discovered, were digging into the palms of her hands. She knew that she had to make allowances for Roberta, who was undergoing a certain amount of strain at the moment, but she could find no excuse for Grant Tyler having butted in to imply that it was a pity that she, Julia Munro, was not doing a job of some sort instead of coming to Umkambo with one thought in her mind – to redecorate while she killed time for one year.

Stan had been waiting awkwardly to introduce Julia to Findlay Kruger. 'My daughter,' he said. 'She's very thrilled to be with us.'

Julia liked Findlay Kruger, who was also very tanned and had a beard which had a reddish tinge to it.

In the quickly gathering darkness insects began to drone. Grant was the first to leave and then Roberta said, 'Well, I suppose I had better go and get Carl something to eat in the line of dinner.'

As Julia watched Grant striding across the lawn, in the direction of his own bungalow, Carl was saying, 'But you're going to eat, honey, aren't you? You *must* eat, Roberta.'

'Well, perhaps a little fruit, if I can find some. It's too hot to eat, Carl. How you can wade through those big, hot meals, I just don't know.'

After the Bramleys and Findlay Kruger had gone Samson came out to collect the glasses and Julia went to stand at the edge of the verandah to try and hide the hurt she was feeling from her father.

CHAPTER THREE

DURING dinner her father told her a little about his work at the Umkambo Game Reserve and then she even willed herself to ask about Grant Tyler's juvenile crocodiles – just to prove she didn't care.

She listened carefully as he explained how Grant would undertake an examination of several clutches of eggs and the nesting sites from which they came. Stan Munro helped himself to some more potato. 'Grant makes a note of the habits of a parent reptile, the sand surrounding the nests is examined and individual eggs are unearthed, at intervals, so that they can be examined and the embryo measured.' He looked up at Julia. 'I don't suppose all this makes much sense to you?'

'It all sounds very complicated,' she replied, dredging up a smile.

'Well, yes, I suppose it does, but it might well give you an insight into the activities of a Game Ranger. My lot revolves around the office, of course, as I explained to you – but I like to get out myself, from time to time, and make my own personal observations.'

'You say that, after hatching, a certain number of reptiles are then selected from a brood and placed in an enclosure? Why?' Julia was still interested in the pattern of Grant Tyler's life.

Her father smiled at her from across the table. 'This isn't exactly Finishing School conversation, is it? But well, if you were to ask any Game Ranger he'd probably tell you that an accurate record of each specimen's progress is made from month to month.'

As she listened to her father Julia was almost prompted, at the end of his conversation, to remind him that the Finishing School had been *his* idea, not hers – but she kept quiet about this.

'Are the baby crocodiles given names?' She found it strange that her world had shrunk from learning all about antiques to learning about crocodiles.

Her father laughed lightly. 'None of them is exactly

cuddly enough to be given a pet name. Actually, they are identified by numbers. These numbers are painted, in bright paint, on each crocodile's head . . . and by the way, it's just ordinary, quick-drying enamel paint and it lasts up to seven or eight weeks, before it begins to peel off. By using this method, a record can be kept of each individual reptile.' He waved aside the paw-paw salad which Samson was placing before him. 'I might mention, however, that several other ways of identifying crocodiles turned out to be flops.'

Julia allowed Samson to place a dish of paw-paw before her. She looked up and smiled, 'Thank you, Samson. This looks very cool. Just what I'm longing for.' She transferred her smile to her father. 'What on earth is there to study about a crocodile?'

Stan gave a small cough behind his napkin. 'Well, more than you think, actually, Julia. There are a number of things to be taken into account – diet, food supply, individual temperament, the growth rate of the body organs in relation to one another. A chart is kept of all these facts. The crocodiles are weighed and measured for Grant's own particular detailed records and a chart is even kept showing details of dentition of juvenile crocodiles, from hatching up until a certain age.' He laughed suddenly. 'What do you think of that one? Roberta Bramley's future baby problems will be nothing compared to Grant Tyler's baby crocodiles!'

Julia laughed politely before she said, 'Do crocodiles grow quickly?' This was also asked more out of politeness than of interest, because her thoughts were busy with the sarcastic Grant Tyler again.

'They grow about six inches a year.'

'That's not very much, is it?' She lifted curious eyes to his and then there was a small pause before she said, 'Your Grant Tyler is something quite outside my experience, by the way.'

'Really?' Stan's voice was poised somewhere between curiosity and irritation. 'Why is this, Julia? Not – sophisticated enough for you? Not,' he groped for the right term, 'not – smooth enough for you?'

'I find his particular brand of sarcasm quite outside my scope, for one thing.'

'You couldn't have had much – er – experience – where you've just come from, could you? That is – a Finishing School for young ladies.' The question sounded tense and anxious.

'Not much, but I met – people, of course.' She noticed how her father's eyes were searching her face.

'One in particular?'

Julia shrugged her shoulders and then she laughed, very softly and with some embarrassment. 'Well, yes, one – in particular, you might say.'

'His name? I don't think you mentioned this man's name in any of your letters?'

'Leon. Leon Ladenza.' Her voice was low.

Absently, Stan Munro had decided to eat the paw-paw salad, after all, which Samson had stubbornly left on the table.

'Ladenza? Curious sort of name, isn't it?' He looked at the spoon detachedly as he raised it to his mouth.

'I suppose so. I met him through the Finishing School, as a matter of fact.' Her father's silence forced her to speak. 'Leon owns three galleries, in three different towns, and they're filled with all sorts of gorgeous things. The kind of gorgeous things we had to learn about at the School.'

'What do you mean by gorgeous things?' Looking at her father, as he asked the question, Julia knew that he was unsettled now and nervous, and she felt a hopeless pang of love for him because she did not know how to cope with it.

'Well,' she explained, 'paintings, a smattering of antiques, modern pottery, hand-woven rugs and so on – the old and new, and all, as I say, gorgeous and exciting and terribly, terribly expensive.' She recognized her own nervousness and went on, 'We were often shown round the gallery in Grovelea because it's only a matter of twenty minutes' drive from Azalea Park. Leon often gave lectures, both at the gallery and at the Finishing School.' On an impulse she added, 'He's a complete contrast to Grant Tyler, by the way. You would probably refer to him as eccentric – let alone smooth.' She laughed lightly at the thought of her father meeting Leon. 'And he also happens to be a ballet dancer, *and* a very good one, into the bargain. He's terribly graceful in a dark, sullen way. He hardly ever smiles, and when he does it's a tragic, pained kind of smile.' She took a quick breath and allowed it to escape immediately while she shrugged at the same time. 'You have to get to know him, to find out just how sweet he is. He's generous to the point of stupidity. He'll give anything away. I think that if one of his friends had to go into raptures over an antique in his gallery he'd give it to them – and give it because he really *wanted* to. He's just very slightly effeminate . . .'

'Effeminate?' Her father sat back and studied her and she was aware of his freshly laundered khaki clothes and his firm mouth twisted slightly at the corners.

'Very slightly. Just enough to make him terribly pleasant to be with. He notices all the *little* things which mean so much to a woman. He knows when a colour is unbecoming to a girl . . .' She broke off helplessly. 'You know what I mean.' She smiled at him with her green eyes.

Her father's eyebrows lifted fractionally. 'I'm not sure that I do. However, I haven't lost sight of the fact that I am,' he shrugged those khaki-clad shoulders, 'a little out of touch.'

Julia found herself wishing that this ordeal was over, but she prolonged it by saying, 'We took a course in ballroom dancing together – just for fun, so that we could really show off at the graduation ball . . . mainly to show off my gown, I suppose. That was one of the things on Floria's curriculum – dressmaking. Not only dressmaking but designing and cutting. My gown took me the best part of the year to make and the coat to match another three months. It's a marvellous gown and coat – even though I say it myself. It's made of slipper satin – the most subtle apricot-pink and embossed with thousands,' she laughed, '*millions*, maybe, I didn't count, of seed pearls.'

The chill on her father's face was not imagined – or was it? She thought about this as she stopped talking and then, feeling all tight inside, she said, 'Would you mind, very much, if he came here for a long week-end?'

'Not at all, providing it comes at a suitable time, of course. Er – is this your reason for wanting to do the bungalow up?' He gave her a small, withdrawn smile.

'No, of course not.' She felt as though she'd spent most of the night opposite her father at the dinner table. Guiltily, she saw her father's shabby bungalow through the pained eyes of Leon Ladenza. Although Leon never removed those dark lenses she had no doubt that the eyes behind them could look pained. 'It's not because of Leon that I want to try my hand at decorating the bungalow,' she went on, and this was strictly true. 'I'm so thrilled at being home with you. I haven't had a real home since – for – *ages*. I'm longing to do things to it. You don't really mind, do you? I mean, I haven't hurt your feelings, have I? I didn't intend to. Please believe that.' She could feel her nerves snapping and, because she did not seem to be on her father's wave-length, loneliness wove its web about her.

'Just you go ahead,' Stan told her. 'Nothing would give me more pleasure – and, by the way, just let me know how much money you want. It was time I did something about this shabby stuff myself. I just didn't give it a thought, that's all.'

Julia smiled her relief. 'I'd thought of cane,' she said. 'It seems to me to be just the right thing. Cane furniture and lots of colour.'

Her father made a gesture which showed his approval. 'You do just whatever you like. We'll see what we can do about a trip into Hlageni where you can make your own choice.'

Later, in bed, Julia tried to relax some of the tension which had built up inside her throughout the entire day but she merely aggravated matters by thinking of Grant Tyler, and this disturbed her, because she didn't want to think about him. She wondered about the girl who had jilted him. Serve him right, she thought, with a sudden viciousness.

For the next three days she was busy sorting herself out. She had tea with Roberta Bramley and she went out with her father early one morning, while the shadows were still long and dew clung to the grass. Molten rays of strengthening sunlight filtered through the green foliage where nyala, zebra, blue wildebeest, kudu, impala, giraffe and warthog grazed.

She had been instructed by her father that, unless she was accompanied by a Game Guide, she was never to venture from the car if ever she decided to go out to spot game on her own. 'That's one of the rules,' he told her.

'But I can drive out by myself to spot game, provided I don't get out of the car, is that it?'

'By all means – provided you don't get out of the car. As I say, that's one of the rules.' He looked at his watch. 'I suppose we had better be getting back. Sorry, but there it is. I meant to tell you a little more about the Game Reserves of Zululand, but anyway you know by now that it's here that the only well-established herds of white rhinoceros are to be found. The Game Reserves of Zululand are the last stronghold of the white – the *square-lipped* rhino – their last natural sanctuary. The black rhino is also to be found in these reserves. Perhaps the black rhino is in even greater danger of extinction than the white. They're both dangerous – don't fool yourself that they aren't, my dear girl. Don't forget, the car is at your disposal – but *keep* to it, will you? Keep inside.'

'I don't have much option, do I?' Julia felt the stirring of adventure and smiled cheerfully at her father.

He smiled back, 'You don't.'

They drove back to the camp in the gathering heat and Stan dropped his daughter outside the office. 'Coming in for a moment?' he asked. 'You haven't seen it yet. It's quite attractive inside. There's rather a magnificent view from the main window on the other side. It was planned that way and sends visitors for a loop. It's a sort of feature.'

'Well, yes, I'd like to . . .' Julia began, when she happened to spot Grant Tyler at the entrance, 'but perhaps another time. You'll be busy now, I suppose.'

'Seeing Grant there on the steps reminds me,' Stan said, 'that he happened to mention yesterday that he was going into Hlageni tomorrow. Sorry I forgot to mention it. I asked him to give you a lift. That all right with you? It's only about forty-odd miles, as you know, and once you toughen up I suppose you could always make the trip yourself. Nothing to stop you, really, if you keep to the rules.'

'Did – Grant Tyler say anything – about taking me into town?' Her face was serious. 'Wasn't Carl Bramley going?'

'Young Tyler was civil enough – but he's not exactly a ladies' man, you know. Bramley, of course, will be away

46

for three days, from tomorrow. That leaves Tyler.'

'It's a pity about Grant Tyler not being a ladies' man,' Julia said hotly, 'isn't it? Who does he think he is? Anyway, *any* lift will be welcome – until I can make my own plans.'

Grant Tyler gave no indication of having heard her as she approached his Land Rover the following morning. He had his back to her, which was very masculine in its khaki shirt. A surge of excitement went through Julia as she thought about the shopping she was going to do in Hlageni, but the excitement gave way to panic as she thought of the trip there alone with Grant Tyler.

'Good morning,' she called, trying to sound very casual and cheerful. 'I hope I haven't kept you waiting?' She said this pleasantly, although she had not really kept him waiting at all. As she came to stand next to him he turned and his blue eyes, with their thick black lashes, which came as a sharp kind of shock in his tanned face, travelled over her. She was suddenly conscious of her slacks, with their pumpkin-yellow and blue stripes, and of the yellow cotton shirt which went with them, and she stood looking back at him, swinging her copper-toned raffia bag.

'Get in, will you?' he told her, in a curt, dictatorial voice. On purpose, she gave him a wide green-eyed look as she went towards the door which he had opened for her, although, at this particular moment, she disliked Grant Tyler immensely.

In the Land Rover she opened her bag and took out her dark sun-glasses and put them on; behind them her green eyes were hurt and her beautiful bronzed face tense.

At the small, square office building, with its thatched roof and white-plastered walls, he stopped the Land Rover and slipped from his seat. 'I want to collect something from the office before I leave,' he told her.

'Fine,' she answered, still trying to sound cheerfully off-handed.

She watched him stride towards the office and then sat back, enjoying the warmth of the sun on her limbs. Parties of tourists were arranging with African Game Guides to go out to spot game while other tourists, the very early risers, were already coming back from this and were arriving in their cars after having been out in the bush since sunrise.

Grant came back and got into the Land Rover, and as they drove off, the African Game Guides saluted him courteously and he returned their salute in the same manner.

The morning air was fragrant with the scents of growing things and it was a kind of acrid but spicy scent, reminding Julia somehow of thatch grass which had been crushed.

'It's going to be a lovely day, isn't it?' she ventured, shaking back her tawny hair and glancing at the trees with their ruffled leaves stirring in the light breeze.

'I don't know about that. All I know is that it's going to be oppressively hot in an hour from now,' he replied, his hands steady on the wheel.

'Yes, I suppose so,' she answered, with an edge of desperation to her voice. She racked her brains for something to talk about, but because she could almost *feel* the indifferent expression on Grant's face, she remained silent. However, after a while she said, 'It seems rather strange, going into town via a Game Reserve to shop. It will take some getting used to.'

'Oh well,' he said, 'you won't have to do it for ever, will you?'

Discouraged, she replied quickly, 'You twist my words, don't you?'

'Do I?' He did not turn to look at her and they sat in unfriendly silence for a few miles.

'Next time I won't bother you,' Julia broke the silence again, 'I'll use my father's car. I'm quite capable.'

'Quite. I don't see why you shouldn't use your father's car – if it's good enough for you, of course.' He spoke almost too quickly and, affronted, she frowned a little and turned away to look at the bush on the side of the road where a haze was rising up to be pierced by the yellow, slanting rays of the sun. At intervals clouds of busy gnats rose up.

They passed game, half asleep in the sun, and Grant answered Julia's questions about them politely enough. For a while a sense of shared peace seemed to fall between them, but it was false, she told herself. She knew Grant

48

Tyler well enough by now to realize that it was false.

An outcrop of rock marked the river below and along the banks of the river spread the trees.

They drove into Hlageni and Grant parked the Land Rover. 'Will you be able to find your way back here?' He gave her one of his searching glances and she peered up at him through her dark glasses.

'Yes. I know now there's very little more to Hlageni than the main street with its straggle of shops. I'm bound to find a suitable furniture shop. I also want to choose yards and yards of material for curtaining and some scatter cushions. I should be able to get them in the same shop, shouldn't I?'

He studied her disapprovingly. 'You really mean to go to town on your old man's bungalow, don't you? Couldn't you even stick it out – *for one year*?'

She was startled by this unexpected intensity. 'It's not a case of sticking it out for one year. I merely intend making my father more comfortable for the next year – making us both comfortable.'

'That's more to the point,' he replied. '*Us.*' His lower lip curled. '*Me, I, myself . . .*'

'What I buy has nothing to do with you,' she told him, wondering how it was that she could still speak, 'but in any case, what I buy will go with us to Pietermaritzburg, when my father retires there. My father hasn't been really comfortable, by the looks of things, or surrounded by attractive things, for a long time. He just doesn't seem to care about himself. As long as the bungalow is clean and his khaki clothes immaculately laundered that's all he seems to worry about.'

'Well, whose fault is that?' Grant challenged her. 'It's rather late in the day to try and make him comfortable now, isn't it?' Grant Tyler had no regard for feelings. He was hurting her and he knew it, she thought bitterly.

Slightly pale, she controlled herself long enough to say, in a small voice, 'I'll thank you to keep your opinion to yourself.' Then when her anger had passed a little she added, 'I didn't come to Hlageni to discuss this with you. It's already been discussed between my father and myself. When do you want me back here at the Land Rover? That's more to the point.'

'I'll meet you here in a couple of hours from now,' he told her, glancing at his watch. 'Just get in and wait for me, if I'm not here.' His blue eyes flicked over her and she felt dismissed.

'Thank you.' Her voice was stiff and so was her back. 'I'll try not to keep you waiting.' She spoke with a calculated increase of sarcasm as she said this.

Her face was thoughtful as she made her way down the main street. She tried to fight back her irritation as she looked in the shop windows. The pavements were lined with trees which cast sheaves of shadow across the street. Several buildings had a rough kind of mosaic work on them and she stopped to look up at the colourful façades. The mosaic patterns were primitive both in respect to pattern and colour.

Eventually she discovered a shop which seemed to have everything from honey-coloured cane furniture to pictures and material. To her delight, she was able to choose several cane chairs, which although shaped like cones, were extremely comfortable, a low, glass-topped coffee table to match and an attractive cane cocktail trolley, glass-topped and moving smoothly on thickly rubbered wheels. For the dining-room she also bought cane and then started on the choice of materials and pictures. She bought two pictures, which had thick white frames and, in both cases, African women, colourfully swathed in jewel-like silk and multi-coloured beads, made a startling contrast to the frames.

From the colours in the pictures she was able to make her choice of scatter cushions and the Indian raw silk for the curtains, and then, because she just couldn't resist the temptation, she splurged some of her own money on an exciting copper coffee service, which she knew she'd never use, but it seemed to belong to the cane and the colour. She also chose a tall copper pitcher which would look good with or without flowers.

A sense of light-heartedness took hold of her as she arranged for delivery and for her father's old, shabby furniture to be carted away. This was money well spent, she thought, visualizing the finished result of her work in the bungalow.

When she got back to the Land Rover she was disconcerted to find Grant Tyler already there waiting for her, but, much to her surprise, he greeted her politely enough and even offered her lunch.

Against all common sense, Julia made her first error and fell for his offer.

'Well,' he said, as they were settled at their table, 'how did the shopping go?' His mouth turned up faintly at one corner, with an irritating hint of quizzical contempt.

'It went very well, actually.' She thawed out a little. 'I'm very pleased with my choice. Everything is cane – very simple.'

'I'm sure it is.' He spoilt her thawing out by being sarcastic again. He passed her the menu. Their fingers touched, by accident, and she nearly dropped the card. His remark had left her feeling resentful and depressed, and today she did not want to feel this way. She wished now that she had not accepted his offer for lunch and that she had insisted on lunching on her own.

'Well, have you decided what you want?' he asked, and she realized that she had been staring at the menu without really seeing what was written there.

She made her choice swiftly. 'Yes. I'll have steak and chips, please.' She gave him back the menu, careful, this time, to keep her fingers from touching his.

With a look that was almost amusement he asked, 'Is that what you feel like?'

'Yes.'

His eyes were mocking her now and she thought that the colour of them was like blue butterfly wings. 'You're not merely trying to prove something, are you?'

She looked for somewhere to put her bag. 'If I *am* trying to prove anything I'm trying to prove that I happen to be hungry.' She placed the bag at her feet and looked up. Her expression was frigid.

'Well, what do you know?' His laugh was startlingly agreeable. He ordered the same for himself.

During the meal he carried on a conversation with a courtesy she mistrusted and so she was careful not to say too much.

While she took her time over her coffee he said, 'Would you mind making it snappy? I want to get back.'

She responded with a loud click of her cup as it hit her saucer and then she reached for her bag. 'I'm ready when you are.' They stared into each other's eyes for a moment and then hers dropped first and, with them, the hopes that she would ever be able to like him.

'Finish your coffee,' he said abruptly, 'and don't sulk. After all, I merely asked you to make it snappy. Was that a crime?'

'I don't want any more coffee,' she answered defiantly, and watched him with rebellious green eyes as he stood up. 'Okay,' he said, 'then let's go.'

She made up her mind, in advance, not to talk to him on the way back to the Reserve, unless she had no option and so she was thankful when he seemed disinclined to talk himself.

They crossed the boundary line and the Reserve smelled of wood-smoke, forest spice and sun-baked grass, which was beginning to cool off now, and Julia couldn't control a certain excitement at the idea that they were back.

'It's marvellous to be back,' she said, unable to keep the thought to herself. She drew a long, deep breath. 'Do you know, *blind-folded* I'd know I was back.' She turned to look at him. 'Couldn't we – would you mind, *terribly*, if we stopped for just one moment, to listen? I'd love to – listen . . .'

'I hope you know what it is you're listening to when you hear it,' he told her, but he surprised her by driving the Land Rover to the side of the road and switching off the engine.

After a few moments, they heard it – the sharp whistle of a reed-buck, and then silence settled again, heavy and mysterious.

'I've noticed,' Julia felt the need to break that silence, 'that zebra and wildebeest always seem to enjoy being together.'

Grant turned to look at her. His blue eyes fell on her mouth and then they met hers. 'They appear to have a strong affinity for each other. Well, have you heard what it is you wanted to hear?'

'Yes,' she answered. 'Thank you.'

He made to start the engine but turned again, instead, to look at her. He was grinning. 'And did you – er – recognize what it was you were listening to?'

'Yes,' she turned away from him. 'It was a reed-buck.'

She held her breath to see if he'd laugh, because she had taken a wild guess and then he said, 'Well, what do you know?'

Automatically, she released the little breath which, for some unknown reason, sounded like the hiss of a pressure-cooker. Grant laughed and the movement, beside her, told her that he had turned to look at her again. 'You weren't quite sure, were you?' he asked. 'That was a shot in the dark – if ever there was one.'

She turned her head so that it appeared that she was glancing over her shoulder at something, but in fact it was so that he would not see the laughter which threatened her. 'We covered that in our curriculum,' she told him, and had to put her fingers over her mouth.

'Yeah,' he answered, 'I'm sure you did.'

Several warthog raised their tails and fled as the Land Rover approached them. 'Oh, aren't they just too sweet for words?' It was a stupid thing to say, but she couldn't think of anything else to say about these ugly but strangely quaint little animals.

'What's so sweet about them?'

Becoming exasperated with him, she said, 'I should have said quaint, I suppose. Would that have satisfied you?'

'I'm never satisfied,' he replied, turning to look at her, and she couldn't help noticing that his eyes were on her mouth again and she turned from him quickly, her eyes blurred with thought and her fingers active at the bamboo handles of her bag. She wondered whether Grant Tyler was slightly deaf and had to do a certain amount of lip-reading.

Nearer the camp they saw visitors still prowling about in their cars looking for the game which, regardless of the cars and the people in them, still followed an ancient pattern of living by grazing up-wind.

Grant slowed down outside the offices and Julia said, 'Thank you for the lift. If my father is there will you tell him that I've gone on home?'

Without glancing at her, Grant said carelessly, 'Certainly I'll do that – if he's there.'

It had been a day of errors, on her part, she thought, as she walked slowly up the grassy 'island' with the looped road going right round it. In the centre of the island were the three bungalows. Grant Tyler's lawn had a tamboti tree growing in the centre of it. She always noticed the tree.

Within a week, the light truck bringing the furniture arrived in the Reserve and Julia lost no time in asking Roberta Bramley over to see what she had bought, but Roberta disappointed her by being tired and listless. 'I started this pregnancy so well,' she was saying, casually fingering the scatter cushions. 'That's what I can't understand, Julia. Now, I just feel,' she spread her hands, dropping one of the scatter cushions, 'well – so awful! I just can't stand this heat. I get all prickly and I feel positively ill.'

'Cheer up, Roberta.' Julia picked up the scatter cushion and then went towards the new cane cocktail trolley where the ice-cubes were dwindling to nothing in the jug of lime juice. She began to pour the juice into tall glasses. 'It will soon be over and you'll have your little bundle of joy on the *outside*.' She turned to pass Roberta a glass. 'Won't that be wonderful?'

Roberta made a face and sighed. 'Soon? It seems like another whole lifetime to me.' She took a sip of her lime juice. 'Even lime juice gets on my nerves,' she said.

'What do you think of this colour?' Julia asked, putting down her own glass and touching the Indian raw silk.

'Colours make me feel bilious, right now.' Roberta made another face. 'Sorry, Julia, it's lovely, of course. I'm just a misery to myself and to other people, especially poor Carl. I'll have to get away from him for a while. I'll let you have my sewing machine. I'll have it sent over this afternoon. I've finished all my nighties for the nursing-home and the things for the baby, so keep it for as long as you like. Apart from that, Julia, I'm definitely going to my parents for a few weeks – or even a bit longer. Carl absolutely insists that I go. He says not for his sake but for my sake.'

Aware of a surge of disappointment at the prospect of losing Roberta, Julia said, 'Oh, Roberta, I'm going to miss you madly. Honestly I am. What am I going to do without you?'

'Oh well, it will give you a chance to do your redecorating in peace.' Suddenly Roberta laughed and Julia had a glimpse of how Roberta could be – or must have been before she began to feel so hot and uncomfortable. 'Actually, I'd only get on your nerves. When I'm well I'm an awful chatterbox, you know.'

It was in the midst of Julia's cutting out and sewing and arranging and rearranging furniture that Roberta left the Reserve, but nevertheless, after Carl had driven her away it seemed very quiet and the shadows and the loneliness moved in from the bush because the tourists, of course, played no active part in Julia's life.

'I'd like to join the tourists this morning, and go out in the car,' she said to her father during breakfast. 'I'll sew this afternoon. I feel all restless at seeing Roberta go.'

'Good idea.' Stan smiled absently across the new cane dining table. 'You know to keep to the car, of course?'

'Yes. Anyway, I don't intend to go far – just down the way and along some of those little loop roads.' As she looked at her father she wondered fleetingly whether it was her imagination or whether his face was, in fact, tired and drawn.

She drove down into the valley and began to feel relaxed in her yellow slacks and shirt, blue rope-soled canvas shoes and her hair under a bright yellow scarf. Then, changing to a lower gear, she took one of the loop roads which led out of the valley and up to a hill which flattened out at the top and offered a marvellous view of the surrounding hills, hazy and far-away in the morning heat. She switched off the engine and, in the silence which followed, she sighed deeply.

There was not a soul in sight, not even the purr of an approaching visitor's car, and she was thankful for this. Nearby, some large boulders shimmered in the sun as they steadily became warmer. With not a sign of game there was nothing to stop her from going over to the boulders, where she would have an even better view. The sun beckoned her as it shimmered and danced on the smooth boulders and she sat pondering – tempted and yet afraid. Opening the door, she slipped one slimly trousered leg out into the sunshine and narrowed her eyes as she looked up into the blue vault of the sky. A vulture poised before it wheeled down in great, slow wide circles to the stunted, flat-topped trees below. Nearby, some leaves rustled in the breeze and Julia turned sharply, drawing her leg back into the car, but when she saw nothing, she smiled at herself and waited until her heart regained its usual slow beat. She wondered what she would have done if she had seen a rhinoceros appearing from behind the boulders and, apprehensively, she turned, then, still seeing nothing but flattened grass, she put out her leg and stood up.

It was thrilling to let the sun and the air have their way with her and she undid the top two buttons of her shirt. She knew that she was breaking one of the golden rules – that of getting out of the car without a Game Guide at her side – but she could see no harm in it – not here, where there appeared to be no animals and no people to report her to the authorities. Her eyes scanned the old grassy paths, trodden flat by animals. Nearby, a harmless little cricket chirped noisily and persistently, but the sound was strangely relaxing; then far, far back somewhere something barked – a querulous sound – and she wondered what it was.

The sun caressed her face and the white strip of flesh which the undone buttons had exposed as she began to walk away from the car towards the boulders.

How it happened she never knew, but when she found herself face to face with a warthog on the other side of the boulders, she nearly collapsed from shock. She held her breath while both of them stood terrified and while Julia's heart thumped in resonance with the warthog's.

Over the short space which divided them, she was aware of the animal's panic and wonder before it turned quickly and fled, tail up. For a few moments Julia stood, alert and excited, afraid to move in case there were other animals about.

'What the devil do you think you're doing out of that car?' At the sound of Grant Tyler's voice she swung round and then her eyes went past him as she wondered frantically why she had not heard the Land Rover. But the Land Rover was nowhere in sight and she knew that he must have walked up the hill, to one side of the boulders. Looking back at Grant Tyler again she struggled to keep the nervousness she was feeling from not showing.

'I asked you a question.' He walked towards her, tall and slender, a lithe, self-possessed young Game Ranger with a tanned, handsome face. 'Why didn't you answer me?'

Partly from bravado and partly for fun, because she knew what was coming, she said, 'Maybe because I didn't like the tone of your voice. You see, I don't like authority.'

Suddenly there was no longer a part for her to play. Those had been his very words on the day he had brought her to Umkambo. In any event, a clash was immediate between them.

'I can't take this lightly,' he said curtly. 'You know the rules here.'

'I know about the rules – but who cares about rules?' Julia asked, who cared the most. 'In any case I ...'

'You what?' The blue eyes had turned to granite. This led her to rashness.

'I don't take orders.'

'Well, you should give it a try,' he replied coldly.

Julia looked at him with grudging respect and felt inadequate. 'It's so silly,' she began to argue with him. 'There's not a thing in sight.' With a stab of guilt she kept quiet about the startled warthog and she felt suddenly ashamed.

'It will be hard on you, Julia,' he said, surprising her by using her first name, 'if you go against advice. Let me tell you how it is here, just in case you haven't acquainted yourself with the rules. African Game Guides have been assigned to show tourists the animals they've come to see, and the rule is to protect the tourists from their own foolishness which might cause their own death – or, quite probably, the death of some animal – but I won't bore you with the details.'

'But I don't see how all this involves *me*,' she said, with a carelessness she did not feel. 'After all, I'm not a tourist, am I? It would be utterly ridiculous for me to expect to have the services of a Game Guide all to myself every time I decided to leave the bungalow.'

A slight flush came over Grant's handsome face. 'I'm only too well aware of the fact that you aren't a tourist. I wish to heaven you were, to be perfectly frank with you, because in that case you wouldn't be here for very long. Get this straight, it's not up to you to lay down the laws in the Reserve.'

With one hand raised, to shield her green eyes from the

sun, she squinted sulkily at him, like a child. 'I think you're being stupid and unreasonable,' she told him. 'I made perfectly sure that there were no signs of game before I got out of the car. This spot seems to be utterly,' she dropped her hand and gestured widely, '*empty* of game. It must be *terribly* disappointing to the tourists. No wonder there are no cars here.'

'Don't fool yourself,' he said.

'Look,' she said, feeling a kind of fear and rage for him in equal parts. Rage won. 'You can see for miles and miles.'

She broke off as he took a step towards her, 'Look,' he snapped back, 'why don't you keep yourself buttoned up?'

He took hold of her shoulders roughly and then began to button her shirt, which she had quite forgotten about, then he exhaled with slow deliberation as he pushed her from him while she hoped that she was not too visibly shaken.

'While you're about it,' she replied in a voice she knew must have sounded absurd, 'why don't you force me back to the car, like a child, and finished with it?'

He gave her a long look before he said, 'That's just what I plan to do, as a matter of fact,' and a shiver of excitement went over her before she dodged him, like a sleek, wild animal.

'I'm quite capable of getting myself back to the car.' Her breath was fast. 'You wouldn't *dare* touch me!'

'I wouldn't rely too much on that, if I were you,' he retorted, as she began to take her time about swaggering back to the car. At the door she stopped to remove the yellow scarf from her head and she flung back her hair impatiently. 'I'm sick and tired of you, *Gordon* Tyler,' she said, deliberately getting his name wrong.

'And that happens to go for me too.' There was disgust in his voice. 'I'm sick and tired of you too.'

She opened the door and then she turned to look at him. 'Yes, so you keep reminding me.' Her face was set and she felt sick inside.

As she put one leg into the car he said, 'Another thing – not that it matters, one way or the other, but the name happens to be *Grant*.'

Julia bit her lip, not trusting herself to reply, and then she slipped into the driver's seat and started the engine.

On her way back down the hill she saw his Land Rover

parked some way off beneath some thorn trees and she realized that Grant Tyler must have been there all along and that he must have seen her drive to the spot where she finally decided to get out.

With a growing despair she began to wonder whether Grant would speak to her father about the shocking scene on the hill.

CHAPTER FOUR

REDECORATING the bungalow took up most of Julia's time for the next fortnight and she was becoming increasingly thrilled with the results. Purposely, she kept away from Grant Tyler and from the office where she might just come face to face with him.

'The bungalow is looking very attractive,' Stan Munro said, before he went out one morning. 'I must congratulate you on a fine job.'

'Wait until you see it when the curtains have been hung,' Julia told him, as she saw him to the glass doors which led on to the verandah. 'Actually, I am going to hang the curtains this morning. I've been meaning to ask you – have you got a step-ladder I can use?'

Her father stroked his chin. 'I don't believe I have. Can't remember ever having to use one myself. You probably noticed my curtains – stretched across on a piece of elastic. To hang them, I merely stood on a kitchen chair. Now it's all ruffle-tape and what-have-you.' He grinned at Julia. 'Try Grant's place. It's possible he might have one.'

'I'd rather do without than ask Grant Tyler.' Her eyes met his and she let her glance fall.

'Quite obviously you have something against Grant.' Her father gave her another searching look. 'What's he done to you?'

She shrugged her shoulders. 'Nothing really, and yet – everything. We just don't seem to get along very well. He seems to be under the impression that he can take his woman-hater feelings out on *me*.'

'Carl's away, of course.' Her father chose to ignore her remark about Grant Tyler. 'It's possible that Carl might have one. Send Samson over. Carl's garage is open. If he has a ladder it will most probably be in there. I'm sure he wouldn't mind your using it.'

'Oh, I'll manage. Don't worry. The kitchen table will do just as well. The windows aren't that high.'

'Well, watch you don't fall. If you care to wait until this evening you can show me what to do and I'll hang them.'

Julia flashed him a smile. 'I'm far too impatient to wait until tonight!'

After her father left, she got Samson to bring the kitchen table through to the living-room for her and then she told him that she could attend to the rest herself. When the knock on the glass door came she was so utterly engrossed in what she was doing that she nearly fell off the table. To her acute embarrassment she saw Grant Tyler standing at the open glass doors.

'If you're looking for my father,' she stared across at him frigidly, 'he's not here. He's at the office. You should know that by now.' She felt at a disadvantage talking down at him from the table.

'I've come over for a file which Stan told me I'd find on top of the bookshelf in his room.' She saw Grant's eyes flicker round the living-room.

'I see. Well, in that case . . .' She broke off as she tried to work out which would be the easiest way to get down from the table. She knew that to Grant Tyler she must appear like a bored child looking for a game to play – housey-housey, maybe – and she bitterly resented his presence.

'You know,' he told her, coming to stand next to the table, 'I could see these moves ahead, the very first day I met you.'

'I haven't the remotest idea what you're hinting at,' she replied, knowing perfectly well what he was hinting at.

'Shall I tell you exactly what I mean? Quite apart from the bungalow not being good enough for Miss Julia Munro, dressing up and sitting around uselessly would be more honest – or simply admitting that you're bored stiff here. Who do you think you're kidding when you say you want nothing more than to make your old man more comfortable? Anyway, what else are you going to get up to when you've finished making your father's bungalow look like something out of a film set? Paint fresh stripes on the zebra?' Their eyes met and there was a stunned silence before she felt a blind rage welling up inside her.

'Have you quite finished insulting me?' she asked furiously, beginning to breathe hard, 'because, if you have, take your file and *get out*! You're nothing but an – insufferable beast!'

Looking up at her, he shrugged that one off and then he grinned. 'I must say that you don't look the Finishing School type just at the moment. I'll hand that much to you!'

'So much the better. I don't feel like a Finishing School type. For that matter, I never have.' She put out one trousered leg and made to step down on to the kitchen chair, which had held the curtains before she had hung them and which she had used as a step-up on to the table. And then, to her horror, she felt the chair begin to slip. She was beginning to fall. She could feel herself falling and there was nothing to hold on to. The chair was sliding away from the table now and she was going with it. She tried to fight the calamity, shaking all over. It needed balance. One got led into these ridiculous situations without thinking – but it could come right. One had simply to collect oneself. Going suddenly cold, though, she knew it was no good. She was going to land on her back on the floor in front of Grant Tyler. She closed her eyes and told herself that she'd *never, never* get in this position again, and as she fell he was by her side and had her by the elbows. She opened her eyes and looked up at him, her face partly covered by a tangle of tawny hair.

Grant's blue eyes were turned full force on her as he looked down at her, as though he was enjoying her shocked and furious expression.

There was a hush and something inside Julia seemed to jump violently, then Grant laughed. She felt her temper go out of control. 'Don't you laugh at me!' Her green eyes flashed as her fury mounted and she wanted, quite suddenly, to lash out at him with her hands. Steadying himself with one hand against the wall, Grant drew her close with the other and brushed her lips with his own. It was a kiss and yet it was not a kiss, and a further show of temper on her part would have appeared almost ridiculous. In fact, as he released her she began to wonder whether she had imagined it and she found herself tensing, as she waited for him to do what he most certainly intended to do, and that was to take her into his arms and kiss her properly – but he didn't. To her shocked surprise she realized that she was not sure whether she was pleased or sorry, and told herself that this was merely because she was not going to be given the opportunity of rebuffing him.

For a moment they stood, slightly apart, looking at one another with a candid gaze that withheld nothing, then he said, very softly, 'Damn you, Julia. Damn you!' She noticed that his breathing was hard. Her expression was childlike and confused and she struggled to think of something to say, but she was beaten and she watched him turn away and stride towards the glass doors.

After he had gone, she stood just where he had left her, trying to compose herself in case her father came for the file himself – or in case Samson came into the room. She felt suddenly hot and exhausted, as Roberta might have felt. Scanning the room with her eyes she let out a long breath and then began, methodically, to stack those curtains which she had not yet hung. Grant Tyler had ruined yet another day. Her face was a set mask. A film set! Pondering this, she pressed her teeth into her soft under-lip, then she walked outside on to the verandah and stepped back into the living-room, in much the same manner as a visitor would do. Then she stood examining the room with a critical eye.

Even though the room was far from finished, it looked attractive and inviting and there was nothing – nothing at all – to justify Grant Tyler's remark, she thought bitterly. The fact was that he was disappointed that it had turned out so well. He would have enjoyed seeing it a hideous flop.

Thanks to him, however, her work inside the house was finished for the day and she went outside and stood in the sunshine, her peace of mind shattered. Grant Tyler had done that for her. What was it he was trying to do to her? Except for him, she was happy here – even without Roberta it had turned out all right.

She turned and went back up to the verandah, keeping her eyes from straying to the tamboti tree in Grant's garden. Samson had closed the glass doors and she opened them, giving them a somewhat stronger push than was strictly necessary.

Going swiftly towards the stacked curtains, she said loudly, 'I don't intend being unsettled by Grant Tyler. Work will go on here – as usual! She grinned to herself. 'Everybody on set,' she said. 'Lights!'

By the time her father came in for lunch she had finished hanging all the curtains in the living-room and she had found the ideal position for both pictures – one in the dining-room and one in the living-room – and because one could take in both rooms at a glance, the pictures were so sited that they made immediate impact.

'Well, well,' Stan said, smiling, 'I take my hat off to you, Julia.' He walked around the living-room and she watched him with wide eyes. 'For a moment I thought I'd come into the wrong bungalow!'

With some of her good humour recovered Julia said, 'It *does* look attractive, doesn't it? And it was all done on a shoe-string. It really cost very little.' She stood with her thumbs hooked in at the waist band of the faded blue denim jeans, which she had worn when gardening at Azalea Park, and she swung her slender hips from side to side, then she went across to one of the windows and lifted a fold of the material and, as she did so, she noticed that she had broken two finger-nails. For a moment she studied them, frowning a little, and then, on an impulse, she said, 'Tell me, does it look like something out of a *film-set* to you?'

'Yes,' he replied, looking around. 'It does, somehow, I think, although it's a damn long time ago since I saw a film. But it does give the impression of a film setting. It's very striking.'

Staggered, Julia looked at him.

'Have I said something wrong?' he asked, and in the silence which followed she sighed deeply.

'Yes.' The word was abrupt and she turned away from him. 'I hoped you wouldn't say that, actually.' She swung round. 'In what way? In what way does it remind you of a film set, apart from being – striking? By striking do you mean – overdone?' She hooked her thumbs back into the waist band of her jeans and her yellow shirt rose and fell as her breathing became quicker.

'It's certainly not overdone. It's just right. It's colourful, for one thing. Exciting – it's certainly exciting, Julia, even to someone like me who is out of touch with things. At the same time, though, you've – very successfully, I think – made it appear casual enough to suit the conditions here.' He smiled and his teeth looked very white in his tanned face. 'For all its suggestion of casualness it looks as though somebody had taken a lot of time working that side of it out, and I suppose that's exactly what you did, eh? It's very clever – it's just right.' He raised his eyebrows slightly. 'Who said it wasn't?' His smile became an amused and questioning grin, and this maddened her.

'Your *bush-happy* Game Ranger Grant Tyler said it wasn't. That's who!' She removed her thumbs from her jeans again and began to pace the room in a workmanlike manner, but looking very feminine, for all her sun-bleached jeans and wild tawny hair and green eyes. Impatiently, she ran her fingers through her hair. 'Oh,' she clenched her teeth, 'he makes me sick, that man – and he'd better just leave me alone from now on! That's all I can say.'

Stan Munro chose to ignore this remark and walked over to the cocktail trolley and helped himself to a drink. 'I'd forgotten how it was to feel like this,' he said, lifting his glass. 'How it was to appreciate *inside* – as well as outside.' His green eyes focused on a point beyond the room, in the direction of the tamboti trees on the other side of the sandy road which looped right round the three bungalows.

'Well,' Julia's smile was slow, 'I'm glad. I'm very glad. That's how I want it to be. This is our home, after all. If only you knew how much I've longed for a home—' She broke off in confusion and noticed how her father had flushed slightly.

He lifted his eyes. 'You're a home girl, all right,' he said, very softly. 'I forgot to take that into consideration when I parted with you.'

'All I've always wanted was to be with you.' Her own response was also soft. 'But you did what you thought was best.' She shrugged inside the yellow shirt. 'I suppose it *was* right.'

She stood regarding him and she knew that he was still a good-looking man – fairly tall, lean and handsome in his khaki clothes. His face was clean-shaven and evenly tanned and his hair streaked with silver at the sides – but he looked tired.

'Are you tired?' she asked suddenly.

He stood for a moment, cradling the empty glass in his hand, and then he went back to the trolley and put it down and it made a little click as glass hit glass.

'Nothing serious.' He sighed very lightly. 'I have to have one or two blood tests done soon. Routine stuff. Have to have it done, from time to time. Should have told you about it, I suppose, but I preferred just to let things ride.'

'What is it?' she asked, in a frightened little voice. 'As you say, you should have told me.'

His voice was suddenly strained. 'If we look at things in the best possible light – it's absolutely nothing to worry about. I guess it's all a case of the correct diet. Somebody has said that living is a matter of glandular efficiency brought about by correct eating habits. Every now and then my doctor pulls me up sharply about not sticking to a fat-free diet, gives me a course of pills and injections and I'm as right as rain again.'

Something took Julia by the throat – an invisible thing called fear. 'Where do you go for this – check-up? Into hospital? You can't possibly travel from here every day.'

'No, I can't. I spend one or two days in hospital in Hlageni.'

'One or two days?' They stared into each other's eyes. 'What do you mean by one or two days? One or two days could mean anything – a week, two weeks, four ...' Her voice trailed away.

'Grant Tyler and Carl Bramley will keep an eye on you. As you say, a day or two could cover anything up to two weeks.' He sounded dubious, and she fought back her irritation which was working hand in hand with fear.

'You aren't sure?'

'No, not exactly – but it's never for very long. The going into hospital is just to save trouble. Under normal circumstances people would have this treatment at home, without undue inconvenience.'

'When are you due for another check-up?'

He slipped his hands into his pockets and stood looking at her unhappily. 'Within the next few days. I'm sorry to have to spring this on you. You'll be all right here, Julia. It's quite safe.'

'It's not *me* I'm worrying about. It's *you*.' Her sun-bronzed face was hurt and her green eyes shadowed with concern. 'I didn't know. Nobody told me.' She moistened her lips with her tongue and swallowed. 'All the time I've been,' she gestured hopelessly, 'fiddling around here, making curtains and moving furniture and this and that – and the next thing I didn't even know.' She expelled a breath and thought for a moment before she said, 'Does Grant Tyler know about this – about you?' The idea was like a shock to her.

'Yes, he knows. You know now.'

'Yes.' She tried not to show her distress – for his sake.

'I want you to know, Julia, that this isn't serious. I have to have these blood tests done and that's all there is to it. If necessary I have a course of injections and some pills, but it has to be done there – at Hlageni. I can't change that.'

'No, of course not. I can see that to have the treatment here would be impossible,' she smiled.

'What about lunch?' he asked.

She grinned at him. 'I'm going to be far more fussy about those lunches and dinners now, believe me. You're a very wicked man!'

In the afternoon, storm clouds began to gather and then later, in the gathering dusk, they rolled and curled over and settled darkly over the Reserve.

On her way back from a stroll, as far as the hut accommodation for tourists, Julia could smell rain. A gust of wind thrust itself through the restless leaves and a lone bird flew high. From time to time the bruised and battered clouds were illuminated from within by braided gold lightning. By the time she reached the bungalow the thunder, which had just been a distant growl and a vague threat, became louder. After one alarmingly loud clap, the rain started.

It was still pelting down and thundering by the time Julia and her father decided to go to bed.

The storm made Julia restless and she roamed about her room, moving first one thing and then another. The lightning worried her, as it flashed through her father's drab unlined curtains, and she vowed that she would start on her own room next – beginning with the new curtains which she intended should have a good lining.

Eventually it was the lightning which drove her to bed, and when she turned off the light she placed her fingers over her eyes. Every time there was a clap of thunder and the lightning seemed to pierce right through her fingers

67

and her eyelids she experienced a moment of panic and tried to take her mind off the storm by thinking of Grant Tyler. Then she tried *not* to think of him – to fight him off – along with the restlessness and the fear she was feeling. She tried to erase Grant, feature by feature, from her mind.

Why did he have to be here at Umkambo? Why was there *always* a Grant Tyler *everywhere*? She took her hands from her eyes and rolled over on her stomach, burying her face in the pillow to try to keep out the lightning. The pillow-slip felt damp and the sheets also felt damp, and she knew that morning was going to be a long time in coming.

It was a long time in coming and, into the bargain, it rained for three days, so to keep herself occupied Julia worked in the bungalow. On the fourth day she awoke to the magical sounds of a sunny day, mysterious and exciting. From her window she could see the changing angles of the sun on green leaves and the greens became exceedingly variable. She lay for a few moments longer, enjoying the fresh smell of damp earth and listening to the birds singing. Not very far from the camp the game would be enjoying the sun too. The rhinoceros, with his long curved horn and his black piggish eyes, would be standing in that almost absent-minded way of his, beneath the thorn trees. The thorn trees would appear almost silver in the strengthening sun. Visitors, going out, would be sure to see impala giving exhibitions of fantastic jumping. Flinging back the sheets, Julia knew that she had to be a part of all this. She would go out in the car, providing the roads were all right, of course, after the rain.

During breakfast she said, 'I think I'll go out this morning – be a tourist, for a change. It would be nothing short of a crime to stay indoors today. Will the roads be all right? I wish you didn't have to go to the office.'

'I'm not going to the office until later,' Stan told her. 'I want to go out myself for a little while. Would you like to join me? I'll be going in a Land Rover.'

'Oh?' She raised curious green eyes. 'Where are you going?'

'I'm going down to the river. By the way, you won't have to get out of the Land Rover. So far as you're concerned, it will just be a drive.'

'Well, that will be fine. I'll have to change, of course. Will you give me time?' He was already dressed, but she was still in her short floral housecoat.

Her father glanced at his watch. 'I'll give you just ten minutes.' He was obviously pleased that she was going with him, and he did not seem to notice the white kid boots she was wearing when she eventually joined him outside.

Julia had bought the boots during the winter months, when they were in full swing. Everybody was wearing them and she had taken Samantha's advice about buying them when she had gone to Johannesburg with Samantha. They had offered Julia's elegant long legs some sort of protection from the wind which seemed to cut right through one as it swept round the corners of Johannesburg's skyscrapers.

The calf-length boots, which she had decided to wear with a cobalt-blue skirt and a fine white cashmere sweater, seemed to be the very thing to wear for a ride in a Land Rover after four days of rain.

'This is fun,' she said, settling down, next to her father.

'Do you think so?' He returned her smile and his smile was very like her own – slow and serene.

Julia nodded. Everything looked beautiful after the rain. Through the rain-washed foliage the molten rays of sunlight strengthened and gleamed.

Stan drove out to a crocodile nesting site, on the river bank, then Julia's heart sank as she saw Grant Tyler's Land Rover parked nearby.

'You – you didn't tell me *he* was going to be here,' she said, thinking about how she had spent half the night seething over Grant Tyler again. She seemed to do nothing else when she was alone.

Her father gave her a shrewd look. 'You don't have to get out. In fact, I didn't intend you to – not down there, anyway. Besides, to put your mind at rest, Tyler is going on somewhere else. He'll probably leave here before we do, as a matter of fact.'

'I hope so.' There was a disconcerted silence and then her father got out of the Land Rover and, from where she sat, Julia was able to watch him disappear from sight, as he went behind a screen of bush and overhanging weeds and creepers.

She stretched her long legs and closed her eyes. The sun slanted across her and she delighted in the feel of it. Some time later she was roused by the voices of her father and Grant, who had left the river and who were now standing near to the Land Rover. Without turning her head, Julia listened to them discussing the fine cracks which had developed on the eggs – because of the rain, no doubt, she thought, with a certain amount of satisfaction. Serve the handsome, bush-happy Game Ranger right. She hoped that it would interfere with his precious experiments and then sat bolt upright. 'But, Julia,' she said sweetly to herself in a secret corridor of her mind, 'you never *used* to be so *spiteful*!' Her mouth twitched slightly. It was true, she thought. Grant Tyler had done that to her – along with bringing out all the worst in her. It was a staggering thought. Apart from a lot of frivolous nonsense at Azalea Park and all the darling this and darling that she was really rather serious-minded and certainly not inclined to be spiteful. A sigh escaped her. She had a temper, of course, and knew how to use it, but then who didn't?

'How many inches were recorded, did you say?' Her father's voice put an end to her thoughts.

'Two – over the three days.' Automatically, she tensed as Grant answered.

They were moving on now, she could tell by their voices and they were coming towards the Land Rover.

Grant gave no indication of having seen her and she felt a rage rising against him.

She looked at her father. 'Did you see – what it was you came to see?'

'Yes.'

A spark of devilry made her ask, 'And did you *recognize* what it was you came to see? Some people don't you know.'

Stan looked puzzled for a moment. 'Yes,' he said. 'Fifty per cent of the embryos in Group Three have died, if that means anything to you, Julia.'

She felt suddenly sorry and guilty. 'Oh.' She blinked as she thought this over. 'Why? Why did they die? The rain?'

'That's right. The rain. The eggs containing the dead embryos had developed fine cracks.' He opened the door.

'Come and get some sun,' he said. 'Here are the binoculars. See if you can find something. Buffalo up there, on the hill – eh, Grant? See them Julia? Able to pick them up? They look just like a dark shadow.'

She stepped out on to the grass, which felt mushy beneath her boots, and began to focus the binoculars on the distant hill, her eyes tracking down the buffalo. 'Oh, I can see them.' She became excited. 'A *terrific* herd! They won't charge, will they?' She lowered the glasses and looked at her father. Purposely, she avoided Grant.

'You'll see better from over there.' It was Grant who answered, and he pointed to a small clearing in the grass. There was a small twitch to his mouth and, not noticing the trap which was being laid for her, Julia started to walk towards the clearing.

She was not quite sure how it happened – but then she never was, she thought bitterly, not when she was with Grant Tyler – but suddenly she was up to her ankles in thick mud. The marvellous morning turned into a flop and she stood, with eyes closed and teeth clenched, while she heard Grant call out, 'Oh, bad *luck* there!' Just as if she had missed a ball in a game of tennis. Slowly, she drew in a breath – and knew that it would be a long one. 'Such nice *white* boots, too. Pity about that,' Grant said again.

The breath was completely drawn now and she felt that her lungs were going to burst. She turned, releasing the breath as she did so, and then her eyes were full of shock when she saw that Grant was studying her with a certain detached amusement, curious to know what her reaction was going to be.

Somehow she managed to control herself – until he laughed. 'Well, there's a thing,' he said, and her eyes rested on the laughter lines in his cheek while she was thinking furiously, 'That type usually do – they usually have twin lines in their cheeks.'

'Why look at *me* like that?' He laughed again at her outraged expression. His eyes were so blue, so shadowed by those thick black lashes – until you saw the lights behind the shadows.

The surge of humiliation she was feeling gave way to temper and, stooping, she removed the muddy boots with some difficulty because the zips at the back would give trouble just at a time like this. When they were off, she walked back to the Land Rover, giving particular care to the kind of swagger she had learned at Azalea Park. She carried the boots in one hand and could feel the mud oozing between her toes.

When she had thrown the boots into the Land Rover she came back to stand next to her father. Mud was still oozing up from under the green grass, and it curled like innocent butter between her toes with their defenceless pink-lacquered nails. She tried not to look at them – to forget them and she could almost *feel* her father's and Grant Tyler's sensible footwear.

'Sorry about that.' Stan Munro added to her humiliation in his concern for her.

'Forget it,' she said snappily. 'I have. It's not serious.' Guiltily, she thought about how she must have sounded to her poor father and so she turned to smile at him, though it cost her much to do it.

'Well, Stan,' Grant said, 'I'm off.' He sounded highly satisfied – the disappointment of the cracked eggs forgotten.

'Don't let us keep you,' Julia retorted. Suddenly she hated Grant Tyler very much.

After he had driven away her father said, almost gently, 'You don't want to take too much notice of Grant Tyler. Even his best friends wouldn't describe him as being subtle.'

Julia shaded her eyes with one hand. 'I didn't think he *had* any friends,' she said, 'apart, of course, from his *animal* friends.'

She saw that her attempt at indifference was not going to work, after all, and she dropped her hand from her eyes. 'I *hate* him,' she said, her voice strangled with anger.

Her father put his arms around her and let her cry there. 'Sorry,' she said. 'It's just – I'm just – so humiliated. Why did it have to happen in front of him – and in those stupid boots?' Stan stroked her hair. 'I'm sorry, Dad.' It was the first time she'd called him that, and it made her cry all the more and she had the feeling, as his arms tightened about her, that he might have been crying himself. Well, that was something else Grant Tyler had done, she thought. Only this time it had paid off.

For the next few days, she concentrated on finishing

decorating the bungalow.

When Grant Tyler came over, to have a drink one evening with her father, she kept out of his way and made excuses when her father invited her to join them.

During dinner, after Grant had gone, Stan Munro sat back and studied Julia for a moment before he said, 'Julia, I'll be going into hospital for a few days. Randle wants to see me again.'

There was a sickening jolt in the pit of her stomach. 'Randle, of course, is your doctor?'

'Yes. I'm going to ask him to have a word with you – to put your mind at rest.'

When she made no effort to answer he said, 'Cheer up. Don't look so stricken, my dear girl. It's all routine stuff, Julia. I've explained it all, haven't I?' Julia had a feeling that he was becoming a little impatient with all this attention focused upon himself. 'A few blood tests to be done, and so on. I warned you this would happen.'

Biting her lip, she said, 'Yes, I know you did, but somehow, I suppose I didn't want to believe that it would happen. When is it to be?'

'Next week, some time. I'm waiting for word from Randle. Grant will take me into town, but you'll come too, of course. When you've spoken to Randle you won't be so worried. Like everything else, it could lead to – things,' he shrugged. 'These precautions have to be taken, from time to time. It's as simple as that, really.' He stood up and smiled down at her stricken face. 'You'll be all right here. I've arranged with Carl and—' he hesitated, 'Grant to keep an eye on you. It's perfectly safe here.'

'I'm not worried about that,' she retorted, stung by the fact that once again Grant Tyler had to be involved in her life. 'I can look after myself.'

On the day that Grant drove them into town, however, Julia realized that it was Grant she would have to turn to if anything should happen to her father, and the thought gave her little comfort.

Stan Munro was admitted into hospital and Julia and Grant went outside into the sunshine. 'My father arranged for me to speak to Dr. Randle,' she told him, glancing at the big clock at the entrance to the building. 'I have to see him in ten minutes' time, in his office, here at the hospital.

'I'll try not to keep you waiting too long.'

'Please don't hurry. I'll be in the foyer.' For once there was no sarcasm in the tone of Grant's voice.

'I want to be told the truth about my father.' Her voice was taut, as she felt the necessity to confide in someone. 'I'm terribly worried. I wish he hadn't kept me quite so much in the dark. I didn't know ...' There was despair in her voice. 'How was I to know?'

'Your father has to undergo certain tests,' Grant told her. 'You – he has acquainted you with the facts. Why don't you accept them?'

The interview with Dr. Randle left her feeling very much more satisfied and the sense of relief was almost too much for her.

'Well?' In the foyer Grant's eyes searched hers. 'Are you satisfied?'

'Yes. I can't tell you how relieved I feel. I couldn't be all that sure that my father wasn't keeping something from me.'

'I'm going to take you to tea,' Grant said. 'You feel like tea, don't you?' He took her arm protectively, surprising her.

'More than you'll ever know!' There was a catch in her voice.

He took her for tea at a small place and he allowed her to talk about her father without interrupting her.

On the way back to Umkambo he said, 'I want you to come and have dinner at my place when we get back.'

She gave him a doubtful look. 'Oh! Thank you – but Samson will have prepared something for me.'

He turned to grin at her. 'He won't, you know.'

'Why not? What's happened to Samson?' She looked enquiringly at him.

'I gave Samson instructions not to cook for you, this morning, before we left. I've decided to be very civil to you and to our friend Carl Bramley, who has returned from the bush after three days, and I've decided to act as mine host to you both. I left word for Carl.'

She was silent for a few moments, then she said, 'That was very thoughtful of you. Thank you.' She was thinking that she had never been to Grant's bungalow, with the tamboti tree on the front lawn, and, woman-like, her mind was groping about inside her wardrobe as she wondered what she should wear to dine with the two Game Rangers.

Grant dropped her off at the Munro bungalow and called after her, 'About six-thirty, then, for a drink first. That should give you time to relax over a hot bath.'

Although Stan Munro was more often than not away from home at this time of the day Julia felt the silence immediately she entered the bungalow. It was something she couldn't explain and she was surprised that the aloof and sarcastic Grant Tyler should have had some sort of insight into what her feelings might have been on this first night without her father.

As a sharp contrast to the day's oppressive heat the evening had grown wonderfully cool. The warm bath soothed and relaxed her and, when she had finished, she went to her wardrobe and was pleased to see the well-filled hangers there, although she had known right from the start that she would not be able to wear half of the things which hung there.

She finally decided to wear another of her slack suits which, although not too elaborate, was, on the other hand, meant for evening wear. It was the orange colour of a burning candle and the top had just a trace of beadwork. Slipping her bare feet into gold-strapped sandals, she wondered what Grant would have to think about them. He would be sure to let her know that, once again, she had done the wrong thing by wearing them. She knew enough to realize that there was always the possibility of treading upon a night adder. Still, she'd be perfectly safe if she took a torch along with her.

When she was ready, she went along to Grant's bungalow where she stood for a moment beneath the tamboti tree, looking up at it. The tree had always held some sort of fascination for her, possibly because she associated it with Grant's bungalow and for the simple reason that Samson had told her a little about the tree which was otherwise known as a sandalwood. He had explained that the wood from the tamboti, if used for firewood beneath a cooking-pot, could cause food poisoning. In fact, many Africans flatly refused to cook food made on fires of this wood. Her father had also pointed out the trees in the Reserve and had explained that beautiful dark glossy furniture could be turned out from the hard wood, while Zulu girls used the powdered wood as perfume and the black wood, running through the centre of the trunk, to make scented necklaces.

'What's so interesting about a tamboti tree?' Carl Bramley's cheerful voice made her look towards the verandah, where he and Grant were sitting. 'We're dying of thirst here!'

A surge of excitement shot through Julia for no good reason at all, except that it seemed suddenly very thrilling to be dining alone with two handsome, sun-tanned Game Rangers.

'I'm coming,' she called back, beginning to walk towards them. 'I was just admiring the tamboti tree. It looks marvellous from our place, at night, with the moon shining through the branches.'

When she reached the verandah Grant was pulling a cane chair forward. 'What will you have to drink?' He turned to look at her. 'How about a long, cold shandy?' He gave her what, for him, was a surprisingly friendly smile.

'Thank you, I'd like that very much indeed.' She sat down, the slack suit accentuating her perfect figure. She looked very conspicuous.

Politely, and shyly, she asked after Roberta and then sat sipping her shandy while she listened to Carl outlining the last three days to Grant, which had something to do with poachers. 'I'm dead beat,' he said, 'and longing to hit the hay, Grant.'

Grant's bungalow awakened a flood of exciting associations to Julia – the furniture, also of cane but of a more conventional style than her own, the attractive lamp, with its intricately patterned pottery base – very much like the lamps she had chosen herself. She wondered at his sarcastic remarks about her efforts at redecorating her father's bungalow.

The lamp had been turned on, although it was not quite dark, and the floor-to-ceiling bookshelves were, no doubt, Grant's handiwork. It was all very unexpected and exciting and she was glad that she had chosen something glamorous to wear. Although this was the first time that she had visited the bungalow it had a certain feeling of intimacy that seemed to calm her nerves.

Before they sat down to dinner Grant's African servant lit candles.

During the meal Carl kept smothering yawns and then finally with an apologetic smile, he asked Julia to excuse his bad manners.

'It's not the company, I can assure you,' he said. 'The fact is I'm half asleep on my feet.'

'That's quite all right,' Julia smiled back, and sipped her wine, which she knew had been brought out by Grant as something special.

It was such a relief to be able to relax in Grant's company for just this once, she thought, almost liking him for being so hospitable when she needed something like this.

Eventually, Carl stood up. 'You'll have to excuse me if I buzz off early, Grant,' he was saying. 'I must get some sleep before I pass out.'

Once again Julia told Carl how much she was missing Roberta, and it was then that she noticed the secret glance which was being exchanged between the two Rangers and she knew without a doubt that, without her father and without Roberta Bramley in the Reserve, she was just a nuisance to these two men.

As though he had noticed what she was thinking Carl said quickly, a bit too quickly, she thought, 'How's the painting going, Grant?'

Shrugging one khaki-clad shoulder, Grant said, off-handedly, 'Oh, I haven't done much. I have to be in the mood.'

Julia looked at him with interest. She had often wondered what Grant did in his spare time. However, she remained quiet, not wanting to fall into the old feminine trap of, 'Oh, do you *paint*? How *marvellous*! I'd adore to see them some time, when you have time?'

There was going to be no falling into traps. Not tonight.

She turned to look at Carl as he began explaining to her about Grant's painting. 'Grant has rigged up a studio for himself. It was to have been the nursery, one day, but ...' he broke off and gave Grant a friendly shove, 'old buddy here was too smart – or was it the other way round? I can't remember.'

Grant's face was like stone. The candlelight gave unusual colours to the amber beadwork on the candle-flame coloured slack suit as Julia's breathing became tight. Disconcerted, she said, 'Well, I must be going too ...'

The African servant passed them, on his way to the living-room, with a tray containing coffee things, and Julia looked after him helplessly.

'Show us what you're busy on, before we have coffee, and then after that I must push off,' said Carl, oblivious to the feeling he had created.

For a moment Grant seemed about to refuse, and then he said, 'Well, come along.' He gave Carl a slap on the back. 'I didn't know you were quite so interested, old boy!'

He led the way into a white corridor where there was a small table with another lamp on it. Then he stood to one side for Julia to enter a room. He turned on the light and she saw that there was a trestle at the far end of the room which was loaded neatly with painting gear. There was also a shadow-board on the wall and various tools were hooked to it. Several paintings were propped up against the walls.

Grant was apparently busy on a seascape and, turning to him, Julia showed genuine interest. 'How on earth do you manage to paint a *seascape* in a Game Reserve?' she asked him.

'I have that kind of imagination,' he told her, not smiling.

She would have liked to examine the paintings, one by one, but something told her that he was tense and anxious for them to leave the studio.

Back in the living-room Grant poured the coffee himself and Julia was secretly amused. Somehow, she had half-expected him to ask her to do it.

When Carl Bramley stood up to go all her nerves struggled for guidance from somewhere and she looked round helplessly for her bag. 'I must go to ...' she began before Carl lifted a hand to stop her.

'Look,' he said, 'don't let me rush you. Your cup isn't even cold yet.' Julia saw that his dark eyes were laughing at Grant and she felt furious at this ridiculous turn of events. 'You're not rushing me,' she stammered. 'I'm also – tired.' She began to walk across the room for her bag, which she had left on the floor next to the chair she had sat on when they had first entered the living-room. When she turned again, Carl had gone. Her eyes met Grant's and there was a sudden hush before she said, 'Why didn't he – wait?'

'Because he felt that there was no need to rush you, no

78

doubt. He knew the general idea was that I invited you here, to save you being alone on the first night your father is away. You'll be used to it – to being alone – tomorrow.'

He remained standing at the glass doors to the verandah and she knew that he wanted her to go, now that Carl had gone.

'Thank you for having me,' she said, passing him on her way out. He followed her and when they were on the verandah he looked down at the gold-strapped apology for shoes. She could sense his disapproval again.

'I'll see you home.' It definitely was an invitation to leave.

'Not at all.' She opened her bag and brought out the torch. 'I've brought a torch.' She did not mention the shoes and switched on the torch, and at that particular moment, a hyena brayed somewhere in the distance and the beam of light from the torch swerved as her fingers tensed. For several seconds the sounds came regularly before they grew fainter and fainter with the distance the animal placed between itself and the camp.

Heavy and mysterious, the silence settled again, except for the sound of human voices which came from the tourist section of the camp.

'That,' Julia gulped, 'sounded a little close, didn't it?' She tried to keep her voice casual. 'Do they ever get into the camp?'

'Animal noises are louder at night,' he told her. 'He was miles away. Noises come through the quiet night air with greater clarity than during the day. You're not nervous, are you? There's no need to be.' He sounded vaguely impatient with her.

'Of course not. Do I – *look* nervous?'

'No, of course not.' She knew that he was smiling his sarcastic little twitch of a smile. 'You look very brave, in those gold sandals, actually.' He took her arm. 'A word of advice here. I'd think twice before I wore them at night, if I were you.'

'I brought a torch along. I'm not that stupid.'

'Okay,' he said, 'you're not nervous and you're not stupid.'

They stepped out on to the lawn and, overhead, the sky seemed to be alive, glowing with the incandescence of millions of stars. Grant's obvious tenseness at being left stranded with her made Julia annoyed.

'I'll go barefoot, if it suits me.' Her voice was tight. 'I can't really see what it has to do with you.'

'I'll leave that entirely to you. But it still wouldn't be very wise.' They began to cross the lawn. She had to have the last word. 'That remains to be seen.'

There was a sudden noise – a noise like a quick dry sigh – and Grant pulled her to one side and she knew, without even trying to look for it, that she had very nearly trodden on a night adder. It was the sort of thing that could only happen to her, she thought when the shock had passed.

'I guess this is your round.' She had difficulty in using her voice. 'But then it always is, isn't it? You always anticipate being in the right, don't you?'

'You should know by now that invariably I always am,' he told her curtly, and with a mixed feeling of anger and frustration she allowed him to guide her back to her father's bungalow.

CHAPTER FIVE

BEFORE Stan Munro had gone to hospital he had spent most of his evenings writing or reading, but nevertheless it was lonely for Julia without him. As she roamed about the bungalow she tried not to worry about him and to have faith in what the doctor had told her because, already, she was mistrusting every word.

She fretted about Carl Bramley and Grant Tyler, convinced as she was that to them she was nothing but a nuisance.

At the back of the bungalow somewhere she could hear Samson and his wife talking continually, and their gusty laughter, in between telling stories, was comforting somehow.

After she had changed into cool pyjamas Julia washed and creamed her face, then lay on her bed with nothing but the sheet over her. Earlier on in the evening Samson had apparently sprayed the room with mosquito-repellent, and the smell caused her a certain amount of discomfort.

Moving her legs beneath the sheet, she tried to relax and she lay, breathing quietly, but every nerve was tense and she was afraid to turn off the small lamp at her bedside.

Outside, Samson gave a loud click of disgust at something his wife had said, then this was followed by a fresh burst of laughter, with Samson joining in. Smiling, Julia turned out the light and tried to settle down, but the idea crossed her mind that there might be a snake in the room and once again she became tense.

That must have given Grant satisfaction, she thought bitterly – her nearly walking on a night-adder this evening after she had told him she'd go barefooted, if she liked. What a fool he must think her – and she was, of course.

The African voices outside were slackening off now and there was the sound of buckets being dragged over the paved area near the water tap and then, soon after, there was silence, except for the insects which whined in the moon-tinged bushes.

Because it had grown cooler Julia sat up and reached for the blanket, telling herself that she would have to learn to relax here by herself. After all, Carl and Grant were close by.

In the morning she felt moody and highly strung, but she tried to keep her thoughts orderly as she went about attending to small domestic chores in the bungalow. From the windows on one side of the house she could see down towards the tourist section of Umkambo, and the sight of the cars lined up ready to go out to look for game and to take photographs made her feel restless and she wondered whether she should go out too. This would never do, she thought. She would have to pull herself together, so she began to cut out the curtains for her bedroom.

Two days later, she was quite desperately anxious to see her father, so, after breakfast, she drove the forty-odd miles into Hlageni by herself.

Her father looked rested – so much so that Julia wondered, as she entered his ward, whether any tests had been done.

'Haven't you had any blood tests done?' she asked, kissing him.

'Yes, several,' he replied, smiling. 'Why do you ask?'

'Well, you look so rested. Somehow I expected to find you pale and worn out from it all.'

He laughed. 'Nonsense! Whatever for? This is a very pleasant surprise. I never expected a visit from you. It's not the sort of drive you're used to taking on your own.'

'I enjoyed it,' she told him. 'I'm an old hand at living in the Reserve now, Dad.'

At the end of her visit Stan said that he would put through a telephone call when Grant could come to take him home.

'There's no need for Grant to take you back home,' Julia said hotly. 'I can take you back myself.'

'I know you can,' her father gave her an amused, ironic glance, 'but after all, that was the arrangement, in the first place. We might as well keep to it.'

On her way out of the hospital Julia was fortunate enough to meet Dr. Randle. 'Oh, hello there,' he said, looking down at her from a tall height. 'I was about to telephone you, you know.'

She widened her eyes at him. 'There's – nothing wrong,

is there?'

'Nothing at all. This is the position. There are tests to be done, results to be waited for, and I want your father to have a course of injections, not to mention a rest. So he'll be in for a while longer. Actually, I would like him in here for another two weeks, *at least*.'

'Another two weeks?' It seemed a lifetime to Julia. There was a tight feeling in her chest. 'And at the end of that time is he going to be all right – or are you keeping something from me? I'd rather know, to be perfectly frank with you.'

'You have my solemn word that I'm being perfectly frank with you.' Dr. Randle studied her face for a moment. 'I had the idea at the back of my mind that you might just want to plan something for the next fortnight – visit relations, or something. It can't be a very suitable arrangement for you being at the Reserve without your father.'

Immediately, Julia's thoughts flew to Carl and Grant. 'Yes, I see what you mean.' She hesitated. 'But what happens if I'm needed here – at the hospital?'

'My dear girl,' Doctor Randle threw back his head and laughed, 'what do I have to do to convince you that your father's all right? Make no mistake about it, I wouldn't be sending you off if I thought you were going to be needed.'

'Is this an order, then?' She smiled up at him.

'Not in the least, Julia.' She was surprised that he had remembered her name. 'Let's put it this way – it's merely a *suggestion*, on my part.'

'What about visiting my father? He'll be lonely. I should be visiting him here from time to time.' She felt at a loss.

'Let him rest, there's a good girl. It's not the sort of trip that you should take too often on your own, anyway.'

'I suppose not – although I enjoyed it. I'd hate to have the car break down, though.' She thought of the game she had seen – impala, with the sunlight fastening itself to their coppery backs and the giraffe splayed nervously over their reflections, as they drank, at a waterhole. Harmless animals – but what about the others?

'Anyway,' Dr. Randle went on, 'that's the position – about your father. The rest I'll leave to you. Think about it, though. I'm sure it would give your father greater peace of mind if he thought you were not on your own with the thought, always at the back of your own mind, that you

83

should be visiting him.'

'I'll think about it. Thank you.'

She did think about it – on the way back through the Reserve, and travelling just that little bit faster than she should because the sun was getting low and she had wasted time in Hlageni buying more curtaining material and searching for a suitable cottage woven bedspread. Glancing at the speedometer, she sighed. 'I suppose I'm breaking another rule,' she thought. She was doing thirty-five miles an hour when she should have been doing twenty-five.

Her hands vibrated on the steering wheel and she could hear the gravel of the dirt road spurting out from beneath the tyres. 'If a herd of impala come bounding across the road in front of the car, either they've had it or I've had it,' she thought, wondering whether she would be able to pull up in time, but she had to get back before the gates closed just outside the camp. That was another rule. *Sunrise to Sunset*. So whatever way she looked at it – she was in trouble.

Relief flooded over her as, near to the camp, she saw several cars still out, driving slowly, an African Game Guide in most of them.

Whew! She let out a long breath because she had made it in time and was suddenly very pleased with herself for all that she had accomplished this day. She looked forward with childlike anticipation to a long bath and a change of clothing. She'd slip into something exciting – even though there would be nobody to see her.

When she had taken her bath and changed into white slacks with a Rajah type top with gold braiding, which she had made herself at the Finishing School, she did something that she had never done in her life before. She went to the new cocktail trolley and poured herself a sherry. Somehow she felt that she had deserved it – and then – Grant Tyler was standing just inside the glass doors, which had been left open to catch the breeze, and it was too late to do anything about the sherry. She placed the glass on the trolley and tried to keep her voice easy as she said, 'Well, hello there.'

One of the lamps had been turned on and her face gleamed like pale copper. 'Apart from the sherry,' she thought with a hollow feeling, 'what have I done now?' One look at Grant's face was enough to convince her that she *had* done something.

The blue eyes left her face for a moment to flicker over the sherry glass on the cane trolley. Her own eyes followed his swiftly.

'Would you like one – a sherry, I mean?' She tried to sound calm and completely sure of herself. 'I – just felt like one after my trip to Hlageni and before I eat a solitary dinner.'

She wished she had not said that. Now, why had she said it? He would think that she was hinting for his company and that was something she didn't want, she told herself.

'No.' His voice was curt and she thought, 'Oh *you*, Grant Tyler!'

'Well, for goodness' sake, come right in!' she said. 'You make me nervous – just standing there. Why haven't these bungalows got an entrance hall, I wonder? Some places have *two*, and I can see why. It's enough to scare anyone out of their wits to look up and find somebody half in and half out of their personal living-room.'

'What you really mean is that these bungalows are not up to your Azalea Park standards.'

She turned on him furiously. 'No, that's not what I mean at all. That was pretty silly, wasn't it? That remark of yours! It's the sort of remark I've heard dozens and dozens of times from you and, quite frankly, I'm sick of it!' Looking at his scornful face, she thought wildly, 'I'm going to shout at Grant Tyler!'

'I'll shout in a minute,' she said, 'honestly.'

'Go ahead and shout,' he shrugged. 'It's just the sort of damn silly thing you would do.'

'Oh, *yes*, I *know*, I'm very silly.' She raised her shoulders and let them drop. The lamp light caught the gold braiding at her neck. 'What is it you want?' she asked, going defiantly towards the trolley and taking a sip of sherry. She put the glass down again with a loud click and turned to look at him again. When he made no attempt to answer her she put her hands on her hips. 'What exactly is it you want?' She saw one corner of his mouth go up. Well, let it go up, she thought.

'Julia,' he said, standing looking at her, with his hands in his pockets, 'was it necessary to go at such a hell of a lick today?'

Disconcerted, she stared back at him before she composed herself enough to say, 'Are you sure your information is correct?' She pretended innocence. 'I wasn't going at such a – hell of a lick.'

'Any damn fool could see that you were exceeding the speed limit.' He took his hands from his pockets. Stupidly, she thought how handsome he appeared in this room; his khaki clothes contrasting excitingly with the cherry folds of the Indian raw silk curtains.

To one side, the huge pottery base of the lamp gleamed like an ancient Egyptian bronze-and-olive-coloured urn. 'It's strange,' she thought, 'but, without realizing it, I've managed to convey a timeless colour scheme – sophisticated and yet timeless enough to conjure up such worldly cultures as those of ancient Egypt and Rome – such colours as bronze, cocoa, mustard, that tiny dash of mauve over there.' Her green eyes went back to Grant and, for a mad moment, she wondered how she would react to his touch.

'I was coming back from the hospital,' she said flatly. 'I'd been to see my father. I was in a hurry to get back before the gates closed. I was late – at least, I thought I was late. I couldn't see myself making it, but as it was, there was no need for me to have worried.' In her confusion, she picked up the sherry glass again and took a swallow, for that was what it amounted to. It certainly wasn't a sip this time.

'What time did you go to the hospital?' He raised his brows.

'I left here early this morning. Very early, actually.'

'Did you spend the day with Stan?'

'No, of course not.'

'How come you were late, then?'

'You mean how come I was pressed for time, coming back?'

'Yes.'

'Well, I did a bit of shopping after I left the hospital. Where were you? To see me coming back?' Her voice was petulant.

'I was about.' Their eyes locked.

'Oh, you're always about. You miss nothing – absolutely

86

nothing. You're always so concerned about your Game Reserve, aren't you?'

'Yes,' he answered softly. 'There's only one thing that counts with me, and that's my work here. I don't intend to change that. Not for the present, anyway. Why do you think rules and regulations are made in these Reserves?'

'I don't know. You tell me,' she replied recklessly. She took up her glass again. 'Um, this sherry is really good. Are you sure you won't have some? You're very welcome.'

'Blast the sherry!' Grant's voice flared into a sudden anger which she was beginning to know how to provoke now. 'Do you realize that had an animal – a valuable animal – bounded out in front of your car this afternoon you would have had no alternative but to hit it?'

'You seem to spend your entire life worrying about your animals and your juvenile crocodiles – poor little things, at the mercy of Grant Tyler – don't you?'

'You're perfectly right. The Reserve is my constant care. I carry its problems – and the problems created by people like you – with me day and night.' He sounded as if he had given the matter more than the usual thought.

'Tut, tut!' Julia took another sip of the sherry. 'I feel so sorry for you, Grant.' She was very conscious, beneath the flippancy she was showing him, of a hammering of her heart – a sadness and dismay that she should have been reduced to this.

'I feel sorry for you too, for that matter,' he retorted. 'What did you buy?' His eyes scanned the room she had created. 'More useless rubbish for your father's bungalow – more sherry, for the sophisticated little cocktail set-up? Trinkets,' his eyes flicked across her wrist, with its bracelet of South African gem stones, 'to emphasize your – so-called polished Finishing School beauty?'

Julia's eyes reflected the lamplight and they seemed to change from green to black and then back to green again as she listened to him.

'Don't you go on at me like that!' Actually, she was making a tremendous effort to control herself from crying. 'Are you satisfied now?' she asked. 'As usual, you've reduced me to nothing.' She tilted her face forward and her hair slipped over her cheeks.

There was a silence, all of a sudden, an unnatural kind of

silence, and then, without warning, Grant had tilted her face upwards. He pushed aside her hair and kissed her full on the mouth, and as he kissed her he placed his fingers on her arms and the pressure of his fingers began to transmit messages through her nerves.

When he released her, he looked into her eyes which had filled with a trusting kind of innocence, then he said, very softly, 'Damn you, Julia – for being so beautiful. I didn't intend this. You could call it a mistake. I'm sorry.'

'Get out,' she managed to say, 'and try your mistakes out on someone else. There must be other girls who would be willing . . .' Her voice broke.

'Don't explain these things to me,' he said. 'I know them all by heart.'

'Yes,' she stormed back at him, 'so I've been told!'

He was about to go through the door when he turned round to look at her again. 'One more word of advice, Julia,' his eyes went to the cocktail trolley. 'I'd cut that habit out, if I were you.'

'I'll please myself about that!' She looked back at him with hurt, wide eyes, wishing frantically that she could control her trembling – and her breathing.

'Have it your own way.' He shrugged his shoulders and strode from the room.

When he had gone, she walked to the glass doors and closed them. Closed them against Grant Tyler and the night with its distant animal night noises and dew-moist vegetation.

Some time later Samson coughed in the dining-room and she took her hands from her face and said in a very small, very tired voice, 'Thank you, Samson. I'm coming.'

In the morning something happened which led her to the final conclusion that she had better telephone her Aunt Bonita, in Pietermaritzburg, to enquire whether she would be interested in spending a few days at Umkambo.

She had gone to the office for a book which her father had left there, but before going inside the building she had decided to walk round to the other side where she could admire the rock garden and the view of the valley and a spur of mountains several miles away.

On this side, the foundation of the building was high

and the side windows of the tremendous picture-type window were open. She was not tall enough to see into the office – or to be seen. However, she heard something which caused her to stand still and her eyes, shaded by a wide-brimmed yellow hat, went wide with the hurt she felt.

'How long did you say Stan is going to be in hospital?' This was Carl's voice.

'Several days, from what I gather. A fortnight – longer, maybe.' Julia stiffened as she listened to Grant's reply.

'Well,' Carl was obviously pondering over this bit of information, 'that's not so hot, is it? Looks like we're going to have to act as a couple of nursemaids for a bit longer. It's okay for old Findlay, being at the other end of the camp – he's not so involved. Anyway, I've got enough on my mind as it is, without having to help act nursemaid to Julia Munro. I'm not saying that she isn't a nice enough kid – but this is no place for her without Stan. I don't know why the devil he didn't postpone her coming to him for a while. He must have known that he was due for another check-up.'

Suddenly Julia could not bear to hear what Grant's answer would be. She went back to the bungalow where she had spent the entire morning brooding on what she should do. The obvious thing seemed to be that she should telephone her Aunt Bonita.

She did this, after making sure that both Carl and Grant were out. There was only Findlay Kruger, who was carrying on without her father.

'I'll phone you back this evening, Julia,' Bonita Munro said. 'I'll have to discuss this at home, of course, when Jake and Gillian and Kathy get back from the office. Will that suit you?'

'That will suit very well. I'll be here at the office, waiting for your call coming through.'

Bonita Munro was the widow of Stan Munro's brother and she stayed with her daughter Gillian, who was married to Jake Feldwood who owned a small printing business in Pietermaritzburg. By marrying Jake, Gillian had been landed with a stepdaughter named Kathy who was practically her own age. Bonita helped to run the home while they were all at work at the firm.

'If you decide to come,' Julia asked, 'how will you come?'

89

Bonita, who owned her own car and who thought nothing about distance, laughed. 'I'll drive there. I'm used to it, since Russell died.'

'I'll be here at the office at five-thirty,' Julia said, before ringing off, 'waiting for your call to come through.'

Her first reaction was to snub Grant and Carl, who were in the office with Findlay Kruger, when she entered the building at five-thirty to wait for Bonita's call, but she knew this would appear ridiculous. After all, they were quite oblivious to the fact that she had overheard their conversation in the morning.

When the call came through her fingers were white at the knuckles with the tension she felt, while she listened to her aunt explaining that it would be perfectly all right and that Tina, the excellent servant, could manage without her for a while and look after the Feldwood family.

It was like a big cloud being lifted from Julia's head. 'Oh, that's *marvellous!*' she said, her face radiant. 'I'm so glad. When can I expect you?'

'I'm going to leave right away,' Bonita replied. 'At the crack of dawn tomorrow I'll be on my way, and by this time tomorrow afternoon you can begin to look out for my car. I've been there before, of course. I know the way and I'll take the trip slowly.'

At the end of the conversation Julia passed the receiver back to Findlay Kruger who cradled it for her. 'Thank you,' she said. Then she turned to where Carl and Grant were sitting in the office. 'By the way,' she said, in a tight voice, breathless with the feeling she had worked up against them, 'I think you both just might be interested to hear that, from tomorrow this time, somebody else will be acting as *nursemaid* to me. Actually, I wouldn't have bothered to even have mentioned it, but I know that it will take a load off your minds.'

It gave her a tremendous sense of satisfaction to see the look of flushed surprise on Carl Bramley's face, before he swung round in his chair and picked up the earphones. Turning to Grant Tyler, Julia said sweetly, 'And by the way, that goes for you too.'

However, it was not Bonita Munro's car that pulled up outside the bungalow the following afternoon, but Leon Ladenza's, and Kathy Feldwood, Gillian's difficult stepdaughter, stepped out of it first and called up to the verandah, 'Don't look so stunned. It's only us!'

Already on her way down to the road, Julia called, 'But I am stunned. Where on earth is Aunt Bonita?'

When they met Kathy embraced Julia ritually. 'It's a long story,' she said, 'but to cut a long story short I had a fight with Wilbur Newton and I persuaded Bonita to stay at home and let *me* come instead to get over him.'

At this stage, Leon joined the two girls. 'Darling!' He placed his arms around Julia and kissed her. 'Stretch out the carpet, will you?'

'What's all this about?' Julia tried to keep her patience. 'It's all beyond me.'

'Of course it's all beyond you.' Leon stepped back on his white crêpe-soled shoes to study Julia. 'Darling, you look like a copper goddess, doesn't she, Kathy?' Kathy shrugged and Leon went on, 'Look, what about Kathy's luggage? Mine, I was told at the office, is to go along to hut eleven.'

Julia was both intrigued and disappointed at this new change of events. 'You still haven't explained what's happened to Aunt Bonita?'

'What difference does it make who keeps you company while your father is in hospital?' Kathy asked. 'But to answer your question, I happened to meet Leon in Pietermaritzburg and he told me he was going to spring a surprise on you by coming to Umkambo. Oh, Leon, *you* tell her!'

'Kathy was feeling ghastly,' Leon explained. 'She's had this fight with this wretched Wilbur Newton – what she sees in him, I don't know, but that's Kathy's affair. I, on the other hand, was bubbling over, wasn't I, Kathy? I had just availed myself of a cancellation booking. Several friends of mine are booked in here, by the way – hut number eleven – and one of them backed down and I was asked whether I'd like to take his place. It seemed like fate, darling. I accepted, and then I had to go and meet Kathy. What a *twist* of fate *that* was ... and here we are. It's as simple as that, really.' Leon gestured and there was something so theatrical about the gesture that Julia was irritated by it.

'I see.' She was surprised at Bonita for allowing Kathy

to have her own way, and yet she was not so surprised really, because that was Kathy all over. Nobody had a chance against Kathy Feldwood.

It was through Julia that Leon had been introduced to the Feldwoods in the first place. He had on several occasions called for Julia at Azalea Park and driven her to Pieter-maritzburg to visit her Aunt Bonita.

'Kathy's coming was all Kathy's idea,' Leon went on, with no regard for Kathy's feelings. 'Don't look at *me* like that, darling. I could quite well have done without *Kathy*, believe me. Finding your Aunt Bonita here would have been bad enough.'

'Shut up,' Kathy snapped, 'and get my bags out of the car and bring them inside.'

Julia led the way up to the bungalow and into the newly decorated living-room. 'Not bad,' Kathy said, sniffing. 'It smells new, though. Is it?'

'Yes, it is. Dad's old stuff was awful. He had to admit it himself. We're very much more comfortable now.'

'I'm sure you are.' Kathy's voice was sarcastic. Her gaze wandered about the room. 'I suppose it wasn't good enough for you – coming from the Finishing School?'

Julia's eyes went wide with annoyance. 'I'm going to have trouble with this girl,' she thought.

Leon all but staggered into the room with Kathy's cases. 'Darling,' he dropped the cases, 'this *is* attractive. Your work, of course!' Like Kathy, he sniffed. The room smelled of new cane, fabric and rugs.

'Bonita once said that, quite apart from what Julia's father spent on her very lavish education, he's hoarded his money,' Kathy said. 'Well, all I can say is that Julia is going to make sure she gets her clutches into it as quickly as possible, by the looks of things.'

'That's not very nice, Kathy.' Leon studied Kathy disapprovingly. Then he went across the room on silent soles, where he stood looking at the Chantal de Cousa painting which Julia had bought in Hlageni. 'You quite obviously had nothing much to choose from, sweetie, when you chose a Chantal de Cousa. Am I right?'

'In one respect you're right,' Julia answered, feeling positively taken over by Leon and Kathy. 'I didn't have much to choose from at Hlageni, where I did my shopping, but on the other hand, I like it. I like them both. Go through to the dining-room and have a closer look at the other one. Afterwards, while I get Kathy settled in, you can go back and get yourself organized in your hut. When you've done that come back for a drink before I give you dinner.'

'Dinner?' Leon swung round. 'Darling, you don't mean to say we aren't going to cook great hunks of meat over hot coals, do you?'

'Not tonight.'

It was while they were having drinks on the verandah that Grant Tyler walked past, and Julia immediately felt her nerves tighten. She knew how this sundowner party must look to Grant.

Kathy sat up in her chair. 'If you tell me that gorgeous hunk of male out there is married, Julia, I'll put an end to myself!' Her voice was excited. 'Who is he? Getting over Wilbur is going to be easier than I thought.'

'Isn't that the fellow who came for you at Azalea Park?' A vaguely disconcerted expression showed itself behind Leon's dark glasses.

'Yes, that's Grant Tyler.' Julia kept her eyes averted.

'Married?' This was from Kathy.

'No.'

'Ask him to dinner.'

'I'm sorry, Kathy, that's out.'

'Why?'

'Well, for one thing, he's always busy, and for another – he happens to dislike women. He's a woman-hater, in plain English.'

'I consider that as a challenge,' said Kathy. 'I want you to ask him over, Julia. If you don't, I will.'

Suddenly Leon got to his feet in one of his cat-like movements. 'I think that is a jolly good idea, Julia. After all, it will give Kathy here something to do – getting over Wilbur.' He turned to Kathy. 'I'll ask him for you, and Kathy, darling, the very best of good woman-hater luck to you.'

'Thank you.' Kathy's smile was slow and, with a feeling of helplessness, Julia listened to them rough-shodding her.

Watching Leon go after Grant Julia felt a rage rising against them both. There had not been one word about her father. Leon must have heard by now. There had not been one word from Kathy to the effect that Kathy was pleased to see her.

'I want to get away on one of these three-day-walking trails I've heard so much about,' Kathy was saying, 'especially if your Grant Tyler is going to be in charge of it.'

Looking at Kathy, Julia noticed how the irritable little lines had already, at twenty-three, fastened themselves around her mouth.

'The object was that I should have company here, while my father is away,' she said. 'Didn't Aunt Bonita tell you?'

'Julia,' said Kathy, 'having company when one's father happens to be away went out with the Ark, or didn't you know that?'

'We've made progress,' Leon told them, coming on to the verandah. 'He's coming, but Kathy darling, I had to do a lot of sales talk to get him to come.'

'Good for you!' Kathy stood up. 'I'll bath now – and change? What clothes, Julia?'

Suppressing her temper, Julia said, 'Anything you like, Kathy. Slacks, maybe, or a frock ... it's not all that important.'

'Oh, but it is,' drawled Kathy. 'It's *very important*, Julia.'

CHAPTER SIX

By the time Grant Tyler arrived Julia and Kathy were in the lamp-lit living-room.

'This is my cousin, Kathy Feldwood,' Julia told him.

'I've been dying to meet you.' Kathy looked into Grant's eyes for a moment longer than was necessary. 'By the way, I must explain, I'm only Julia's cousin by marriage. My father married Julia's Aunt Bonita's daughter Gillian. My father also happens to be old enough to be Gillian's father. Another thing I feel I must stress is that I'm not a Finishing School type, like Julia.'

'Thanks for filling in the gaps,' said Grant, but he was smiling.

'I made up my mind in such a hurry, about this trip,' Kathy went on. 'When I heard that Leon was coming – well,' she shrugged, 'I felt, with Julia's father away, it would look better if I came along too. Leon happens to be Julia's boy-friend, by the way, not mine.'

'You over-estimate my interest in Leon,' Grant answered, while Julia sat stunned by Kathy's casual insolence. 'However,' he went on, 'welcome to Umkambo. We're very pleased to have you with us.'

'Thank you. I'm very pleased to be here – now.' Kathy's voice showed her pleasure. 'I wasn't, at first.'

At that moment Leon arrived from the tourist section of the camp. He was freshly shaved and dressed in casual but expensive jeans and a cashmere turtle-neck sweater. He completely ignored Kathy and Grant. Instead, he went straight to Julia and hugged her. 'Darling,' he said, 'I hope I haven't held up that jolly little soufflé in the oven?'

'Not at all,' Julia replied, 'since it doesn't happen to be a jolly little soufflé.'

Leon dropped with the ease of a ballet dancer into one of the cane chairs, and throwing one elegant leg over the other he looked about the room. 'Julia's marvellous, you know,' he said. 'It's miraculous, really.' All his gestures were larger than life and Julia, conscious of Grant's blue eyes on him, felt herself stiffen.

Obviously enjoying the situation, Kathy asked, 'What on earth did your father have to say about this little effort, Julia? It must have set him back a cent or two. Trust you to double up on everything!'

Julia's temper erupted at last. 'My father happens to like it, Kathy, and so do I, for that matter, and as we have to live here, I guess that's all that counts.'

'Darling girl, you need a copper plate over there,' Leon cut in, completely oblivious to the tension, 'and I have the very one for you. I'll post it to you, along with the ikon.'

'The ikon?' Suddenly, recklessly, and completely *with* him, Julia laughed. This was just like Leon, she thought with a pang of joy, and to show Kathy and Grant Tyler that she didn't care what they were thinking she said, 'Darling, what ikon?' She fell into the darling this and darling that tone of the past.

'The one I'm sending you. You must have it. I insist.' He got up from the chair and came over to Julia. He took her fingers and pulled her up to him – he was a figure of grace. 'Come here,' he said. 'Now stand there – no, here. Can you see it? In that light? Next to those colours?'

'The ikon?' Her eyes were tantalizing. 'Darling, you're so right. I must have an ikon.'

'Marvellous,' Leon replied. He turned to look at Grant. 'Julia does have this exciting touch of bohemia, you know.'

'How much is this going to set my father back?' Julia asked, for Kathy's benefit.

'Accept it, with my very best love, as a house-warming gift.' Leon kissed her ear.

'You're very sweet,' she murmured, with a calculated increase of tenderness. 'Very sweet, darling.'

There was a loud sigh and then Kathy said, 'I know I'm being terribly silly, but what is an ikon?'

'Kathy!' Leon's face went blank with shock. 'An ikon, Kathy dear, happens to be an image. I have the very one in one of my galleries.'

Julia tried not to look at Grant Tyler, who was sitting looking about the room with an infuriating bored indifference.

'What about dinner?' Kathy stood up. She was looking attractive in some kind of sand-coloured hunting jacket with embroidered pockets and more embroidery on the trousers. 'Although you're always on a diet, Julia, I happen to have a healthy appetite and, right now, I'm starving.' She laughed. 'Remember the time you had a crush on young Doctor Laurens? You used to drive him up the wall asking him for slimming pills.' Kathy spoke with casual amusement.

Julia felt completely staggered by Kathy's remark. 'You're mixing me up with somebody else,' she retorted, sick of Kathy and the whole lot of them. 'I don't happen to know young Doctor Laurens.'

'Aah, come off it, Julia!' Kathy laughed outright, and Julia wondered how one could rake up such a genuine *false* laugh.

During dinner Kathy got going again. 'What a wonderful meal, Julia. I'll hand it to Samson, he cooks like a dream.' She looked at Grant. 'Doesn't he? Doesn't Samson cook like a dream?' Cool and mocking, her eyes met and held Julia's again. 'Ooh . . .' she looked down at her plate. 'Sorry, trust me to put my foot in it. I forgot that you were supposed to have cooked it.'

'As a matter of fact, I did cook it, Kathy. Samson only prepared the vegetables – but don't let it worry you. I'm sure you're just trying to be terribly kind,' Julia said while Kathy turned on a look of amused disbelief.

'That's right,' she said, 'I – forgot.' She turned to Grant. 'By the way, I want to ask you about one of those three-day walking trails.'

'Go right ahead.' His eyes met hers.

'I want to go on one. I'd also like to see what it's like to grill meat with a handsome Game Ranger one night. May I?'

'You'll be able to find out about the trails at the office.' Grant spoke with casual amusement. 'And there's no reason why you can't grill meat with a handsome Game Ranger one night – if you can find yourself one.'

'I regard that remark as a challenge.' There was a mocking tone to Kathy's voice.

'Well, good for you,' answered Grant.

'Why?' She gave him a long look. 'Are you interested?'

'I'd be interested to know where you're going to find a handsome Game Ranger who'd be free to do this with you. Still, you could always give it a try. Don't let *me* put you off,

Kathy.' Julia noticed the ease with which Grant handled Kathy's name. He might or might not have been making fun of Kathy.

Depressed and resentful, she noticed how the elaborately carved orange-coloured candles in their copper containers which Leon had brought along with him as a gift stood out on the table. So did the silver ice-bucket which went along with the wine he had also brought with him. She was thankful when the meal came to an end and Grant went back to his bungalow and eventually when Leon left them to go along to hut eleven.

In the morning, after a night of nightmares, she went out game spotting with Leon and Kathy. They were back in time for lunch and then Kathy went over to the office to make enquiries about the three-day walking trail. She eventually came back with the news that she had put her name down for a trail, which Grant would be conducting, in a day's time.

'I thought you came here to be company for Julia, while her father is away?' Leon asked, looking around for a place to put his glass of lime juice. 'Wasn't that the general idea? After all, I can't very well sleep here, can I?'

'The general idea was for me to get away from everything,' Kathy snapped, 'and that's just precisely what I intend to do.'

'Look, don't let's have any more arguments,' Julia cut in, trying to keep what little peace there was left. 'Kathy must go, if she wants to. You too, Leon. It would be a shame to miss it.'

'We'll both go,' said Leon. 'I'll go and add our names to the list.'

'No, don't include me. I have to be on call here, in case a message comes through to the office from the hospital. You needn't worry about me.'

'Darling Julia, if you stay, I stay.' Leon was emphatic. 'I came here to see you, after all. Actually, it will be a relief to get rid of old Kathy here. She is a pain in the neck.'

'Thank you,' Kathy said.

'You're very welcome.' Leon turned back to Julia. 'If you are nervous at night I'll come and sleep on the verandah outside.'

'Oh, ha-ha, listen to our brave hero!' drawled Kathy. 'If

you heard an owl hoot you'd die of fright.'

'Kathy, you're so *evil*.' Leon gave her a disgusted look.

The following evening Kathy said, 'I'm going over to Leon's hut.'

'But I thought he was going to play cards with the fellows he's sharing it with?' They had just finished dinner together and Julia was straightening the chairs.

'I know he's playing cards – but does that stop me from joining them? Is there a rule about this?'

'Kathy,' Julia's voice was sharp, 'there's no rule about this. I understood you were leaving early tomorrow morning. Leon, for one, said that he was having an early night – cards or no cards.'

'Where's the torch?' Kathy looked round the room.

'Next to your bed.' Julia turned away, afraid she would say too much. She had made up her mind to tolerate Kathy while she was here – partly for Leon's sake. She did not want to spoil his little holiday. Leon, for all his eccentric ways, was a hard-working young man. He had only got where he was through hard work and he deserved a break.

A moment later Julia stood watching the night being marked by Kathy's torch and Kathy's cigarette, as she went down the road in the direction of the tourist accommodation.

Struggling to stop the restlessness which had taken hold of her, Julia took up a magazine and sat down and tried to concentrate on the glossy pages in front of her, but her mind kept revolving around Kathy and Leon and the fact that they had only succeeded in adding fat to the fire by coming here.

There was a slight knock on one of the glass doors and it made her jump. 'Julia, it's Grant!'

As she went to open the doors she could feel her nails digging into her palms. 'I suppose you've come to discuss the trail with Kathy?' She didn't feel as if it was her own voice speaking. She had had so much of everything, she thought bitterly, and it was telling on her. 'Kathy's over at hut eleven, with Leon. You'll find her there. She left only a few minutes ago.'

'I didn't come to see Kathy. I came to see you.'

'Oh?' As casually as possible, Julia asked, 'What have I done this time?'

'You aren't coming tomorrow?'

'No. Of course not.'

'Why of course not?'

Thinking about her father, she said, with some heat, because *he* had apparently not given Stan Munro a thought, 'Well, I should have thought the reason was perfectly obvious.' She was quite unaware of the impression she was making on Grant.

'It is quite obvious.'

'Well, why ask, then?'

'Mind you,' Grant went on, ignoring her question, 'it's probably just as well. I don't think your boy-friend could stand up to a three-day trail.'

Julia felt her temper rising. 'Is that so? Well, for your information, Grant Tyler, Leon Ladenza happens to be a ballet dancer, and a very good one at that.'

Grant's lower lip curled sarcastically. 'Well, what does that make me?' he asked. 'A talent scout?'

'No, not a talent scout. What I'm trying to get across to you is the fact that Leon is far stronger than you think. He's probably a lot tougher than you are, although it's a – hidden kind of strength.'

'You don't say?' His lip curled again. 'Well, he certainly knows how to keep it hidden – I'll hand that to him.'

'You don't have to hand anybody anything,' she stormed back at him.

Kathy saved what might have been another row by turning up at that very moment. 'Hello there,' she said in her best voice, and Julia was never certain how she did it, but in a moment Kathy had manoeuvred herself in front of Grant. 'I came back for my cigarettes. Mine are finished – the ones I took with me – and I can't smoke their strong cigarettes. Were you looking for me?'

'Yes, come to think of it, Kathy, I was,' Grant replied, and Julia was fascinated by the boldness of the lie. 'All set for tomorrow?'

'I'm all set.' Kathy, apparently wanting all the excitement she could get, hugged herself. 'I'm thrilled about going with you, Grant. Automatically, you're the type I'd give my life to. Tell me, is it very dangerous? Fortunately, I'm not one of these Finishing School types – I know how to rough it, and enjoy roughing it.'

'Can you climb a tree?' Grant was smiling. 'That's what counts most.'

'Grant, you should just see me,' Kathy replied, with mock pride. 'One thing I did learn was how to climb a tree, but I guess you don't have to go to Finishing School to do that, do you?' She laughed and then turned to regard Julia with the spiteful attitude with which she always regarded most girls.

'You're quite a girl, Kathy,' Grant said, laughing; the laugh was low and genuinely amused and, listening to it, Julia thought that it had not been a bold lie after all. Grant Tyler *had* come looking for Kathy.

'What about food and bedding for the trail? We don't have to carry all that stuff ourselves, do we?' Kathy sounded worried.

'Don't worry about that. Your roughing it effort won't have to stretch that far. Donkeys will take care of that side of it for you. They leave before we do, along with a couple of Game Scouts and using a different route from us – but we all meet up in the end. We've got everything worked out to a fine art.'

For reasons she could not explain, Julia made a point of not being anywhere around to see them off when they left on the three-day walk through the bush on a selected trail. However, in her room, she could imagine them setting off in the direction of the valley, walking silently, and expectantly, along a track still wet with dew. There would be a constant rustling of life unseen, she thought, which would cause Kathy, and the other girls in the party, to tense up and look to Grant for reassurance.

The party of six would possibly come face to face with animals, on a natural footing, as they followed the game trails. As her mind raced on and on she could visualize Kathy beside Grant as they rested on a fallen tree, maybe, and then, at night, there would be the protection of the camp fire.

Later on in the morning Leon called to take Julia out for a drive into the Reserve, and during the days to follow he was always eager to please. One day, despite a notice board warning to the effect that a steep, pot-holed road was out of bounds to visitors, Leon turned off and used the road to get to a reed-infested area where they could scan the river for crocodiles. 'This must surely be the result of the year of the great floods in Zululand,' Leon said, as he manoeuvred the car out of the small clearing. He pointed to the great trunk of a wild fig tree which lay decaying in the sun and then again to straggling bunches of débris which clung to the forks of trees.

At night they grilled meat together, and once they joined a number of other tourists to do this.

Although Julia tried desperately to enjoy herself with Leon, depression kept harping at her as she thought about Kathy on the trail. Visions of Kathy, always with Grant, of course, keeping up with him as they trudged along, sitting next to him, as they rested and ate the food and drank the steaming coffee made for them by one of the African Game Scouts, kept niggling at her. At night there would be the stars, millions and millions of them above the burning embers of a camp fire, and in the day there would be that dry harshness and brilliant colour all blending together.

The party arrived back from their walk through the bush, on a selected trail, late in the afternoon.

'You're looking marvellously tanned, Kathy,' Julia said, with complete sincerity. 'Did you enjoy it?' She tried hard to disguise her curiosity as mere politeness.

'After being with Grant Tyler for three days, what do you think?' Kathy asked, and Julia found that she was unexpectedly hurt. 'I'm dying for a bath, Julia. My feet are practically killing me.'

'Let me run a bath for you and then I'll give you some ointment my father has – for your feet.' On her way to the bathroom Julia paused again. 'How did everybody stand up to the trail, Kathy? Was there – any excitement?'

'Oh, for Pete's sake,' Kathy said irritably, 'I'm too tired to want to talk. I don't feel like going into everything now – but yes, everybody stood up very well. Once a black rhino charged, but Grant was in superb command.'

'Did – you have to climb a tree?'

'Actually, Julia, I did have to climb a tree, and seeing that you're so interested, I'll tell you a little more about the trip. Grant was marvellous, of course. And he looked marvellous. But then you know that side of it. He was madly thrilling. I saw a couple of the girls giving me spiteful looks, which was damn silly. I couldn't help if Grant would persist in – well, you know, fussing over me, and all that sort of thing, could I? Before we left Grant said, "You'll notice that I – er – carry a rifle, but I've never had occasion to use it on trail, and if I can help it, I don't intend to." Well, of course, everybody just tensed up with excitement. And then Grant went on to say, "I'd like to point out that you are intruders in a sanctuary of white rhino." Well, as I say, right from the start, he had us all in the palm of his hand. We would have died for him, but with him around, of course, there was absolutely no reason to.' Kathy's eyes met Julia's. 'Actually, Grant stays on guard throughout the night, did you know that? A couple of times, exhausted as I was, I just had to keep him company. He's a honey – an absolute honey! He gave *me* none of that woman-hater treatment, I can assure you. I just adore him.' This was strange, coming from Kathy, who usually ended up by criticizing everybody after a few days.

So the woman-hater had been finally broken down – and by Kathy. Well, this was how Kathy had invited it – right from the first minute she had met Grant.

Much to Kathy's irritation they saw very little of Grant for the next few days and he only arrived back from where-ever it was he had been on the day before Leon and Kathy were due to leave the Reserve. Kathy, who was obviously put out about everything, did the next best thing by inviting Grant to have drinks with them.

This was the first time that Julia had actually come face to face with Grant since before the walking trail and he gave her a careless look. 'Well, how's it?' he asked, before his blue eyes scanned the room which Julia and Leon had been working on again and which had been rearranged.

'You might as well look,' said Kathy, coming into the room. 'Our two interior decorators have been at work again. Our two *perfectionists*. Do you think Julia will ever get this bungalow to her satisfaction? I don't. She'll probably need more money spent on it.'

'Kathy darling, you don't need money to create an exciting room,' Leon cut in. 'Let's face it, *you* might – but people like us,' he looked across at Julia, 'don't.'

'Oh no – just a few copper plates and ikons and Chantal de Cousas thrown together.' Kathy's face was spiteful. Her nostrils moved imperceptibly and she gave a tight-lipped smile. 'And of course, *they* don't cost money, do they? It's a good thing our Julia here doesn't have to live in our shabby old house.'

'Actually,' Leon was all set to argue with Kathy now, 'your old house has wonderful potentialities, do you realize that? It *could* be one of the show-places of old stately homes of Pietermaritzburg. It needs somebody with imagination to turn it into one. I know I'd like to get my hands on it.'

'Well, you're welcome to it, so far as I'm concerned.' Kathy's voice contained hostility and petulance. 'It will take more than imagination, though, to get it going. It has to have *money* spent on it, and I'm afraid my father isn't as generous with his money as Julia's father is. Perhaps I should get Julia to work on him. She'd get blood out of a stone. In no time she'd have my father selling his wretched printing business to get the money to transform Chiyana into a stately home.'

Julia had been wondering how long she could stand this, and at length she burst out, 'Kathy, would you mind? This is getting rather tedious.'

When they had finished their drinks Grant stood up, ready to go. The rest of the conversation had been about three-day walking trails and Julia had noticed how Kathy always got around to speaking as though it had been only herself and Grant involved. She had a knack of isolating everybody else in the party from the trip.

'Will I see you in the morning before we go, Grant?' Kathy went to stand next to Grant and touched one of his shirt buttons as she looked up into his face.

'I hardly think so.' He took her hand away from the button and held it for a moment before he dropped it. 'I'll be out, at the crack of dawn – before the crack of dawn, if it comes to that. So it will have to be goodbye now. Cheerio, Kathy.' He grinned down at her.

'Not, not just like this!' Kathy's voice was strained. 'I'll – I'll walk back with you to your place.'

Grant's eyes dropped to her sandals. 'Too many snakes about, Kathy.' He turned to look at Julia, who felt like a shadow in the room, 'Julia knows all about those snakes that lurk about.' His tone was mocking; then he went over to Leon and held out his hand. 'Well, cheerio, Leon. I hope you enjoyed your stay in our Reserve? Too bad you couldn't make it on the trail.'

'I've enjoyed every minute of it,' Leon answered. 'I'm positively sick at the thought of tomorrow.'

'I'm sure you are.' Grant's voice had changed slightly. 'Partings are always so nerve-racking, aren't they?' His eyes went back to Kathy. 'Well, look after yourself, Kathy . . . and cheer up about Chiyana.'

'You'll get in touch with me, won't you?' Kathy was having trouble trying to conceal her disappointment in Grant.

Grant was looking vaguely unhappy now. 'I'm not a letter-writer, Kathy. But I'll be in touch, of course.'

Kathy was slipping her feet out of her sandals. 'Anyway, I'll come outside with you. Wait for me. I'll go and put on a pair of closed shoes.'

When Kathy and Grant had gone Leon said, 'I'm going to miss you, darling. Terribly.'

'I'm going to miss you, too.' This was not strictly true. Julia was only too thankful to have Leon and Kathy go. There had been so much tension attached to the whole visit that it had been nothing short of a disaster.

'How am I going to bear travelling back with Kathy? She's so *evil*.' Leon raised a hand to his forehead. 'Darling, you've been wonderful, the way you've coped with her – you honestly have.'

'Hush,' Julia cut in quickly, 'she's coming back. I wonder why?'

Parting with Grant had obviously upset Kathy because she went straight to her room.

Because Julia didn't want to hurt Leon she allowed him to take her into his arms and to kiss her.

They broke apart suddenly at the sound of Grant's voice. 'I'm sorry to cut in on this,' he said, and then there was a terrible silence. He held out Kathy's large chiffon handkerchief and then dropped it into a cane chair where it fluffed up like a scarlet plume of smoke before it slithered to the black slate floor. 'Kathy's,' he said, and turned away.

Thinking about it later, in bed, Julia felt angry and helpless.

With Grant Tyler around life would always be like this. He would always be there to look upon everything she did with disapproval. There was always something he would have to say, or do, to make her feel guilt-stricken and upset. He was spoiling her life at the Reserve with his sarcasm and his disapproval of her, and now she was going to be left alone with him again – until her father came back. If Kathy had not interfered and if she had allowed Bonita Munro to come here in the first place, this impossible situation would not have cropped up, even with Leon here, because of course after Leon had left Bonita would have stayed on.

In the morning before Leon and Kathy left Kathy said, 'I forgot to give you this on the day we arrived.' It was a letter from Bonita Munro in which she explained how upset she was by the scene which Kathy had created at home. 'Kathy is always packing her bags and leaving home,' Bonita wrote, 'when things go wrong for her as they have done now with this Wilbur Newton lad. Everything has just played right into her hands, isn't it strange? Her meeting with Leon Ladenza in town, who was set to surprise you with a visit, and then her arrival home from the office to discover that you had invited me to Umkambo. Jake worries so much over Kathy, and when Jake is worried Gillian is upset. It's a vicious circle, and for Jake and Gillian's sakes I've given into Kathy and let her come in my place. If your father is going to be away longer than you expected, get in touch with me, Julia, and I'll make a plan. Dear, why don't you come to *us* for a little while? You could take the train and Jake would meet you at the station here. Do let me know how things are with you.'

Julia folded the letter. Leon and Kathy had gone now. The deserted bungalow filled her with such a surge of despair and restlessness that she decided to take the car and go to Hlageni to see her father.

'You're a long way from home,' he said, when she walked into his ward. 'This is a surprise, Julia.'

'I was missing you,' she told him frankly. 'I was unhappy.'

'My dear, I'm sorry.' There was a new tenderness in his voice. 'It won't be long now. Cheer up.'

She had decided not to tell him everything, but in the end she told him about the arrangements she had made with Bonita Munro and how Kathy and Leon had turned up instead.

Some time later he said, 'Are you nervous back there on your own?'

'No,' she said. 'It's – not that.'

'What, then? What is it?'

'It's just – well, I don't want Carl Bramley and Grant Tyler,' purposely she put Carl's name first, 'to feel that they have to – to be responsible for me, and I think *they* think that they have to be.'

'Look,' he sounded faintly upset, 'Julia, do me a favour, will you? Get in touch with your Aunt Bonita and this time you arrange to go to her. Go to her for a little holiday. When I'm finished here I'll get in touch with Grant to come for me and then, once I'm settled back home again, we'll make arrangements about getting *you* home. We should have thought of that, right from the beginning. It was selfish of me to leave you there on your own, in the very first place.'

Julia felt guilty. 'We didn't know your tests and injections were going to take so long. I've been stupid – I shouldn't have worried you. I'll be all right now.'

'I'll feel much happier if you go to Pietermaritzburg,' he said.

'All right, I'll go.'

Her father looked anxious. 'You'll let me know what happens, won't you? Ring the hospital.' He gestured towards the telephone in the ward.

'I'll ring you,' she said. 'I promise.' He looked much better, more rested, somehow, and she knew that his stay in the hospital was doing him good. 'Is everything going according to plan?' she asked. 'How do you feel?'

'Randle is more than satisfied,' he told her. 'Blood tests satisfactory.'

Before she left he said, 'Take those roads carefully, will you, Julia?'

'Don't worry,' she answered. 'I'm quite used to handling corrugations now.'

Grant Tyler looked surprised when she told him, the following day, that she was going to Pietermaritzburg. 'Will you be going into Hlageni soon? I'm going to ask you for a lift, if you are.'

'Are you going away?' he asked.

'Well, it would appear so, wouldn't it? I wouldn't be

trying to cadge a lift if I wasn't.'

'Look,' he snapped, 'sarcasm is almost always lost on me.'

'Are you or are you not going into Hlageni within the next few days?' she asked, ignoring his remark.

'As it so happens, I am.'

'When? I'd like to make arrangements about the train and so on – telephone my father and – Pietermaritzburg, as a matter of fact.' She did not tell him where she would be going. He could find that out for himself.

'Make your arrangements,' Grant said, 'and let me know the exact day and time of your train and I'll work in with your plans. It doesn't really matter when I go – the fact is that I have to go into Hlageni, anyway, sooner or later.' He sounded vaguely anxious. 'Are you coming back?'

She felt tempted to lie to him to say no, just to see how he would react, but she said, 'Yes. That's a blow, isn't it?'

He reacted with a quietly impatient gesture. 'Let me know your plans, will you?' She stood watching him as he strode in the direction of his Land Rover and noticed how his hair was still damp from his shower.

It was a relief when all her plans had been made and she had spoken to her father on the telephone.

And then she was on her way to Hlageni in the Land Rover with Grant. Her tawny hair stirred in the breeze. 'No doubt you'll be visiting the Royal Show in Pietermaritzburg?' Grant said pleasantly enough.

She put up a hand to her hair and brushed a strand from her eyes. 'Yes. As a matter of fact I shall most probably be working there, during the mornings – or the afternoons, maybe, or both – while I'm there.' This was strictly true. She had telephoned Leon at his gallery in Pietermaritzburg to tell him that she was arriving. Originally, she had telephoned his gallery in Grovelea and was told that Mr. Ladenza could be reached at his gallery in Pietermaritzburg and at the Richmond Hotel where he was in residence until after the Royal Show. Leon was delighted, of course, to hear that she was arriving, but mentioned how busy he was, because of the Show where he was exhibiting. Immediately Julia had offered to help him, and readily he accepted her offer.

Grant Tyler was silent for a moment. 'Oh? At one of

the stands, you mean?'

'Yes. Leon is exhibiting.'

'I see.' There was another pause. 'And that's the whole point, then?'

She turned to look at him. 'The whole point of what?'

'The visit. I can guess the rest.' His voice was cool ... distant.

Julia moved her shoulders irritably. 'Well, go ahead and guess, if it will give you satisfaction.'

At the station Grant said, 'Well, I suppose I might just be seeing you, one of these days?' It sounded like a question.

'Well, naturally.' She tried not to look at him. 'I'd better get on the train – there's the first bell.'

She was no sooner on the train when the second bell went and the train began to move slowly. She and Grant waved an embarrassed goodbye and then she sank back against the seat. Hurt and disappointment had their way with her and she cried a little, and then, when she had herself in hand she even began to feel excited and considered *what* she would wear and what she would wear with it and *where* she would wear it.

Jake Feldwood was at Pietermaritzburg station to meet her.

Julia smiled at him. 'I could have taken a taxi,' she said. 'This is very kind of you.'

'Not at all,' he replied. 'It's getting late, and quite apart from that, it's a pleasure. Come along. I can manage those two light cases. No need for a porter. Can't see one, anyway. Never can, when you want one.'

'It must be the peak hour,' Julia replied. The hustle and bustle seemed terrific, after the tranquillity of the Umkambo Game Reserve.

'The mail train has just pulled in,' Jake told her. 'Lucky blighters all off to Cape Town. The car is just outside, Julia. Fortunately I was able to get parking. That's nothing short of a miracle, these days, I can tell you.'

'We don't have that problem at Umkambo.' She was nearly running as she tried to keep up with Jake.

In the car Julia had to struggle to disguise her relief when Jake said, 'Kathy's not at home, by the way. She threw up a perfectly good job at the office and went off to the Transvaal somewhere. She went with some girl. She was no sooner home from your Umkambo Game Reserve than she cleared off. In the first place, she and that Wilbur Newton fellow had a row. *That* upset her. Now she's upset about something else. Next week it will be something else again.' Jake's mouth tightened in a gesture of irritation. 'Damned if I know what to make of my own daughter. She resents Gillian, of course.'

Julia listened politely and when Jake finally asked about her father she was glad to change the subject. By the time she had given him the news they had arrived at Chiyana.

As Leon had said the house was one of those old show-places – or rather, it could have been if only Jake's business flourished enough to allow the money being spent on the home. It was a large house, sturdily built, but it required bold, imaginative treatment to turn it from a solid, sombre structure into a show-place. It would have been a challenge to someone like Leon.

Bonita and Gillian met them in the large hall and it was plain to see why Jake Feldwood had swept Gillian Munro off her feet in place of a much younger man. There was a quiet beauty about Gillian, who was short and had the Munro tawny skin and tawny hair, whereas Jake was tall and fortunate enough to have turned completely silver at the temples.

It was relief not to have to face up to Kathy and Julia knew that she had done the right thing by leaving Umkambo for a while. She found herself hoping that Kathy would not return until after she had left Pietermaritzburg.

Later, when they were together in the room which Julia was to have, Bonita said, 'How are you going to stand it for a whole year in a Game Reserve, Julia? You poor child, you've never known a proper home, have you?'

'I love it at Umkambo. I'm going to be sorry to have to leave it.'

'Kathy came back raving about one of the Game Rangers there,' Bonita went on. 'I don't think she was too happy about leaving him behind, so she just cleared off to Johannesburg. That's just Kathy all over. How poor Gillian puts up with them all, I just don't know.'

What Bonita meant of course was *Jake and Kathy*. 'Jake's very good to Gillian, but – well, he is old enough to be her father, isn't he? I think Gillian married him to get over her affair with Burton Walker. Burton Walker let Gillian down badly – there's no getting away from that. I don't think she'd ever trust another man, except Jake.'

'At least she trusts Jake,' Julia replied hotly. 'That's always something. Some people, once they've been let down, never trust another man – or girl, as the case may be. Gillian could have ended up by being a bitter – *man-hater*, couldn't she?' A little embarrassed by her outburst, she added, 'There's nobody quite as insufferable as a *man-* or *woman-hater*.'

CHAPTER SEVEN

THE following day Julia went straight to Leon's gallery. Leon was there, along with his assistant, who was wearing a yellow organdie cavalier shirt and satin-lined slacks of bronze lace leaves. That was the kind of gallery it was.

Leon, dashing in white turtleneck cashmere sweater and narrow white slacks like a fencer, came rushing at Julia from across a shimmering expanse of bronze and white mosaic tiles. 'Darling,' he folded Julia in his arms and kissed her, 'this is marvellous. Marvellous!' He led her towards a long line of elegant storage units.

'It is,' she said breathlessly, thrilled for the moment at being back in the swing of things again, 'isn't it?'

'Come and meet Nicolette, darling.' Leon led her across the bronze and white floor again to the vision in yellow organdie and bronze lace leaves, and afterwards he said, 'Julia darling, you're going to come along with me to the show ground to see what we've been doing there, and then you're going to have lunch with me.'

Leon, with an expert's know-how, powered by a brilliant imagination, had changed a depressing stand into a magnificent mock gallery which held the visitors' eyes, and interest, at every turn.

Looking at it, Julia was aware of the watchfulness and thoughtfulness of the decorator. No wonder he was making such a name for himself.

Carefully he had managed to create something fabulous, which was going to make every visitor to the mock gallery go away feeling vaguely restless, with the thought that something had to be done about getting to work back home to create the kind of atmosphere that went with the kind of things Leon Ladenza had to offer.

Here, Leon's assistant's name was Ronny and she was every bit as glamorous as Nicolette. Apparently the girls took it in turns to be at the stand, with Leon dashing from the gallery to stand in between.

To begin with, Leon guided Julia to a sensational peacock blue swivel chair. 'Just look gorgeous for the moment, darling,' he told her.

The Royal Show had been open for two days, but the crowd was thick. Fashions ranged from the sublime to the ridiculous but there was a smattering of elegant suits and suitable shoes.

The mock gallery was never vacant for a moment. Leon and Ronny were plied with questions, and at one stage Leon came over to the sensational peacock-blue swivel chair and muttered, 'I'm a physical wreck, darling. Ronny has gone to lunch. When she comes back we'll go and have something to eat ourselves. How's that?'

'Fine,' Julia answered.

'One has to watch every move here. What some of these people lack is *feeling* – and as for their brats, darling – ! Heaven forbid that I should ever become a father.'

Julia's eyes followed his dark lenses to a spot in the exhibit, where one small boy was busy eating ice-cream which was joining forces with the grime on his face and hands. As he licked and sucked he was contemplating several ceramic panels, and it was obvious to the casual onlooker that this small boy was living in a world of colour and form.

Julia laughed softly, 'Oh, isn't he cute? You can't tell me that you wouldn't like to be the father of a little son like that? I just refuse to believe it.'

Leon turned a pained face to her. 'You can't be serious, Julia?' She stiffened at his tone and felt disappointed in him.

By the time Ronny came back from lunch Leon was irritable and even inclined to be stand-offish with the people who were visiting the stand, although he was too smart to be downright rude.

'Let's go for lunch,' he said. 'If you want to powder your nose first, darling, there's a powder-room just round the corner. I'll be with you in a moment.'

On their way to the restaurant they passed the stand of the Natal Parks Board. 'By the way,' Leon's voice was off-hand, 'Kathy's boy-friend is here. I've heard, of course, about Kathy's great departure. If our Kathy only knew what *we* knew, she'd kick herself, wouldn't she?'

A wave of apprehension washed over Julia. 'I didn't know that *he* was to be here in Pietermaritzburg. I take it that you *do* mean – Grant Tyler?'

'Who else, darling?'

And then at the back of Julia's mind she remembered Grant's words on the way to the station at Hlageni, 'Well I suppose I might just be seeing you, one of these days?' It had sounded like a question, and she had said, 'Well, naturally.'

'Let me show you around very quickly,' said Leon, cutting into her thoughts, and because it seemed stupid to protest, she allowed him to take her hand and guide her up the steps which led into the Natal Parks Board stand.

The foyer was banked with shrubs and rocks on one side, and a tremendous curved desk on the other. There were two Game Wardens behind the desk, and at the far end a young Game Ranger was using the telephone next to a girl who sat watching the crowds go by.

From the foyer they went into a small hall where women clerks and Game Wardens were busy advising the public about holidays at various Reserves and answering questions regarding their work as conservation officers for the flora and fauna of the Natal regions.

'Through here,' Leon told her, leading the way through to what could only be described as a mini-games park.

In this area there were several hartebeest calves, wild duck and eland. There was a high fence to prevent the otters behind it from escaping, while further down several juvenile crocodiles basked in the sun on the banks of a man-made river.

At that moment Julia froze, holding her breath, as she spotted Grant Tyler, looking more handsome than she remembered him. He, too, was busy answering questions from curious visitors. Standing next to him was a small boy who waited patiently for Grant to answer his own questions, from time to time. Whenever Grant did have a moment to spare he would incline his head to listen to this small, freckle-faced child, and several times he laughed and ruffled the boy's untidy hair.

'We'll go and say hello to Tyler, darling,' Leon looked at his watch, 'and then we really must go and eat.'

Grant, however, had spotted them and was coming towards them. 'Hello,' he said, and then, to Julia, 'So you made it?'

'Yes.' Her manner was stiff. 'I didn't expect to find you here, though. I'm surprised that my father didn't mention it, even if you didn't.'

He gave her a slow, amused look. 'Didn't I mention it?' His blue eyes were mocking. 'I was sure I had.'

Julia felt annoyance surfing to the top. This was an old game, she thought, and began to play it with a certain amount of viciousness.

'Well, you possibly did. I can't remember, actually Those, of course, would be yours?' She looked towards the crocodiles.

'Uh-huh.' He ruffled the boy's hair again. 'So you want to be a Game Ranger, huh?' he laughed. 'Well, good for you!'

'Where do you find the patience, Grant?' Leon looked frankly bored. 'Didn't think you had it in you, somehow.'

'I'm really very patient,' Grant replied, looking at Julia. 'Far more patient than you think, actually.'

'Well, I suppose you can afford to be,' Leon answered shortly. 'After all, the little brats can't harm your crocodiles, can they? When I think of the damage these people do at my place I get positively sick.'

'Now I can see why you were always having to dash into Hlageni,' Julia said to Grant. 'I suppose you were making arrangements about getting your crocodiles up here to Pietermaritzburg? How *did* you get them here, by the way?'

The look he gave her was maddening. 'In a taxi, Julia.'

'Really? It's astonishing what taxis can do, isn't it?' She sounded polite, rather than furious.

'Darling,' Leon said, 'we must go. You'll have to excuse us, dear boy, but we were about to have lunch. We just dropped in to see how you were coping with these ghastly crowds.'

'It's all in the game, dear boy,' replied Grant, and Julia knew by his smile that he was trying to annoy her – and succeeding.

They had to find their own table at the restaurant and Leon flung himself into a chair. 'I'm sorry about this, darling. This is a positively loathsome place. Whenever I have to come here, I feel utterly invaded by sheer *bad* taste.'

'It's not serious, darling. Don't make yourself sick over it.' Julia found herself falling into their old jargon. Give her Leon's eccentric blunderings, she thought, they were far better than Grant Tyler's sarcasm, any day.

She knew that, while they were in this particular restaurant, however, nothing would put Leon in a good mood. He had to be surrounded by sheer *good* taste.

'They have to cater for hundreds of people, you know,' she ventured. 'People who come and go all day long. It's that kind of place, after all. I think they do jolly well, taking everything into consideration.'

Leon turned his dark lenses full on her, 'Julia,' he said coldly, 'let's not talk about it, shall we? It pains me to have to eat in the place, let alone go on and on about it. I only eat here when we have been so busy that I have no other option. Tell me, have you brought a gown to dance in?'

'Yes, I have. I brought the gown I wore to the graduation ball, as a matter of fact.'

'Good, because we'll be dancing, of course, when all this hectic rush is over.'

While the waitress hovered around Leon, Julia, watching him, was aware of the conflicting feelings he was arousing in her as he virtually cringed away from the possibility of any kind of personal contact between himself and the waitress. While one part of her was faintly amused that Leon could be so positively eccentric, the other part was aware of a slow mounting anger that he should be so bad-mannered.

The waitress dropped a spoon and it fell on Leon's lap. 'Sorry,' she said.

'Don't give it another thought.' Leon placed the spoon on the table. 'I want you to feel perfectly free to consider my lap as your off-loading zone, while I'm here.'

Julia felt her face go hot.

'Humanity at its very worst,' Leon said, through clenched teeth, when the woman had gone. He looked down at the grill in front of him. 'I doubt if I am going to be able to stomach this, darling.'

'Well, do you mind if *I* go ahead?' Julia's voice showed her displeasure. 'I'm looking forward to it. I'm famished. I had an early breakfast before I came into town with Jake.'

'Go ahead – but take my advice and be careful of your teeth. I happen to speak from experience. The last time I was forced to eat here my face was one vast pulsating ache. I'm sorry about this, darling, I really am. Circumstances and all that sort of thing, you know.'

'Oh, darling, it's not so bad, really.' Julia was provoked into laughter and then, in confusion, she broke off as Grant Tyler, handsome and cool in his khaki gaberdine, approached them.

He came straight over to their table and stood next to the vacant chair at their table. 'I was told to find myself a table,' he gave them a pleasant enough smile. 'May I share yours – the place is just about packed out, as you can see. It's the most popular restaurant at the Show and serves the best grills.'

Leon waved a languid hand in the direction of the third chair. 'My dear fellow, make yourself at home. But you can't really mean that – about the grills?' He began to pick at the grill in front of him. 'My senses are all completely assaulted and ravaged. Terrible place, isn't it? Unexpectedly, Julia doesn't seem to mind it.' A nerve twitched in his cheek. 'How you've changed, darling!' He gave Julia a chilled look.

'Nonsense.' The tone of his voice changed the tone of hers. 'I haven't changed at all.' She gave him an angry look and then bit her lip as she told herself that Leon's remark was too trivial to be worth this unreasonable anger on her part.

Eventually Leon gave up all pretence of eating and pushed back his plate and his chair and then sat with one elegant slim leg thrown over the other.

'Darling,' Julia forgot about Grant, 'it's not serious. What have you got to worry about?' Although she was being flippant she was annoyed. Frankly, Leon was maddening!

Leon uncrossed his legs and then eased his position to fold one leg over the other again. The tips of his fingers met. 'I'm not worried,' he answered. 'I'm depressed. I'm sick of feeling tired and dirty. I shall be glad when this beastly Show is over. Places like this have the power to caused me the most hideous distress.' He glanced around the restaurant and then looked at Grant. 'What about you?'

'I'm easily pleased. I'm out of touch, I guess.' Grant stopped cutting his steak, for a moment, to look about him. 'It serves my purpose. Actually, that's what counts here. After all, all that people want in between tramping round from stand to stand is a quick meal.'

'Talking about stands, have you seen Leon's exhibit?' Julia asked, anxious to get the subject away from the restaurant. 'It's a sort of mock gallery and it's absolutely fabulous.'

'I'm afraid not. I've been too busy keeping the crocodiles from getting homesick,' Grant replied. His smile just bordered on being sarcastic.

'By the way,' Leon asked unexpectedly, 'apart from the Umkambo Game Reserve, where is your home?'

'This is my home town – Pietermaritzburg.' Grant's tanned face was bent over his grill.

'Really?' Leon looked frankly bored. 'Where were you educated, old boy? Went to Tulbagh House myself.'

The babble of voices was very loud. Somewhere in the distance there was music, loud and restless.

'What do you know?' Grant's head was still bent over his plate. He did not look up. The thick dark lashes threw into relief his tanned skin. 'I went to Tulbagh House myself. From then onwards it was the Townes Agricultural School.'

Some of Leon's energy returned. 'Bit of a comedown for a Tulbagh House boy, wasn't it, old fellow? Plug or something?'

'Surprisingly enough, no. I worked for a year as a stockman and then joined the Natal Parks Board.'

'As you say, you're easily pleased, old boy.' Leon regarded Grant with a ruined expression. His sensitive hands moved with continued tension and he kept looking in the direction of Julia's plate, anxious for her to finish eating so that they could leave.

Grant looked up. 'I did what suited me.' His voice held a hint of amusement in it, but his eyes were cold.

'Will you ever come back here to Pietermaritzburg,' Julia asked, 'or are you going to spend the rest of your days in a Game Reserve?'

'Seems a futile business to me,' Leon cut in. 'Still, I suppose we *do* have a need for Game Rangers.'

'I might *have* to give up my work in the Reserve,' said Grant and a strange shock went through Julia as he met her eyes. 'I might have to become a farmer.'

'A farmer? You're not a very ambitious type, are you?' Leon sounded played out now, as though he had given up trying to find Grant Tyler interesting. He yawned, without flicking a muscle of his dark face. 'So tell – why a farmer, Grant?'

'For the simple reason that I happen to have a farm at my disposal.'

'Not here, of course? You mean in some frightful little part of the Karroo, or something?'

'No, here – just outside 'Maritzburg, actually.'

Julia's eyes widened. 'That sounds marvellous! Personally, I'd love to live on a farm.'

Leon laughed then. He changed the position of his legs with quick, sharp movements. 'You? You – on a farm, darling? Oh, come off it, Julia. Who are you trying to kid?' He looked at Grant. 'This girl would go *mad* on a farm.' His dark lenses concentrated on Julia again. 'Don't talk rubbish, darling.'

Flushing a little, Julia repeated, 'I'd love to live on a farm.'

'Well, maybe you would – if it had a freeway into town at the foot of the farm gates and the house was of the finest architecture and riddled with gorgeous things, but I guess you don't get farms like that. Frankly,' he permitted himself a little smile, 'I wouldn't know a farm if I saw one. Not that it particularly worries me, I can assure you.'

'Let me show you my farm.' Grant smiled a pleasant boyish smile, but he did not look at Julia. 'Then you'd always know a farm if ever you saw one.' He cut into his steak. 'Well, what do you say?'

'Well, that's – very kind of you, dear boy.' Leon looked down at one swinging shoe. Julia drew a suffocated breath as she watched him. 'Would I have to tramp around the cow fields and all that sort of thing?' He lifted his chin and the dark lenses were aimed back in Grant's direction.

'Not necessarily,' Grant's reply was casual. 'I'd give you lunch.'

A passer-by bumped against Leon's swinging foot and

apologized. Leon looked up. 'Not at all. The floor is all yours.'

Today Leon had a strange capacity for arousing anger in Julia. Suddenly he looked at her and said, 'What about it, sweetie? Would you like to see Grant's farm?'

'I'd like to – but I haven't been invited.' She smiled recklessly at Grant.

'Julia,' he said, also smiling, 'would you like to see my farm? You're very welcome.'

'You're not joking?' Her face was serious now. 'Is there – *really* a farm?'

'Of course there's a farm.'

'Well, then, thank you. I'd like to – very much.'

'When are you going to be free?' Grant's glance embraced both Leon and Julia. 'Speaking for myself, I'll be free from midday tomorrow. We could leave here and go to my farm for lunch. It would save Leon having to eat here.'

'Well, yes, that would be perfectly all right.' Leon sounded doubtful, now that there really was a farm. 'I could make a plan, I suppose. Julia?'

'Your plans are my plans.' Her smile was wide now, and happy, although why she should be so happy about going to Grant Tyler's farm she didn't rightly know.

Grant arranged to meet them the following day and on their way back to his exhibit Leon asked, 'What is that fellow trying to do to me?'

Julia looked at him curiously. 'Why?' Her hair was burnished by the sun to a glowing golden brown and there was a wide excited look in her green eyes.

Leon stopped walking to say, 'Darling, imagine me tramping round a dirty old farm! How do you see it?' He sounded sarcastic and nervous.

'Well, you sounded as though you wanted to go.' Julia discovered that her temper was in a dangerous state.

'Oh, I admit that, in a moment of mad weakness, I wanted to go. It sounded fun, and then suddenly the stupidity of it struck me. I'm not interested in farms, darling. I'll get us out of the arrangement, if it's the last thing I do.'

'Leon! You can't.' Brush strokes of shadow fell across the show-ground as people milled around.

'What is this word can't? I'm going to. I'll think up an

excuse for both of us.'

'Not for me. I'm góing. I'd never dream of being so rude. Grant Tyler is probably making arrangements at this very minute with his manager, or whoever it is that looks after the farm for him.'

Leon looked at the crowds with distaste. 'I can't understand you,' he said. 'You'll be bored stiff – so why go? You must learn, darling, to do only what you yourself would like to do.'

'Well, I'd like to go to Grant Tyler's farm.' Her lower lip was thrust out defiantly.

'Something must have been left out of me, because I, on the other hand, should loathe to see Grant Tyler's farm, and what's more, I don't intend to see it. You'll offer my apologies, seeing that you're so set on going. Besides, I'm pressed for time. The fellow had no right to do this to me. Actually, I'm pressed to the point of a physical and a mental breakdown. I feel ghastly.'

'I'd rather the apologies came from you.' Julia's voice was stiff. 'I'm no use at telling lies.'

'What you don't seem to understand, darling, is that they're not lies. However, I'll do that. I'll apologize for myself.'

When they reached the exhibit Leon said, 'Does it look like lies to you? Look at the people. It's been like this since the Show opened. Apart from all this, there's the gallery in town and two others to think of. Somehow I have to manage all three. Things await my constant attention. My life is riddled with trunk calls.'

'I don't want to argue with you,' Julia turned her face away.

'Oh, I agree,' Leon said swiftly. 'This wretched argument has progressed beyond the limit of sanity. So let's just call it off, shall we? You go to your Ranger's farm – I'll offer my apologies and I'll stay behind.' He nodded his head disdainfully in the direction of the Natal Parks Board Stand. 'I don't believe the fellow went to Tulbagh House.' His face was a vague pallor now beneath the dark lenses.

At the end of the day, after helping to answer questions at the exhibit, Julia went back to the Felwoods' to change and then Leon picked her up in his car and took her to the exclusive air-conditioned restaurant in town.

'About tomorrow,' she said, after Leon had driven her back to the Feldwoods'. 'Have you made up your mind what you are going to do?'

'I told you,' he sounded impatient, 'I think I made it perfectly clear. I'm not going. That's all there is to it. You go, by all means.' He gave a sarcastic smile. 'You're playing with fire, aren't you, darling? I can't imagine what dear Kathy will have to say about it when she finds out. Anyway, leaving Kathy out of it, the fresh air should do you the world of good. Make the best of it and forget about everything else.'

Suddenly exasperated, Julia said, 'Have you made your excuses to Grant?'

'I'll make them in the morning. It will be easy enough just to dash over to see him at the Parks Board stand. Perhaps I'll even do my bit by offering to let him have Nicolette to baby-sit for his crocodiles.' He laughed. 'Darling, imagine it! Nicolette in her bronze lace slacks!' His next remark came after a pause, veiled with caution. 'By the way, darling, what do you think of Nicolette? She's – devastatingly beautiful, don't you think?'

'Completely devastating.' Julia's expression suffered very slightly.

'Anyway, I think you're being marvellously sporting about this ghastly farm business and I hope a miracle happens, darling, and you have a simply wonderful time. You deserve it.' Leon sounded cheerful now that he had decided not to go.

'Thank you.' Julia's voice had an edge to it. 'And, Leon, thank you for a lovely meal.'

He shrugged elegantly. 'Not at all. It was really *very simple*, darling, but I'm so glad you enjoyed it,' he answered modestly.

This was not strictly true, so far as the meal was concerned.

They'd both had fish, which had been marinated for an hour or two in Winterhoek white wine and wrapped individually in foil and placed amongst embers to bake. With the Galjoen they'd drunk chilled Theuniskraal. Then Julia had ordered grilled chicken and with this she had sipped Witzenberg Winterhoek. Leon's succulent T-bone steak had been marinated for three days in a tangy sauce made from oil, Villa Rosa, finely chopped garlic, salt and pepper. The steak was served with jacket potatoes and green salads and Villa Rosa wine.

Finally they had both decided on braaied fruits – grilled banana, served with whipped cream and glazed apple brushed frequently with sugar and white Winterhoek wine. The apple was served hot with a glass of Drostdy Full Cream sherry.

At the Feldwoods' door he said, 'Isn't this a hideous fright of a door, Julia? What they need here, of course, is . . .'

Julia cut him short. 'It's not just as simple as that. Jake hasn't got the money. All Jake's money is tied up in his business.'

'Let's face it – Jake just hasn't got the imagination,' he said, and Julia refused to argue with him.

'I'll see you tomorrow,' she said. 'I'll be in at the exhibit all morning to help you. How did I do today?'

'You were marvellous, darling, and I do thank you.' He took her fingers and kissed them. 'In the afternoon you will go to Grant's farm?' He stopped kissing her fingers.

'Yes.'

'Very well.' He released her hand. 'Oh, one thing, Julia – don't forget to wear sensible shoes, will you?' He placed his arms lightly about her and kissed her.

She moved out of his embrace. 'I won't . . . and I won't ask you in, darling. I know how this old house *depresses* you.'

'How right you are – and yet it could be a show-place, with a little imagination,' Leon answered, and Julia took a steadying breath. 'Goodnight, darling,' she said. 'Drive carefully going back to town, will you?' She opened the old panelled door and went inside.

In the morning, she helped at the mock gallery and then, at twelve o'clock sharp she went along to the place where she and Leon had arranged to meet Grant Tyler. He was already there, and because she never quite knew how to take him, a pulse started hammering in her throat.

He smiled a quick smile and this time he looked as though he meant it. 'Hello.' He sounded cheerful.

'I – I hope I haven't kept you?' Julia asked. Her green

123

eyes were hidden behind outsize sun-glasses. Then she took off the glasses and frowned a little because of the glare of the sun.

'I've just arrived, as a matter of fact,' he told her. He was dressed in a long-sleeved khaki shirt, with a tie, and khaki gaberdine pants.

'You know, of course, about – Leon?' Julia's manner was suddenly nervous. 'I mean, he *did* come over to your stand to explain, didn't he? About – not coming ...' her voice dragged to a standstill.

Lifting one khaki-clad shoulder, Grant said, 'No. No, he didn't come over to – explain. What was there to explain?'

She felt exposed and was at a loss how to cover up for Leon's bad manners. 'Well, something must have detained him. He was going to come over and – to tell you all about it – he was so busy, he ...' she shrugged and gestured with one hand, 'Leon moves around – he *entertains*. He's never free ...'

'All right. You've made your point and to use one of your own corny expressions, Julia, it's not serious, darling.' Grant's voice was caustic. 'You don't have to explain. What about you? There's absolutely nothing to bind you, you know. You're a free agent. Just say the word – if you don't want to go and we'll call the whole thing off.' He almost sounded as though he didn't want her to come to the farm, after all.

'Well, *I* had intended coming, all along.' Her face felt stiff. 'But if you'd rather not ...' She felt furious with Leon – betrayed.

'Come along, then.' He slid his tie up into position, although it didn't really need the adjustment. 'My car is in the parking ground. No Land Rover, this time.'

As they walked towards the parking ground, Julia tried to match her step to his long, loose-limbed stride and their shadows moved directly before them and were getting shorter all the time.

She fingered the buttons of the jacket of the light suit she was wearing. 'I should have come over to your stand to ask you,' she said, 'whether it would be all right to come dressed like this. You see, I've been helping at the stand all morning and I had to wear something suitable.'

Grant gave her a quick, careless glance and then looked away again. 'You're quite all right as you are.'

'I brought a pair of flat-heeled shoes. They're in my bag.' She held out the large raffia bag she was carrying. 'I know slacks would have been better . . .'

'You can relax,' he told her. 'I am not going to take you tramping about the cow fields. We won't have all that much time. We'll be having lunch, and anyway, to put your mind at rest, my mother should be dressed very much the same way as you are yourself.' There was an undertone of irritation, crossed with amusement, in his voice.

'Oh.' She was surprised, because somehow he had given her the impression that there would be a manager at the farm. It had not sounded as though parents were involved in his farm.

When they got to his car she stood next to him while he opened the door for her. A sudden gust of wind started to blow her tawny hair about and she tried to do something about it by taking her scarf out of her bag, but Grant said, 'Let it blow!'

His presence excited her, actually, and this she put down to the fact that he looked very masculine and handsome in his khaki and that she had never been out with a Game Ranger before. She could not really count the previous times.

'Too bad your boy-friend couldn't manage it,' he said, spoiling her thoughts for her. He slid into the car beside her. 'I hope I won't bore you too much – on my own.'

For a moment she gave him a long look and then, with a slow blink of her eyes she said quietly, 'You won't bore me at all.'

He drove fast, but not nervously, like Leon, and they soon left the hill-rimmed city of Pietermaritzburg behind and began to climb the long hill out of it.

'It's quite the ideal farm, in a way,' Grant said, 'because as a matter of fact, the dual highway does go right past the old farm gate. That's not so bad, for a start, it is it?'

'No.' She felt a strange and quickening annoyance. 'I'm quite aware that you're trying to relay a message, by the way.'

'Oh? What is the message?'

'Well, you seem to think that I weigh everything up by

125

these standards – the dual highway, gorgeous furniture and the things that go along with it, swimming-pools making cobalt shapes upon green lawns and flagged terraces decorated by glamorous garden and pool-side furniture – just because the Finishing School had them.'

'Well, don't you?' There was something about the question.

'No.' She took a breath. 'I'd live in – in an antheap, if I *had* to!'

'Well, I guess we'd all live in an antheap – *if we had to*.' He turned to look at her. 'Wouldn't we?'

When she made no attempt to answer him he said, 'Green eyes.'

From where they were now they had a magnificent view of Pietermaritzburg in the valley. The hills surrounding it looked hydrangea-blue behind a screen of haze.

The road had straightened out a little, although they were still climbing and then, when they had run out of things to say, Grant slackened speed and turned off at a point where two large white posts, half hidden under a bank of purple bougainvillea, apparently showed the way to the farm.

CHAPTER EIGHT

THE Cape-style house was a genuine example of the Cape Dutch architecture that was popular two hundred years ago. In another two hundred years from now, thought Julia, it might well be declared an historical monument. This was a house which, although it cherished the past, was also aware of the present.

Julia, viewing the house from the outside, felt a sense of expectancy about what it was going to look like from the inside – and what it must be like to live in such a house.

White, gabled and gracious, it stood in a magnificent setting of flowering bougainvillea, hibiscus and other flowering shrubs. A low window-box ran the length of the verandah and it blazed with red and pink geraniums.

'Surely this can't be the farmhouse?' she said, without thinking, and then blushed. 'I'm sorry,' she said. 'It seems so beautiful – I hadn't quite pictured it this way.'

It wasn't surprising, she thought, thinking about Grant's sneering remarks at her efforts of decorating 'on a shoestring' in her father's bungalow at the Reserve.

He gave her a careless look. He seemed to be giving her an awful lot of careless looks, she thought, since their meeting in Pietermaritzburg. 'Well, I'm glad you like it. I – was sure that Leon would like it. Pity he couldn't make it – but I realize, of course, that he gets around a lot, that he's busy, that he *entertains* . . . still, another time, maybe.'

Julia let this slide.

Grant parked the car in a spacious area for this purpose which led Julia to think that the Tylers must *entertain* quite a lot themselves.

He switched off the engine and turned in his seat to look at her. His blue eyes travelled lazily over her face.

'The house is almost – like a painting, isn't it?' she said, to destroy the silence.

'You will see a painting of it, in the hall, as a matter of fact. My mother commissioned Simon Caister to paint it and, having been to the Azalea Park Finishing School, you will know all about Simon Caister.'

Her next remark was made in a small, contained sort of voice she did not know she possessed. 'You are obviously wealthy,' she said. 'Why, in that case, did you show such contempt towards my attempts at redecorating my father's bunglow? I find that rather puzzling.'

He gave her another lazy blue look. 'My parents are wealthy. *I* am not. I don't suppose you'll understand this, but I had to escape from it – quite apart from the fact that I'm essentially the outdoor type.'

'Why?' she asked. 'Why did you have to escape?'

'Because it was the result of money – hard-earned – by my father. However, the time is coming when I shall be expected to take over the farm, being the only son – the only child, as a matter of fact.' He rubbed a hand across his chin. 'My father is packing up, for health reasons. He and my mother intend to take a holiday – abroad somewhere. After that, when they return, they'll build a smaller home, here on the farm somewhere. It's going to be my lot to carry on here. This will be my home – where my son, if I ever happen to have a son, will carry on, when *I* pack up.'

Her smile was hesitant. 'I see.' She was so surprised that he had thawed out sufficiently to tell her so much about himself that she did not want to do or say anything which might spoil it.

He had slid his arm along the back of her seat, and as he removed it now she tensed as his fingers just touched the back of her neck.

'Come along,' he said. 'It's a wonder my mother hasn't dashed out to meet us. She must be under the shower.'

They walked round to the front of the house which commanded a beautiful view of the garden with its lawns, flower-beds and shrubs. Beyond retaining stone walls and steps, fitted with wrought-iron lamps, the ground dropped down to more lawns and flower beds, a tennis court to one side, and a rose garden. As a backdrop to the tennis court and the rose garden there were tall trees, which did not interfere with the view from the house, because of the slope. It was from this point, surmised Julia correctly, that the farm lands would continue. 'What kind of farm is this?' she asked, looking at Grant.

'Dairy. That's the main concern here. Are you afraid of a bull?' he grinned at her.

'I suppose I would be, if I came face to face with one. My big fear happens to be snakes.'

'Snakes?' He gave her a puzzled look. 'And yet you wear gold-strapped sandals at night at Umkambo?'

Suddenly the Umkambo Game Reserve seemed part of another life. She laughed. 'I'm never afraid of the snake I don't see – it's the snake I *do* see that I'm terrified of. I suppose my fear stems from when I was a small girl. My mother was always afraid that I'd be bitten by a black or a green mamba. They were always about.' She stopped talking. Near the house there was a blue and yellow mosaic-lined swimming-pool and the sun made wavering streaks of yellow light beneath the water. Grant told her that the old loft, complete with ladder, was really a very well equipped change house.

Sally Tyler met them in a hall where gold damask curtains toned with Persian rugs which were enhanced by a magnificent crystal chandelier. Simon Caister's impression, in oils, of the house dominated one wall.

'Hello there!' Grant's mother's eyes went from Grant to Julia. They were what could only be described as smiling eyes, and Julia couldn't imagine them ever not smiling.

'I thought there were to be three of you?' It was obvious to the casual visitor that Grant and his mother were good friends.

'Julia's boy-friend couldn't make it,' Grant said, and Julia thought bitterly, 'Oh, so there we go again?' but she kept on smiling.

'By the way,' Grant was saying, 'this is Julia Munro. You've heard me talk about Stan Munro. Well, as I explained to you, this is Stan's daughter.'

'Hello, Julia. I'm so pleased to meet you. I'm glad you happened to be in Pietermaritzburg at the same time as Grant. Come upstairs and prepare for lunch.'

'Thank you.' Julia liked Sally Tyler immediately.

'Your father is in the study, by the way,' Sally said, looking over her shoulder at Grant.

Taking Julia's arm, she then led her towards the ruby-red carpeted yellow-wood staircase. 'I've been looking forward to meeting you, Julia,' Sally Tyler said, while Julia was overcome by the magnificent pieces on display and Grant became more of a mystery to her. 'How do you like living in the Reserve?'

'Oh, I love it. I'm going to be terribly upset when my father's year is up and we have to leave – which will be at the end of December. He's retiring, of course. Grant probably told you.'

The staircase wall was hung with original paintings and prints and Persian rugs. 'You've just finished a year or so at a Finishing School, Grant tells me?' The smiling blue eyes which went so well with prematurely silver hair and a young face travelled over Julia.

'Yes, that's right.' Julia's voice immediately indicated that she was on the defensive now. 'I have.'

They were in a hallway now, furnished in the Italian Renaissance style, and this room was obviously the heart of the upper storey, with entrances to all the other rooms leading from it.

Sally led the way into what must have been her bedroom. 'I always had a longing to attend a Finishing School, but of course, in my day it was practically unheard-of, unless one went overseas somewhere. I used to read all the books I·could lay my hands on about girls going to Finishing Schools.'

Smiling politely, because this was Grant's mother and she did not want to go getting all involved, Julia said, 'Really?'

Sally Tyler's bedroom was extremely simple with its fitted Ambassador-blue carpet maintaining its continuity through to a luxurious dressing-room and on to her bathroom. She took Julia into the dressing-room and Julia was stunned by the sweep of built-in cupboards with their exquisite filigreed fittings.

Glass doors, with traditional small panes to match the architecture of the house, were open to a black-railed balcony and a light breeze stirred ivory satin floor-length curtains.

'I'd love to live in this house,' said Julia, on an impulse.

'Would you?' Sally sounded pleased. 'Although it's not far from town it can be lonely. We have no immediate neighbours.'

'I know – but that wouldn't worry me. I don't get bored easily. I – like doing things about a house.'

'What kind of things, Julia?' Grant's mother sounded a little on the amused side, as if she were trying to compare notes.

'Well,' Julia felt suddenly slightly ridiculous, 'I like — fiddling about . . .' She could feel the thump of her heart.

'Tell me about it.' Sally's smile was inviting. 'I like fiddling about too.'

Julia laughed then. 'I haven't had a real home since I was seven – since my mother died. It's just been – schools, but when I *do* have a home I like moving things about, experimenting with colour and so on.' She spread her hands. 'I've learned all about these things, but I've never had them. I like collecting things, although I've never had a chance to collect much. I've never had anywhere to put anything.' She shook her hair back. 'Grant, for some ridiculous reason, keeps referring to Leon Ladenza as my boy-friend. It's the way he says it that irritates me. I met Leon through the Finishing School. Leon has the sort of things in his galleries that we had to learn about. He often gave lectures. It's a pity he – couldn't come. He would have been interested in your collection because, of course, I can see that you have a priceless collection. I noticed the Martaban jar on our way up here which dates back to the Ming period . . . that's an example of the kind of things he lectured us about.'

'You don't want to take too much notice of Grant, Julia. He has a big chip on his shoulder. The first girl he ever had turned out to be a little gold-digger.' She laughed. 'In fact, that was some time ago, but if she were still in the picture today she'd probably have said, "I dig this place." She was more in love with this house than she was with Grant. Grant was still fairly young, but it didn't take him long to find out that his little girl-friend only clung to him because she had visions of a good marriage in her mind. Then,' she shrugged, 'poor Grant – he met another girl. He met her at Hlageni, I believe – *we* never met her, and although she never saw this house, she seemed to be madly in love with Grant, according to his letters. They actually became engaged, but before he had the chance to bring her home here the engagement fell through. Apparently Philippa decided that she couldn't take being a Game Ranger's wife, after all. The idea of living in a thatched-roofed bungalow in a Game Reserve didn't appeal to her. And so ...' she went on, but she was still smiling, 'Grant became a woman-hater. I thought they went out of existence years ago, but I was wrong. Frankly, Grant got over these two girls long ago – he just seems to think he owes it to himself not to trust another girl.' Sally glanced at the clock. 'Let's go downstairs. I'll get Grant to show you over the house – but, Julia, we really must try to get together again while you are here. I'll try to think of something. And before we go, don't let Grant get you down. By the way, I've been to the Leon Ladenza Gallery in Pietermaritzburg.'

They went back down the stairs. Grant was in the hall below looking up at them. 'What do you two get to talk about?' he asked.

Sally's laugh was soft. 'Oh, lots of things. We discovered that we have a lot in common. Grant, show Julia around, will you? But first introduce her to your father. Then give her a drink, and by that time lunch will be ready for serving. Will you do that?'

'Yes, ma'am. Julia, come and meet my father.' Grant seemed to be a different person, and Julia, not trusting his good mood, gave him a shaky smile.

Grant's father was in a book-lined, leather-filled study. When Grant opened the door he stood up behind his imposing stinkwood desk.

Tall, tanned and handsome, like his son, he said, 'So you've arrived?' He greeted Grant with the somewhat distant courtesy which led one to feel that Grant and the tawny-haired girl beside him did not quite belong to his world.

The entire wall, facing the garden, consisted of small-paned floor-to-ceiling glass windows with French doors, to one side, which opened out to the terrazzo-tiled verandah with its pink and red geranium-filled window box.

'I'd like you to meet Julia Munro,' said Grant. 'Stan Munro, her father, lives next door to me at the Reserve.'

'Ah yes, so you've told me. How do you do, Miss Munro? So you're busy helping at the Parks Board stand too, are you?'

'No,' Julia replied, 'I'm not. I – just happened to be in Pietermaritzburg while my father is in hospital. I'm staying with an aunt.'

'Oh, I see. Yes – er – Grant was telling me about your father. On the mend, though, isn't he? Nothing that diet can't check?'

'He's getting along very nicely, thank you.'

An elderly African manservant, in white trousers and jacket buttoned up to the neck, came into the study and put a silver tray with ice, bottles and glasses down on a side table, near the French doors.

'You'll have something to drink before lunch, of course?' James Tyler gesticulated towards the tray. 'Or would you two young people prefer to have it elsewhere?' He sounded as if this was what he hoped they'd prefer.

'Mother's orders are that I'm to show Julia around the house and then we'll have something long and cold to drink before lunch. We'll have it on the verandah, most probably.'

'Good.' James Tyler flicked his fingers against some paperwork. 'Just want to get these figures into some sort of shape,' he said. 'Good, then – I'll leave that part to you, Grant.'

When they were back in the hall again Grant said, 'Well, what shall I show you first?'

'I don't know.' They were becoming quietly friendly now. '*You* tell me.'

He grinned down at her. This was a Grant she had not known existed. 'Through here,' he said, 'to the lounge.' Julia smiled back. She was beginning to enjoy herself with him. He bowed, very formally, and because the next move was up to her Julia went through to the lovely room where more small-paned French doors led out to the verandah on two sides.

'It's beautiful,' she said, looking at the low, white fireplace which was flanked by handsome Louis chairs upholstered in wine satin.

'My mother preferred a low white fireplace to a great hulking hearth,' Grant said. 'I think I do too.'

'It's beautiful,' Julia repeated, looking around. She moved right into the room. The colours of the Louis chairs linked with the upholstery of a delicate blue and mushroom-pink button-backed suite and floor-length curtains which brushed an expanse of off-white carpeting upon which Persian rugs were scattered and made a pleasing contrast. Lovely lamps with pale pink shades were everywhere.

It was a quietly dignified room – a long way from the cane furniture of Grant's own living-room at the Umkambo Game Reserve – and, looking at it, Julia was at a loss to understand the handsome young Game Ranger who was standing with his hands in the pockets of his khaki slacks, watching her.

'This would be right up your street,' he said. It was a statement made in a studiously flat way.

Julia gave him a level look. 'Is it wrong to admire beautiful things?'

'What about outside?' He took his hands from his pockets and went to stand at one of the glass doors.

'It goes with the inside,' she told him. 'It's all beautiful – extremely well thought out and maintained.'

'From here you can't see the rest.' His voice was clipped almost. 'Past the swimming-pool, the tennis court, the rose garden. Sometimes it causes a headache – the dairy and, of course, the land, both with their problems and never-ending work. My father doesn't always spend his time sitting behind that stinkwood desk of his with the silver tray, bottles, glasses and clinking ice to one side of it. I won't either, when I take over. I'll work harder, probably, than I do at Umkambo.'

'What is it you want me to say?' Julia asked. She tried to suppress her temper. 'You want me to shudder away from the idea of a dairy and, as Leon would have said, the cow fields – and all the rest of it, don't you? You'd like me to do that, wouldn't you?'

'You don't have to shudder away from it. It's there. Most girls would hate to be involved in the work and worry that goes with running a farm, even a – an exceptional farm like this, and I guess you're no exception.'

'Did Stan – did *my father* tell you that he used to be a farmer?' she asked, when her anger passed a little. 'Farmers and Game Rangers seem to go hand in hand, don't they? Up until the time that my mother died I was brought up on a farm. For that matter, I wish I was still there.'

'Stan never talks about himself.' There was curiosity at the back of Grant's voice, but quite obviously he was not going to ask about it.

Julia could not contain herself any longer. 'No,' she said, in a tight little voice, 'you're right. He doesn't talk about himself.' There were shadows in her green eyes. 'He withdrew from life – *from me* – after my mother went out of his life – our lives. He forgot about me – what was going on inside me.' She took a deep breath. 'He sold the farm, the lovely old white house, and packed me off to a boarding school.' She shrugged her shoulders and went to stand away from him, by herself, near to the fire-place, where the books stood out in their bright jackets. There was a collection of blue and white porcelain, she noticed, in a cabinet against one wall. 'Of course,' she went on, 'it had to be a *plush* boarding school. He felt he owed me that much. He had to do the right thing by me.' She lifted a hand and rubbed her neck beneath her hair, as if the muscles were pulling there and she wanted to ease the tension a little. She dropped the hand and sighed. 'I suppose he was lost – but then he found himself again. He was lucky, far luckier than I've ever been. He found peace in the new kind of life he chose. After that, *I* was the one who was lost. Alone. No home. Just one plush school after another.' She swung round. 'I don't know why I'm telling you this – but yes, I do know. There is one thing I'd like to ask you. Can you blame me for wanting to decorate the very first home I've ever had since –' she shook her hair back, 'since I've almost forgotten when? The Finishing School, after Varsity, was his suggestion, not mine. To please him, I let him have his way. I've always tried to please him. Sending me to Azalea Park was *his* way of keeping me tied to him – he didn't want to lose me, although he didn't really have me. He was afraid that he would lose me, like he lost my mother. He became fear-ridden – just as you've become a woman-hater!' She stopped abruptly and she did not move. She could have bitten her tongue out, and she stood staring at the bright jackets of the books which didn't clash with the quiet colours of the room, only fitted in – because they belonged there.

There was a sickening kind of silence and then he said, 'Who said anything about a – woman-hater?' His voice was cold and it dragged.

Julia turned to look at him. 'I'm terribly sorry. It was a ridiculous thing to say and – I'm sorry. I really am. I'm a little on edge, I guess.'

There was another silence, and it went on and on, and all the time it went on Julia was conscious of the perfume of the flowers in Sally Tyler's vases, of the peculiar Oriental smell of the Persian rugs on the off-white carpeting. The floor-length blue and mushroom-pink curtains brushed the carpeting with their expertly stitched hems as the light breeze stirred them.

'I'm just a fool,' she murmured. 'I shouldn't have said that.'

'No,' he said. 'It's all right. What kind of farm was it? What kind of farmer was Stan?'

'Cane – on the north coast.'

'That would have accounted for the snakes?'

'Snakes?' She looked at him, puzzled.

'You mentioned that your mother was always afraid that you'd be bitten by a snake – a green mamba or a black mamba. I wondered at the time . . .'

'Oh!' She released a small breath. 'Yes. There were always snakes about – there was even a python once, I believe, although I didn't see it. The python was in the cane. The house – was cool. It had thick walls and it had a colonnaded approach to the huge six-panelled front door . . .' she covered her eyes with her finger tips. 'I've tried not to – not to think of it – for a long time.' She took her fingers away and knew, with a sudden fright, that they were wet. Somehow, Grant had moved and he was standing in front of her, only a few inches away, and she heard a sigh, which could have been the hems of those elegant curtains, as they brushed the thick-piled carpet – or it could have been Grant sighing – or herself sighing – she didn't quite know.

'I'll – I'll show you upstairs,' he said, not mentioning the finger tips, which he must have seen, or the white house that she had tried not to think about – for a long time, 'when you're ready.'

'I'm ready,' she said, in a small voice. 'I've already seen your mother's room. It's gorgeous – and the dressing-room, with all its cupboards and vanity units.'

'When my parents rebuild, the room will be there –

waiting for the bride they're waiting for me to find. At the risk of disappointing my parents, that room should be unoccupied for a long time.' He shrugged. 'I guess they all expect something of us.' His face was serious. 'After you've looked around upstairs – we'll have that drink and then, after that, it will be back to the juvenile crocodiles, so far as I'm concerned. And – *you*?'

The question hung on an invisible thread. 'Me?' Julia blinked. 'It's all mapped out – I'm helping Leon again, this afternoon.'

'I see. It's all mapped out. Well, come along, then.'

Later they had drinks on the side verandah, just the two of them, sitting side by side on cane high-stools with coral cushions. The cane bar was placed near the French doors to the lounge and Julia could still smell the Persian rugs, even though they were not new. Grant poured her a shandy and himself a beer, and she held the long, slender glass to the sun which filtered through a creeper which grew against a trellis, nearby, and which flecked the white terrazzo-tiled verandah with rapid black shadows. 'It looks marvellously cold and inviting,' she said, 'after all that heat and dust at the Show. Thank you.'

After lunch, he took her back to the show-ground, and when he had parked the car, he turned to look at her. 'Well,' he said, 'it's practically three o'clock. You'll get the sack.'

She smiled. 'Thank you for the lunch. I enjoyed it – and I adored visiting your home and meeting your parents.'

'I'm glad you enjoyed it.'

She was conscious of him – of his lean, tanned good looks. She could sense a change in him, but she couldn't quite make up her mind what it was. He seemed moody again. Perhaps he was thinking of Kathy. It should have been Kathy, after all, who should have been with him today – Kathy, who had not known that Grant was going to surprise her by being at the Natal Parks Board Stand and who had gone away . . .

Suddenly she didn't want to look at him. She didn't want to care about him.

'Well,' he said, 'let's get back, shall we? Better late than never, I suppose.'

They began to walk across the dusty grass, in the direction of the colourful hive of activity. It seemed strange to think that, all the time they had been in the tranquil atmosphere of the farm, this had been going on. It was just a case of coming back in where they had gone out.

'You'd be amazed,' Julia told him, 'how busy Leon is kept at his exhibit. He's made a marvellous name for himself, you know. Your mother knew it immediately.'

'You don't say? Well, good for him.' The sun sliced through the air, which was getting crisper every day now. At the Agricultural section Grant paused. 'This is where you'll usually find my old man, when he's here. You'd probably find my mater at the Leon Ladenza Stand.'

'Well, good for *her*,' Julia replied quickly. 'Why shouldn't she? Just because she happens to be married to a farmer it doesn't mean that she should be immune to lovely things. How awful to have a wife like that!' She turned her head away from him. 'I'd hate to have a wife like that.'

'Did *I* say I'd like a wife like that?'

'No, but . . .'

He surprised her by crossing round to the other side of her where he could brush her chin lightly with his knuckles, and then he spoilt this friendly gesture by saying, 'You'd better be getting back to your boy-friend.'

'Yes.' Stung by the tone of his voice, she said, 'I'd better be, hadn't I?'

At Leon's mock gallery there were people everywhere. 'I don't know why I bother with this sort of thing,' he muttered, not bothering to greet Julia or to ask about the lunch at the farm. 'People grabbing, touching, plying us with a lot of stupid questions.'

'These are your potential customers,' retorted Julia, still smarting over Grant Tyler. 'That's the object of your exhibit, isn't it?'

Leon ignored the question. 'Well, did you have a simply *ru*-ral time, darling?'

'It was marvellous. You should have come. It came as a complete surprise. Cape-style house, filled with antiques and gorgeous things. Actually, Sally Tyler – Grant's mother – has visited your gallery in town.'

'Really?' Leon's voice was indifferent. 'Well, a lot of people visit my galleries, darling. What surprises me, though,

138

is that the Game Ranger's mother should be one of them.'

He took her out to a very late meal and then they danced at an expensive little place that was just as eccentric as Leon was himself. And then, when he took her back to the Feldwoods', he expressed his usual horror over the house. 'I can't understand it,' he said. 'Why doesn't Jake *do* something?'

'Money!' Julia replied. She was shocked at the snappy tone of her voice. 'Honestly, the way you go on and on over Jake's house! It really is a very nice house.'

They were standing beneath the verandah lamp and he gave her a pained look. 'Well, it is *nice*, I'll grant you that, darling – but who the hell wants a *nice* house?'

'I won't ask you in,' she knew she was being treacherous, 'I should hate to have you suffer, darling. You do understand?'

As she stood watching his low-slung car roaring down the drive-way a flicker of a smile crossed her face.

The following day Grant's mother came to the Show and Julia met her at Leon's exhibit. As a result of this visit to Leon's mock gallery Sally Tyler invited Julia to the farm again. 'Drive back with me now,' she said. 'I came in my own car – James had to come in early, so he used his car. I'll drive you back later this afternoon. Or you might like to have dinner with us? Grant, unfortunately, won't be home.'

'Thank you.' Julia felt strangely flattered and pleased. 'I'd love to come back with you. I – don't know about dinner, though. I had promised my aunt to be home. I dined out last night – it would seem rather unfair to do so again this evening.'

They spent the afternoon talking, and Sally was able to show Julia more of the house and the various treasures which she had collected over the years.

Towards the end of Julia's visit she said, 'I've enjoyed this, Julia – just the two of us. I'm going to be sorry when you've gone back to Umkambo. When do you go?'

'Frankly, at any time now. I've been in touch with my father, of course, by telephone, and he's getting on famously and should be allowed home quite soon now. But perhaps we'll meet again at the Reserve? I suppose you do come to see Grant there occasionally?'

'I can't say off-hand,' Sally told her. 'The farm demands a lot of us, of course, although you wouldn't think so to look at it. Anyway, if you don't go back for a day or two yet, and if Grant can leave his crocodiles for a while, perhaps we can all get together here again? Grant could drive you out.' Sally hesitated. 'When did you last see him, by the way?'

Julia was startled by the unexpected intensity of Sally Tyler's question.

'Not since I was here last, as a matter of fact.'

'Oh, I see. Make allowances for him, will you, Julia? He's not so bad, really. Actually, I think he's fallen in love. It's only a guess on my part, actually. He has mentioned the girl's name several times – and it's not like Grant to do that.'

For a moment Julia wondered whether she should tell Grant's mother about Kathy and the misunderstanding which had caused Kathy's ignorance as to Grant's activities in Pietermaritzburg, but she decided against it. Sally Tyler would find out sooner or later.

On the last day of the Show Leon said, 'By the way, Julia sweetie, what kind of gown did you bring to dance in? Anything I've seen?' They were having lunch together at a smart little place in town.

'I told you,' she said. 'I brought the gown I wore to the graduation ball. The apricot-pink one which is embroidered with a million seed pearls.'

'Oh, of course. How stupid of me! You were a genius to have designed, cut and made it yourself, darling. Normally I can spot a homemade frock a mile off, but yours is fabulous. You have a gift there, darling. No two ways about it.'

'I worked hard enough,' Julia told him. 'I suppose it is a gift.' She said this modestly. 'Some of the girls had to give up. Their gowns turned out to be hideous flops and they had to buy gowns for the graduation ball. Floria said that either you can or you can't do this kind of work. According to Aunt Bonita, my mother had a flair for dressmaking. Actually, Aunt Bonita thought the apricot-pink was a model, when I showed it to her. I was flattered.'

'I'll pick you up about eight,' said Leon. 'Be ready on

the dot, will you, darling? I couldn't stand waiting around in that depressing old house.'

'I can't think why you keep calling it hideous and depressing.' Julia was suddenly annoyed. 'It's all been re-covered – the sofas and chairs, I mean. They had it done when they were married. Gillian really has very good taste. She saw to everything. What they kept, they re-upholstered, and what no longer fitted in, because it was Jake's second wife, they got rid of and bought several rather nice pieces.'

'That might be, but – all that chintz, darling? How *ghastly*! I loathe chintz, darling. So – *suburban*.' Leon signalled the waiter irritably. When he had finished with the man he said to Julia, 'How are you getting back, by the way?'

'Jake is picking me up outside the show-ground gates, on his way home from the office.'

'So there's no need for me to worry?'

'No need at all.'

'No word from dear Kathy yet?' He sounded tired and bored.

'No word. Jake says she usually just walks into the house again, as though nothing has happened.'

'Well, if she doesn't walk in soon she's going to miss her Game Ranger, isn't she?' Leon stood up and came round to Julia's chair. 'Let me help you with that jacket, darling. What did you have to take it off for, anyway?'

As arranged, Jake picked Julia up in town and they drove home through the nagging peak-hour traffic.

On her way to her room, Julia passed Kathy's and, even though Kathy had been gone some time, her room was redolent of stale perfume and cigarette smoke.

Tina, the maid, knocked on Julia's door, which was open, and peered into the room. 'A gentleman, he telephone this afternoon,' she said, smiling.

'Oh?' Julia's thoughts flew to the hospital and she tensed immediately. 'Was it my father, Tina? Did he leave a message?'

'He leave a message to ring him.'

'Oh. Well, thank you. Where's the number, Tina?' Julia glanced at Tina's hands.

'I didn't hear the number, ma'am. The wire was no good.'

'Did you try to write it down? I might begin to recognize it?'

'I didn't write it down. The pencil was broken, ma'am. No point.' Tina's dark-skinned face was serene.

'Oh.' Julia bit her lip, trying to think things out. 'Well, that's all right, Tina.' She smiled, trying to hide the disappointment and frustration she was feeling. 'Er – by the way, did you say anything? Did you speak to him? Did you tell him when I'd be back, maybe?'

'No. I tell him you ring him this afternoon when you get home.'

A small sigh escaped Julia, but she kept on smiling. 'Well,' she laughed suddenly, 'that was very thoughtful of you, Tina. Thank you.'

When she spoke to her Aunt Bonita about it Bonita laughed. 'I know it's no laughing matter,' she said, 'but I should have warned you. Tina cooks like a dream, she's a marvellous housekeeper – nothing escapes her eye – but, Julia, she's hopeless on the phone. We always try to answer calls ourselves – but sometimes that's impossible. I must have been in the garden. Anyway, were you expecting a call?'

'No. I had lunch with Leon. Our arrangements for to-night are all sorted out. That leaves Dad. I hope nothing has gone wrong.'

'Oh, I don't think it's that at all,' said Bonita. 'It was probably for Kathy, from somebody who doesn't know she's away. It usually is for Kathy. I certainly don't get many calls and Jake and Gillian are away all day. Put your mind at rest, though. Put through a call to Hlageni. It shouldn't be difficult to get through.'

The call was quicker than Julia imagined it would be and she felt relief wash over her to hear that everything at the hospital was all right. The call was, of course, put right through to her father's private ward. After putting Julia's mind at rest, Stan promised to ring Pietermaritzburg directly he was given the exact date of his discharge.

When Leon called for her he said, 'You really are gorgeous, darling.'

'Thank you.' She squirmed away from him as he

142

tried to kiss her on the ear.

'By the way, what do you think of Nicolette, darling?' he asked. 'She's quite devastating, don't you think?'

The remark seemed to click and Julia said, 'Yes, she is. I should have thought that you'd be seeing a lot more of her, Leon.'

'Aah . . . there's a snag there, darling.'

'Oh, I see. Well, I'm sorry.'

'Be sorry, darling, if it will please you.'

The red car wound down into the sparkling collection of jewels that was Pietermaritzburg at night.

CHAPTER NINE

JULIA'S mood improved when they got to the hotel where they were going to dance and when she saw all the cars parked beneath flaring lights in the parking area.

Cars were arriving all the time and crawled round the ground in search of a white-coated parking attendant, who, with torches, guided them into parking lots.

Doors closed with that particular expensive thud peculiar to particularly expensive cars. Women laughed softly as they looked up into men's smooth-shaven and lotioned faces. Wisps of perfume were snatched up by a playful breeze to mingle and compete with the scent of flowers growing in white tubs nearby.

Leon locked the car and tipped the attendant. 'I can't say I'm sorry the Royal Show is over,' he said to Julia. 'I'm exhausted, darling. You'll have to forgive me.'

She gave him an amused look. Beneath the blue-tinged flaring lights his face looked white, his eyes blocked out by the ridiculous dark lenses. 'You look on top of the world,' she told him.

They went up the steps towards the foyer of the hotel which was screened by palely illuminated obscure glass against which several palm trees made Japanese-like art designs. Above them, lanterns swung in the breeze.

'You should have left your hair shoulder-length,' Leon gave Julia a critical look, 'not coiled it up. You look just that weeny bit taller than I do – with it up. Still, it doesn't matter, darling, you look devastating as it is. But remember next time, will you?'

They moved out of the glimmer of lanterns into the discreetly lit foyer with its expensive flowers, thick carpets and long linen-fold reception desk near the entrance to the dimly lit patch of dance-floor and surrounding tables with their white cloths and scarlet napkins.

Outside, the traffic droned steadily, but they were not aware of it.

An excellent dance band caused a flicker of pleasant tension to shoot along Julia's nerves as they were shown to their table. There were small nervous lights in her green eyes as they scanned the room.

The floor had not yet filled up, so when she and Leon danced they performed almost an exhibition as several couples stood swaying on the edge of the floor to watch them.

At one end of the dance-floor, there was a sophisticated bar, where couples sat talking and sipping drinks. Here and there a lone man sat waiting patiently for the woman in his life to finish doing things to her face in the powder-room.

The whole atmosphere – perhaps it was the result of the end of the Royal Show – was one of keyed-up excitement, somehow. The cocktail bar, with its low arrangements of flowers, glasses, snacks and half-filled ashtrays looked hazy behind the cigarette smoke which curled lazily around it.

Suddenly Julia felt reckless and excited. 'Darling,' she said, arching her back a little, 'why don't you take off those dark glasses? Why must they be dark, even at night? You've never really told me. Are your eyes really so bad?'

'I'd be as blind as a bat without them,' he said. 'Darling, you *know* that.'

'I should have thought you'd have been as blind as a bat *with* them.'

'You sound like Kathy now,' he said in a difficult voice. 'Don't be evil, darling.' He guided her expertly away from a couple who were really swinging on the floor. 'Concentrate, will you, darling?' he said.

'Why?' she laughed up into his face. 'Why must we always concentrate when we're dancing? I want to relax and be a little reckless.'

'You can't be both,' he told her. 'Either one or the other. Besides, Julia, I don't like to be prodded and poked about.'

She laughed again. 'Darling,' she was finding it very easy to fall into their old jargon for the simple reason that she felt like teasing him tonight, 'I'll concentrate now, really I will.'

'Good,' he said. 'I'm relieved to hear that.' He led her into an intricate succession of steps which she followed effortlessly.

By now, most of the couples on the floor were merely

swaying together on one spot to watch them, and Julia's green eyes slid round them with a lazy kind of amusement. Normally such observations would have filled her with discomfort, but tonight she was actually enjoying the sensation of being admired in her apricot-pink slipper satin beaded gown which fell in a straight sheath to the tips of her gold shoes.

At the bar, several men had swivelled round on bar stools to look at the dance-floor, and Julia was not unaware of several lazy and admiring glances.

The music was slow now, so slow and dreamy, in fact, that those couples still dancing were at a loss to know how to cope with it, apart from trying to do a kind of midnight shuffle. It was almost what could have been described as 'their' kind of music – the kind of music where Leon expertly guided Julia with slow steps one moment which gave way, the next, to a flourish of small intricate steps.

When the number drew to a close they were right next to the bar and came apart amidst friendly laughter and light hand-clapping. 'Darling,' Julia was a little embarrassed now, 'do you have to put us through our paces *quite* so much?'

As she spoke, she half turned to face the cocktail bar and looked right into Grant Tyler's face. He was alone, glass in hand and immaculate in a dinner suit. Their eyes linked and then she watched, fascinated, as his blue eyes, hazed by cigarette smoke, travelled from the top of her tawny head to the hem of her elegant gown and then back again – taking their time. By the time they came back to her face his smile was just a small flip of the lips – hardly noticeable and, she noticed, it did not reach his eyes.

'Oh,' she exclaimed, caught completely unawares, '*darling,* look who's here – *Grant Tyler*.' Automatically, she took Leon's hand. 'Hello, there!' she called.

The music had started again, so she and Leon had to move close to the bar.

'What, all on your o-n-i-o, old chap?' drawled Leon.

'Just for the moment, yes.' Grant left his bar stool to stand up, and then, at that very moment, Kathy came through the linen-fold door right at the end of the bar.

Julia made no attempt to hide her surprise. 'Kathy,' she

exclaimed, as Kathy joined them 'when on earth did *you* get back?'

'Just after you left with *sweetie* here – this evening.' Kathy's eyes were like feasting vultures on Julia's gown.

'I've never met a more evil girl,' said Leon. 'Truly I haven't.'

'To be evil is only to be feminine,' Kathy answered, not looking at him. 'I'm no more evil than Julia here. And by the way, what are you doing here? I suppose it amounts to the same thing, doesn't it?' While she was speaking Kathy went to stand next to Grant. She rubbed her cheek against his sleeve. 'Did I keep you waiting long?' she asked. 'I had to practically re-dress myself in there. I've never had to dress in such a rush before. I kept Grant waiting an age back home – but that's what he got for trying to keep his visit to 'Maritzburg a surprise. I'd never have gone away, had I known.' She turned her back on Julia and Leon. 'I'm ready to go back to our table,' she said to Grant, and took his arm.

'Where is your table, old boy?' Leon took Julia's hand.

'Right behind your own,' Grant answered.

'We didn't notice you when we came in,' Julia said.

'Perhaps you were too busy to notice,' Grant answered. 'Anyway, I was alone. Kathy had gone to the powder room by then. We'd not long arrived.'

Kathy drawled, 'Trust Julia to make me feel like a poor relation! That creation must have set your father back a packet, Julia.'

Julia chose to ignore Kathy's remark.

The four of them began to walk in the direction of the tables which formed a horseshoe round the dance-floor.

'Well,' Leon looked at Grant, 'what are we going to do – make this a party by moving in together?'

A waiter had noticed them and was coming forward. 'Perhaps you would like the two tables to be put together, sir?' he said, but already he had begun moving the tables and he was soon joined by another waiter.

'But isn't this too much trouble?' Kathy cut in quickly, looking at the waiters.

'No trouble at all, madam. We like to see our patrons happy.' The waiters went on moving the tables, rearranging the cloths, transferring the scarlet napkins – everything together in an intimate little huddle.

Looking at the tables, joined as one now, and looking at Leon's dark lenses, which seemed to be appealing to a point beyond the table for patience, and looking at Kathy's frigid face and Grant's mask of indifference, Julia knew that this evening was going to be a disaster.

As the evening wore on it looked as though Leon was not going to put himself out by asking Kathy to dance, and it was obvious that Grant Tyler was not going to make the first move in changing partners.

Suddenly everything was giving out, and Julia felt tired. She was tired of listening to Leon's comings and goings, his perpetual exciting parties. She was tired of Kathy's perpetual sarcastic remarks, with their double meanings, and of Grant's silences and cold expression.

She was not sure whether she was pleased or sorry when Leon asked Kathy to dance.

Grant politely asked Julia to dance and on the edge of the floor they hesitated briefly. Through the thin soles of her shoes she could feel the floor vibrating in time to the drums. Grant took her into his arms and they circled the floor, which was packed now, to the slow music. He did not speak, but she could hear his breathing, very slightly, and the sound of it caused an elastic tightness in her throat.

He made no apologies for not being a good dancer. He had a good sense of time but no particular style to speak of – no fancy flourishes – and she knew that this was not just because the floor was packed.

Patrons had reached the sentimental humming stage now, because of the period of time which had elapsed between eating, drinking and dancing.

After a while, because she was unable to bear the silence between them another minute, Julia said, 'How – are the crocodiles?'

'Bearing up,' he told her, looking down into her face. 'They go back tomorrow.'

'Oh? And – you?'

'I go back with the crocodiles, naturally.'

'In a taxi?' she smiled.

'Yes, in a taxi.' He gave her a faint grin, but his eyes were still cool.

'Have I done anything?' she asked.

148

'What you do in Pietermaritzburg is entirely your own affair,' he told her.

'Jake and Gillian must have been terribly surprised,' she said, deciding to ignore his sarcasm, 'when Kathy turned up like that. They didn't know when to expect her. You nearly missed her, didn't you?'

Somebody bumped into them and, quite reasonably, Grant held her half an inch closer.

'I got Kathy the second time I phoned,' he told her. 'I'd phoned the Feldwoods in the afternoon – late afternoon.'

'Oh, well, it was wonderful to have phoned a second time and to have found Kathy back, wasn't it? Did you know that I spent yesterday with your mother?'

'Yes.'

A kind of desperation made her go on talking. 'It must have been a disappointment that you weren't able to take Kathy to meet your parents. It will be too late now, won't it? I mean – you go back tomorrow.'

'As you say, I go back tomorrow. And you – when do you go back? Unless you've changed your mind about going back?'

'I had occasion to speak to my father on the telephone today. He expects to be discharged soon now, within a day or two. I'll be leaving here accordingly.' She kept the tone of her voice cool to match his own.

At the end of the night they parted company on the flagged terrace beneath the lanterns.

'Are you going straight home?' Kathy looked at Julia and then at Leon.

'Let's be frank, Kathy. Why don't you mind your own business?' Leon answered, in his usual insulting way.

'It makes no difference to me what you do,' Kathy snapped back. 'I merely wanted you to know that we aren't going straight home.' She looked at Grant. 'Let's go, then, Grant.'

Beads of dew hung to the palms with their bold sculptured fronds and on the leaves and flowers in the tubs surrounding the terrace.

Julia held the skirt of her gown in her fingers as she allowed Leon to help her down the steps which led down to the parking area. She listened to Grant and Leon saying good night and making last attempts at small talk.

149

The cars looked like slinky shadows washed silver by the moon. One or two had already pulled out of the area and others were revving up, preparing to leave. A small sports car growled round a circle of parked cars before its owner found the way out.

Out of the corner of her eye, Julia saw Grant holding the door of his car open for Kathy. Kathy had not looked like a poor relation this evening, she thought. She had looked stunning in black with her hair coiled up on top of her head and crystal drop earrings which reached half way down her neck.

'Where would you like to go?' Leon asked, when they were in his car. 'Park somewhere, terribly high up, to watch the lights before we say nightie-night?'

'No parking,' she said emphatically. 'I don't want to watch the lights.'

He shrugged his elegant shoulders. 'Okay, darling – so no parking. What do I feel for parking, anyway? What then? Home?'

'Yes, please. I'm terribly tired.'

Leon shrugged again and started the engine which had an unfamiliar beat to it – and not its usual purr. There was a small silence.

'Is something wrong with the car?' she asked.

'Sounds like it, doesn't it, darling?' Leon's voice grew sarcastic as he became more tired. 'If there is, I'll positively scream! I know absolutely nothing about engines and, like you, I'm terribly tired – exhausted, in fact. This Show has taken something out of me that I'll never be able to put back. Was it worth it?'

'What are we going to do, then, about the car?' Julia's voice was taut. She saw Grant's car slide out of the parking bay, slowly and with confidence before it gathered speed as it left the hotel grounds.

'It might work itself out,' said Leon, reversing out into the white-lined aisle. 'Don't they say that these things do? Especially in the case of a spot of dirt in the jolly old carburettor. It could clear itself, I suppose.'

'It sounds awful.' Julia huddled herself into the folds of the apricot-pink slipper satin coat which went with the frock. She flicked the collar up so that she could feel its expensive slippery touch against her chin.

'Look, Julia, don't keep on and on about it.' Leon was terse, irritable. 'I know damn well it sounds awful – but not half as damn awful as I feel. I also know that I did without this car all afternoon while it was serviced.'

'Sounds like a loose plug.' She pressed the collar of the coat closer to her skin as she listened.

'What the devil do you know about loose plugs? You shouldn't know anything about them.'

'I happened to do a course at Azalea Park, very elementary, of course, but enough to keep me going if I broke down somewhere. Darling, let's face it, we're about to break down.'

'Shut up, will you?' He swore softly. 'We'll go on and hope for the best.'

They were climbing out of town and now and there was a lot of unnecessary gear work going on.

'If you didn't want to do it yourself, you should have pulled into a garage while we were still in town,' said Julia, looking back at the collection of jewels in the hill-rimmed basin below.

'Look, Julia, stop nagging, will you? I'm not in the mood for nagging.' He flicked back one white cuff. 'A garage, at this time of the night or, what's more appropriate, the morning? Who do you think would be on duty? This isn't a job for a night watchman, sweetie.' He drew up to the side of the road and got out and opened the bonnet. 'No loose plugs,' he said, coming back to the car and reaching for a duster. 'I know that much.' He began to wipe his hands.

'How do you know?' she persisted stubbornly. 'You were very quick about it.'

'I wobbled them about, that's how I know. Now shut up, Julia.'

'Give the engine a good rev. That might just help clear the dust out of the carburettor – if it is dust.' Julia sounded faintly impatient.

Leon flung himself into his seat and looked at her through the darkness. 'You can be very domineering, can't you? Sometimes, darling, you can be just a bit too damned efficient. I noticed that at Azalea Park, as a matter of fact.'

'Is that so? Is there anything else you noticed about me?

People seem to notice an awful lot about me, I'm beginning to think.'

He started the car again and revved it until she thought something would explode. 'If anything should move that dirt, that should,' he said.

The car managed to crawl to the top of the hill where Leon stopped again. Below the lights sparkled with a maddening kind of frenzy, impatient for the last of the revellers to be gone.

'Tell me what to do.' Leon, she knew, was speaking out of the corner of his mouth.

'Well, let's *both* get out and have a look.' She opened her door and stepped out into the blackness.

'Julia,' he called after her, 'you'll ruin that gown.'

'So what. It's not serious. It only took one year out of my life. Unless this whole wretched car is falling apart, I might just know enough to get us to the Feldwoods' – where you can spend the rest of the night.'

'Well then, don't do it,' he said plaintively. 'The rest of the night in that shabby old house? Darling, I couldn't stand it – particularly the way I feel now. Spare me that, please. Why the devil Jake doesn't . . .'

'Oh,' now it was her turn, '*shut up!*'

She stood next to him while he opened the bonnet again, 'Leon,' her voice was muffled as she peered beneath the bonnet, 'get back into the car and start her up, will you? I want to listen to something – but pass me a torch, will you?'

'*A torch?*' His voice was high. 'Darling, surely you don't think I can go round carrying *torches* about? How *rural* can we get? Anyway,' he went on, 'don't be ridiculous.' She straightened up to look at him and he took off his glasses. This was the first time she had seen him without them, and even in the light which came from the parking lights, which he had left on, his face looked almost naked without them. He was a stranger to her.

'Put your glasses on,' she snapped, 'and why am I being ridiculous?' She watched him wiping his lenses with a white handkerchief and then he put the handkerchief away and put the glasses back on. 'You admit that you know nothing about an engine. Well, I happen to know a little about them. That makes sense, doesn't it? So you do the starting up and I do the checking up.'

Turning on his heel, Leon got back into the car and started the engine.

'Rev it a bit more,' Julia shouted. 'A bit more . . .' When the revving stopped abruptly she wondered why; then she was aware of the lights and before either she or Leon could do a thing about this ridiculous situation Grant Tyler was drawing up beside them.

'Well,' his voice was gloating almost, 'having a spot of trouble?'

Julia could feel the oil and grit on her fingers and she wondered where to put her hands. 'What appears to be the matter?' Grant's voice was downright mocking and sarcastic.

'Well, that's what I'm—' she corrected herself quickly, 'what we're trying to find out.

Grant's car was facing the opposite way to their own, facing the lights, and Kathy was not in it, which meant that he had taken her straight home to the Feldwoods', after all. Julia wondered why they had not gone on somewhere first. Their parting, seeing that it really was their parting in the true sense of the word, had been very short.

'I'll get my car out of the way,' said Grant, 'in case another car comes on the scene and then I'll come and see if I can be of any assistance. I should hate to see that gown ruined – and those beautiful hands.'

He parked his car a little way off and came back to them.

'Frankly,' said Leon, 'I'm in no mood for roadside repairs. How about towing me back into town, Grant? Actually, I do have a jolly good tow rope in the back.'

'It's a pity you didn't have a torch,' Julia told him, feeling furious at this turn of events – quite apart from feeling the biggest fool this side of the Equator.

Grant was already looking beneath the bonnet. 'It might not be much,' he was saying. He looked up and demanded for Julia's benefit, 'What the devil were you doing with your head under this bonnet, anyway? You'd better wipe your hands on something. I take it he *does* have a duster?'

'Look,' said Leon, 'get me to Wally's Garage, old chap, that's all I ask. I'm ready to fall apart at the seams.'

Grant slammed down the bonnet. 'Suit yourself, old boy.

If that's the way you want it I'll get you to Wally's.' He turned to Julia. 'You'd better get into my car. I'll drive you back to the Feldwoods', where I happened to find out you were staying, after I've got Leon here organized.'

In Grant's car Kathy's heavy perfume mingled with the smoke of the cigarettes she usually smoked. It took some time to get organized and then, when the two cars were on their way into town, Julia said, in a small voice. 'It was fortunate for us that you happened to come along – but not so fortunate for you. It means another trip back here for you.'

'That's all right.' His voice was curt, but she didn't care. He was like that – moody, sarcastic – and she hated him.

'I thought you and Kathy were going on some place else?' she asked.

'Well, the point is, we didn't.'

'I forgot you didn't know that my Aunt Bonita is Kathy's stepmother's mother. That sounds complicated, doesn't it? I hadn't mentioned it, had I? How did you find out? You said a little while ago that you'd happened to find out.'

'It's not important,' he replied. 'The fact is that I did find out. You can put it down to a remark your boy-friend passed, if you like.'

'You're always so bitter about him, aren't you?' she flung at him.

'Am I?'

'Yes.' She sighed. 'This must be infuriating for Leon. He only had his car serviced this morning.'

'Tut-tut – too bad.'

Julia decided to give up and turned away from him. Some time later, he said, 'We're making progress.' He kept the speed easy and his voice was quite impersonal. The lights were no longer just an impatient huddle scooped up in a black basin. They were something which caused Grant's aloof face to show up, from time to time, until, at last, the car was invaded by the light from a perpetual string of street lights.

Julia remained in Grant's car, as the rope was untied and Leon's car pushed into Wally's Garage, where it would receive attention in the morning.

'I'll sell it,' said Leon, as he got into Grant's car. 'I'll sell the damn thing – first thing in the morning.'

'You'll feel different in the morning,' Julia told him.

'No, I won't. I'll never trust that car again. I'm like that, darling. You should know.' He withdrew himself from them into his own little corner.

'You talk like a woman-hater,' said Julia. 'You'll get over it, darling. It's not serious, after all.' Illogically, Grant became the object of her fury: Right now, she hated Leon's car with all her heart.

'Where to?' Grant asked.

'Oh, sorry, old chap.' Leon moved slightly, painfully almost, as though his bones had grown suddenly stiff and terribly old. 'It's the Richmond. It's not a bad place – except that they always starch the sheets so that they're like cardboard. However, I make it my headquarters whenever I happen to be working in Pietermaritzburg. Why *do* some places persist in starching the sheets? I've never been able to work that one out, you know.'

Outside the Richmond Leon said to Julia, 'Darling, I'm terribly, terribly sorry about this. I'll ring you, of course.' To Grant he said, 'Take care of her, will you – on the way back?' He cupped Julia's chin and kissed her.

Julia's hands were clenched fists of tension.

'I'm sorry about all this too,' she said, when they were on their way again. 'But I couldn't think of another thing to do.'

'You tried to fix it,' he replied. 'That was always something, I guess. Anyway, forget it. It's quite all right. I was glad to be on hand.'

'Yes, I'm sure you were,' she said bitterly. 'You *loved* seeing me trying to fix that car, didn't you? As it happened, I was only tinkering. I happen to know a little about cars – not much, but enough. Leon *had* been trying. He'd just got into the car when you came along.'

'You don't have to explain anything,' he said. 'He's your choice, after all.' His voice was offhand and infuriating. 'By the way, I was sorry to have to be in on the good-night kiss. Too bad.'

'Leon kisses everybody,' said Julia. 'He used to kiss Floria, even – *and* call her darling. It means nothing. We all used to talk like that.' She was in a conflict of emotions and wondered why she should feel like this just because

155

Grant Tyler was there to see the kiss. After all, it had nothing to do with him. There was no reason why she should have to offer up excuses.

For a while Grant did not speak. He was concentrating on the small, quiet streets that would finally link up with the main street which would lead them out of town. 'I thought this was known as Sleepy Hollow?' he asked. 'There's not an awful lot of sleep going on tonight, is there?' He used the dip switch as another car approached them.

The lantern, with its yellow insect-repelling globe, was still burning on the Feldwoods' verandah.

'Grant,' said Julia, keeping her voice quite casual, and deciding to overlook a lot of things, 'you've had an awful lot of running about in the car to do – so won't you please come in and let me make you some coffee? Perhaps you'd like bacon and eggs? You still have a long way to go back to the farm – and then there's your trip to Umkambo in the morning, with the crocodiles.' She gave him a smile which he did not acknowledge. 'I don't want you to fall asleep at the wheel. Perhaps Kathy might still be up. Won't she be amazed to find you back on her doorstep?'

The flowers in the garden scented the air. Grant's eyes were on her mouth and she wondered uncomfortably whether the yellow globe had turned her lipstick into some hideous colour.

'Thank you,' he said. 'A cup of coffee would be welcome – if you're sure it's not going to be too much trouble.'

'Not at all. Frankly, I'd love a cup myself and this is such a big, rambling old house that we won't disturb a soul. I have my Aunt Bonita's key. They all have to have keys here.'

Grant stood slightly to one side while she unlocked the door.

The entrance hall was huge and wide and against the walls there were such pieces of furniture as a carved kist, a chest of drawers, with copper fittings, a half-moon table, upon which burned a tall lamp with a tremendous drum-shaped shade which looked perfectly at home in the old house. In the light, Julia's eyes looked big and luminous, and she caught a glimpse of Grant's own blue eyes in the copper-framed mirror above the lamp.

'Through here,' she said hurriedly, and led the way

through into the dining-room with its almost church-like proportions and then, finally, into a large white tiled kitchen. 'Would you like bacon and eggs?' she whispered, although there was no need to whisper.

'Just coffee,' he told her.

'Well, I'll switch the kettle on and then I'll go and see if Kathy is still awake. She might just be. You'll want to see as much of each other before you go back, won't you? This will give you another chance.'

'Kathy – can wait.' There was an edge to Grant's voice.

'As you like.' Her voice was tight. With him nothing she ever did was right. 'Out there,' she said in a stiff little voice, and pointing to a door, 'you'll find a small porch with a lovely view of the lights – if you'd like to look at them while I make the coffee. Just turn the key and go out. I'll call you when the coffee is ready.'

To her relief he followed her suggestion and left the door slightly open. Immediately a small, pre-dawn breeze nudged her long skirt against her legs. Startled, she realized that it was nearly time for the sky to start to get lighter.

That was when Kathy turned up, wearing a shortie gown. 'Well,' she drawled, 'that's not Leon's car outside, is it? It's Grant's. How did you work *that* one? You're terribly clever, aren't you?'

'Hush!' Julia began to gesticulate.

'Oh, hush yourself. He can't hear us here from the lounge. Well, why Grant? Where's Leon?'

'Look, Kathy, Grant happens . . .'

'You don't have to whisper. You want Grant Tyler for yourself, isn't that so?'

'Kathy, please *listen* – Grant Tyler is everything I *don't* want, and he doesn't happen to be in the lounge – *he happens to be out there!*'

How it happened she didn't know, because one minute Grant was out on the porch while she did her whispering, and the next, he was there, standing in the big, old-fashioned white-tiled kitchen. Julia thought she'd be sick if he didn't say something because she knew he'd heard, then Kathy said, 'Sorry if you heard something you shouldn't, Grant. In case you're wondering what all this is about – well, I happen to *know* Julia. She's quite a character, once you get to know her.' She made an elaborate pretence of trying to give the impression that she was laughing off this description of Julia to save Julia's face and not her own. 'Actually, Grant, Julia has to be watched. I'm sorry to have to say this, but it's true.'

'I don't know what put that into your head, Kathy.' Julia was aware that she could be on the way to allowing herself to become over-excited. She knew that she had to get out of here, so she said, 'I don't feel like coffee, after all, but perhaps you'd finish what I've started and give Grant some, Kathy?'

'That makes two of us, actually,' Grant cut in. 'I don't feel like coffee, either. Besides, it's pretty late for coffee. I'll get going, if you don't mind.'

Kathy laughed again, but with much less show this time. 'But I do mind, Grant. Please have coffee with me. I'm upset. I'd been lying awake, wondering where Julia was — what she was up to. Stay, please! Just to save my face, if nothing else. I feel awful for having shown Julia up...' There was a smile of defensive mockery on Kathy's face now.

In a passion of bewilderment Julia said, 'I can't understand you, Kathy, really I can't.'

'But I understand you, Julia,' replied Kathy softly.

Julia reached for the satin coat, which she had taken off and thrown across a white bentwood chair. She looked at Grant. 'Thank you,' she said. 'I'm sorry to have been such a nuisance.'

CHAPTER TEN

Two days later Jake Feldwood brought the car round to the front of the house where Julia stood on the steps saying goodbye to her Aunt Bonita and Gillian.

On the way into town, Kathy, who was going shopping, sat in front with her father while Julia sat pensively in the back of the car. Her green eyes rested on the distant mountains which were almost powder blue in the early morning air.

Jake did most of the talking, trying his best to draw the two girls into a mutual interest, but in the end he gave up and, apart from asking Julia one or two questions about the Umkambo Reserve, fell silent. He dropped Kathy off in Church Street and continued on to the station with Julia before going to his office.

'I'd love to buy some flowers to take back with me,' said Julia, looking in the direction of several flower-sellers. 'I'll be with you in a moment.'

At the station Jake said, 'Well, Julia, it's been nice having you. I know your Aunt Bonita and Gillian enjoyed seeing you again – that's for sure.'

'Thank you for having me,' Julia smiled at him.

'I'm just sorry about Kathy, clearing off like she did and then walking in on the evening of the dance.' There was a pause and then Jake added, 'That was the night young Tyler telephoned you.'

Julia's chin came up. 'The night Grant Tyler phoned *me*?'

'Yes,' Jake said, 'I answered. He said that he'd rang the house earlier on in the afternoon. I didn't mention this to you because – well, to be quite honest, when I mentioned that you'd just gone off with that Ladenza fellow he said it didn't matter. He said, to use his own words, "it's not serious." Kathy overheard the conversation – she'd not long got home – and took the receiver from me. Afterwards they seemed to come to an arrangement, because young Tyler took her dancing. Kathy was in a fine old paddy when she discovered that all the time she was away the Game

159

Ranger was in 'Maritzburg.'

Julia did her best to keep on smiling while she pondered over what Jake had just told her about the telephone call from Grant.

'I'll have to get on the train now,' she said. 'It's due to leave at any moment. Besides, you'll be wanting to get to your office, won't you?'

'No hurry,' Jake replied. 'Who's going to meet you at the other end?'

'My father was going to arrange something,' she told him. 'He told me on the telephone. It will probably be Carl Bramley. Carl was going to collect Dad from the hospital, as a matter of fact. Dad might even drive to Hlageni station himself, for that matter. Anyway, all I know is that there *will* be somebody there to meet me.'

'Ah, well, that's the main thing,' Jake laughed, taking her hand while she managed to hold the bouquet of flowers and her bag in the other. The petals of the flowers brushed her chin and she could feel their moistness and smell their perfume. She wondered whether they would stand up to the train trip.

'Mind the bee doesn't sting you,' said Jake, taking a stem between his blunt, tanned fingers.

'Bee?' Hastily she moved the flowers away from her face and peered into the flowers where a bee was busy with his legs, in one of them. Then he came out of the flower backwards and flew away.

'Well, there's a thing,' said Jake, still laughing. 'He just missed going to the Game Reserve, eh?' He cleared his throat. 'Well, Julia, be good!'

'I have no option,' she told him, keeping her voice light. 'At Umkambo Grant Tyler sees to it that I keep to the golden rules – no getting out of the car, no speeding, no golden-strapped sandals at night – oh, I could go on and on, but I won't!' She laughed just to put the remark right with Jake.

'Well, rules or no rules, I know that Kathy would give anything to be in your golden-strapped sandals.' Jake thought that was very funny and laughed again. 'She's fallen for that Game Ranger like a ton of bricks. I feel sorry for him if Kathy has her way with him, that's all I can say, daughter or no daughter.' He picked up Julia's two white cases, which stood at their feet. 'I'll pass these to you through the window,' he said cheerfully.

Julia got in and there was just time for a little more small talk before a bell shrilled which was followed shortly by another and then the train gave a great jolt before it began to move. Julia stood at the window, leaning out. 'Goodbye,' she called to Jake, 'and once again, thank you!'

The station slipped past and she waved to Jake until a curve in the platform hid him from sight. Soon the train was in the suburbs, rattling and jolting over the points.

She looked down at the flowers and then placed them on the seat beside her, wondering what was in store for her at the Reserve.

At the back of her mind somewhere was the thought that the mystery call which Tina had bungled must have been Grant Tyler. To her surprise she found that she was a little out of breath. It all seemed to click, somehow. Grant's sarcasm at the dance – but then he had expected her to ring him back – after all, Tina had said that she would convey the message. She had given the false impression that she had made a note of the number – not intentionally, but nevertheless the damage had been done. She couldn't think why Grant had phoned – unless he had a message from his mother.

At the end of the journey, a small shock went through Julia when she saw the khaki-clad figure on the platform at Hlageni, but then she saw that it was Carl Bramley.

'How's it?' he asked, when he had helped her from the train and gathered up her two white cases. 'What are the flowers in aid of? Some kind of celebration?'

'No,' she looked down at the flowers and then glanced up at Carl again. 'Well, yes, I suppose you could call it a celebration. I'm celebrating coming back home.' She stumbled over the word home, knowing how Carl Bramley felt about her presence in the Reserve. 'How is Roberta?' she asked hastily, almost praying that Roberta would be back at the Reserve.

Roberta was. 'Oh, that's wonderful,' said Julia, and suddenly everything seemed to be all right again. She was back where she started. Roberta would be there to help solve so many things.

'Well, let's get going,' said Carl, beginning to lead the

way from the platform. 'Your old man's fine, by the way. Home and all that.'

'Yes, he sounded just fine on the telephone the other evening,' Julia answered, trying to keep up with Carl.

'Anyway, he's back and that's the main thing,' Carl said over his shoulder, and it sounded to Julia's sensitive ears like the full-stop after a particularly trying paragraph.

As Carl drove the Land Rover through the boom type barrier Julia found herself thinking how the Reserve always seemed to be full of mystery and vague movements.

Stan Munro certainly looked much more rested. 'Well,' he said 'so we're back to normal?' Julia stood in the living-room, and as she looked at her handiwork, it suddenly seemed a long time since she had redecorated the bungalow. 'You've even brought flowers,' said Stan, after Carl had gone.

'Yes,' she said. 'I couldn't resist them. They've hardly wilted and yet they've been out of water a long time. I'll have to arrange them.'

'By the way,' said Stan, 'we've been invited out to dinner.'

She turned. 'Oh!' She could almost feel the blood drain away from her face. She had hoped that she was not going to have to come face to face with Grant Tyler just yet. 'Who has invited us?' She knew that her voice was strained.

'The Bramleys. Roberta's back, of course. Carl would have told you that. Did he?'

'Yes.' Frantically, Julia wondered if Grant Tyler was going to be in on the dinner party.

'I'll – have to change,' she said. 'I feel grubby after the train journey.'

'Of course,' her father replied. 'There's no hurry.'

At the Bramleys', some time later, Carl offered them a drink before dinner. Roberta was looking much better and her parents, who had brought her back to the Reserve, were also there. Apparently they were going to spend two weeks with the Bramleys before going back home.

There was a lot of talk going on, and in between it, Julia's eyes kept going towards the glass doors which led on to the verandah. Carl said, 'Grant got back yesterday, but went out almost immediately again,' and, for Julia, a danger seemed past – for the moment, anyway.

She did not see Grant for the next three days. Because of Roberta's parents, Julia did not see much of Roberta either, except to go over to the bungalow for tea and to have a preview of all the baby clothes.

She gardened a little and when the sun got too hot in the afternoons she went on with her work inside the bungalow, moving this and moving that, sewing more curtains and so on – generally improving the house all the time.

On her way back from the office, late one afternoon, she came face to face with Grant Tyler.

'Well,' he said, cordially enough, 'so you're back?'

'Yes,' she replied, also cordially enough, but with the memory of that last night in Pietermaritzburg between them. 'Have you been looking for poachers?'

'Well, that would be telling,' he answered, 'wouldn't it? But we're working on that, of course, all the time.'

'Were you in – any kind of danger?' Suddenly this seemed important. It was strange, she thought, but the idea that the Game Rangers might be in some kind of danger had never entered her head before.

'If I said that I was in danger *all* the time, what difference could it possibly make to you?'

'That was a stupid remark on your part, wasn't it?' Her voice sounded small.

'Was it? Well, it was just to let you know that I don't expect you to feel that you've got to *make* conversation. What have you been doing with yourself, since you got back? More house decorating – a few little car repairs?'

The effect of his remark was, as he probably intended that it should be, inflammatory. She had intended explaining to him about the telephone call mystery, but instead she said, 'What difference could it make to you? I don't expect you to feel you've got to make conversation either.' She shook back her hair. 'If you'll excuse me, I'm on my way back to the bungalow. I'd just been to the office to see my father.' To her surprise Grant fell into step beside her. She gave him a sideways glance. 'Aren't you going the wrong way?' she asked. 'I thought you were going *into* the office as I was coming *out*?'

'I've changed my mind,' he told her, and she stopped walking.

'Well, that goes for me too. Isn't that a strange coincidence?' As she walked back to the office she knew that Grant's blue eyes were following her and her mind seemed to stagger beneath the weight of the frustration she was experiencing.

Grant surprised her again by coming to the bungalow in the evening. Stan Munro had just gone to bed and Julia had decided to listen to a radio play.

When Grant arrived, she turned down the volume. 'If you've come to see my father,' she said, 'he's just gone to bed. Go through to his bedroom. He won't mind. He'll probably be pleased to see you.'

'I came to see you,' he said, and she noticed that his hair was still damp from the shower. She wondered why it was that he never seemed to bother to dry his hair properly.

Without waiting for an invitation from her, he sat down. His eyes scanned the room, which she knew was looking quite spectacular with the lamplight emphasizing the colours.

'That's new,' he said, 'isn't it?'

Her eyes flew to the abstract sculpture which Leon had given her before she'd left Pietermaritzburg. 'Yes, it is.'

'From – Leon, of course?'

'Yes.' There was a silence and then she said, 'It came from his gallery in Pietermaritzburg. Leon knows how to combine the best of both worlds.'

Grant's mouth, so firmly moulded, mocked her. Her eyes rested on that mouth. Many girls must have made mention of Grant's mouth in their time, she thought.

'How's Kathy?' she asked, lifting her eyes:

'I won't bore you with details,' he replied. 'I had a letter from my mother, though. She was asking after you. She has asked me to convey her – compliments – love, I think is what she called it.'

At the mention of his mother Julia smiled at him appreciatively. 'Oh, thank you. Please will you give her my – my love when next you write?'

They looked at each other for a moment, while Julia tried to think what could have caused the tension to tighten up between them again.

'I'll do that,' he said. It seemed to strike him, suddenly, that he had butted in on her radio play. 'I'm sorry,' he said, 'were you listening to that?' He nodded in the direction of the transistor set.

'It doesn't matter. For some reason or other I seem to have run out of something to read.'

'I have a stack of magazines,' he told her. 'A fair selection of books. Take your choice. Come over any time.'

'Thank you.' His offer gave her a sharp kind of pleasure. 'My father goes to bed early and sometimes I – I . . .'

'Get bored?' he finished for her.

'No, not bored.' She felt disappointed in him again. 'Lonely.'

He stood up. 'Is there a difference?'

'Yes, of course there's a difference. I love it here. I like the life. I'm not bored.'

'Who are you trying to kid, Julia? Yourself? Or me?' He thrust out his bottom lip again. 'Most girls would soon grow tired of this kind of existence – and I guess you're no exception.'

They were silent for a moment as they listened to the faint, faraway sound of thunder. She hoped that there was not going to be a storm. Grant Tyler had unsettled her nerves too much to have to endure a storm into the bargain.

'I am the one exception, then,' she told him, 'but I would prefer not to argue with you, because I'm not all that lonely.'

She did not try to keep him when he went towards the door. 'My bungalow is open any time you want those books,' he said, before he stepped out to the verandah.

The storm by-passed the Reserve and Julia went to bed and tried not to let Grant Tyler's remarks upset her.

The following afternoon, when it had cooled off a bit, she decided to do some more gardening. After having transplanted a number of little plants that had come up on their own in unexpected places, she concentrated on weeding beneath a small shrub. It was then that she noticed the snake coming towards her.

At first she could hardly believe it was happening. She had never seen a snake making for her before. It was not very long, but it was unusually shiny and black, even to her inexperienced eyes, and she could not even begin to try to place what kind of snake it was.

Her eyes were caught and held, as she watched it coming

towards her, and it seemed to be performing a sinuous exotic dance, especially for her benefit, writhing in a frenzy with its forked tongue darting in front of its shiny black eyes which fastened themselves coldly on her face.

Once she had recovered her first horror Julia scrambled to her feet and backed away from it, then, with relief, she saw the snake veer to one side and it was gone, flattening out along the ground before it was hidden from view by a pile of weeds which she had thrown together on the lawn.

For a few moments she wondered what she should do and then decided that the sensible thing to do would be to go and work in another part of the garden. She went on her knees again, her tawny hair hanging over her cheeks, and began to weed again, but with more care this time.

As the sun beat through the honey-coloured shirt she was wearing with green slacks, she knew sheer bodily contentment. Close to where she was working a spider was weaving its web which was tinged with gold from the sun, turning it from a web into some intricate piece of gold filigree work. The birds, silent during the heat of the day, burst into song now. When she felt tired enough Julia stopped work and went inside to take a shower, then when she was ready for it, she had her tea on the verandah.

At the first attack of giddiness her eyes showed astonishment, and then, when the giddiness passed, she put it down to too much sun and too much bending. When it happened again, however, she lay back in her chair with closed eyes. Slowly she opened her eyes and began to study her nails, to clear her mind for action. She noticed how the rough work had chipped and cracked her nails.

Her breath caught in her throat suddenly, as she noticed the swelling near her thumb. There appeared to be two tiny puncture marks on the skin. 'No,' she whispered. 'It can't be! It mustn't be.'

A vision of the snake, dancing its exotic dance as it came towards her, hypnotizing her, flashed across her mind, and she was instantly galvanized into action.

As she got to her feet she bumped against the table, spilling a little of the milk from the jug. How was it possible to be bitten by a snake and not even be aware of the fact until long afterwards – until that first sign of giddiness, the swelling, the tiny puncture marks

In the panic which whirled about her, she remembered that Grant had passed the bungalow some time ago, on his way to his own bungalow.

By the time she reached Grant's bungalow she was completely out of breath. 'Grant!' she panted, and she saw him look up from the small desk where he was writing notes. 'Please help me. I think I've been bitten by a snake!'

He was up in a second, pushing back his chair and coming towards her in long strides. 'What makes you *think* you've been bitten? You don't just think these things – you either know or you don't know. Show me. Where?'

She held out her hand and he caught it between his own. 'Here,' she said, 'look, it's red and swollen, and I've been feeling terribly giddy. There are also two tiny puncture marks, if you look carefully. I was gardening this afternoon when I saw the snake. It came out of the weeds and it had its tongue out.' As she spoke the sinking sun, sliding through Grant's open glass doors, gilded her face. 'Please,' she said, 'Grant, I don't want to die. You've got to do something, quickly. Don't just stand there! I've showered and changed and had tea – all since it happened. Time is getting short.'

'It didn't happen,' he told her, 'so you can put your mind at rest.' His voice, for once, sounded gentle, and because she had never heard it like this before, she wanted to cry.

'You – mean I – haven't been bitten?'

'This is probably only a spider bite.' He smiled down into her eyes.

'But how can you be sure, Grant? How can you be sure about a thing like this?' She didn't want him to see her cry.

'I've treated one or two snake bites in my time,' he said, 'and this isn't going to be one of them. Let me put something on it. Spider bites can be nasty. Don't look so stricken, Julia. I promise you, you aren't going to die. It's not serious, darling.' She knew that he was mocking her when he said that, but maybe he was mocking her just to put her mind at rest.

He took her hand and led her across the living-room. 'I got such a shock,' she told him, 'when I remembered about the snake. There were spiders, though. I remember now looking at the most magnificent spider web which was being woven right before my eyes.'

In Grant's bathroom she said again, mainly because she *had* to say something in this confined space with him, 'I thought I was going to die.' She watched him washing her hand with disinfectant and he kept on holding it, even when he had washed it and was reaching in the medicine cabinet for some ointment.

'That's a very lonely thought, Julia,' he said. His mouth mocked her and she took her eyes off it to watch him rub the ointment on to her inflamed skin. 'I'm sorry I'm – I'm shaking,' she whispered. 'I can't seem to help it.'

The silence in the bathroom was quite suddenly unbearable and she disengaged her hand from Grant's while he continued to search in the medicine cupboard. She made a big show of studying her thumb.

Grant was very silent – and very separate, somehow. She couldn't explain it to herself any other way. Then, without turning to look at her, he said, 'What are you crying for?' because, by now, she had caved in and was crying softly. 'I've told you you're not going to die.'

He turned to look at her and she felt his lean, khaki-clad presence like a physical impact. 'I'm sorry. I seem to be – strung up,' she said.

He took her hand again. 'Perhaps we're both just a little – strung up,' he said very softly. She did not reply and he said again, very softly, 'Julia?'

'Yes?'

'I said – perhaps we're both just a little strung up.'

'I suppose so.' She bit her lip.

Grant was tense and dedicated to the task of dressing her hand now. There was nothing else in the expression of his handsome face to give any particular meaning to the words and yet they were there – hanging about the bathroom like an invisible energy.

'This will draw the poison from those little punctures,' he said. 'The spider made a neat job of those.'

'It was the sight of the two little punctures which terrified me,' she told him. 'Don't two punctures show after a snake bite?'

Broodingly, he rubbed the ointment into her skin and

then he laughed. 'Who told you that, Julia? A little knowledge is a dangerous thing, you know.'

'Yes, I know. Anyway, I can't remember who told me. Perhaps I read it.'

He grinned down at her; there was a definite change in his voice and his attitude towards her, and again she was aware of him.

Close to the open bathroom window some kind of shrub gave off a heavy perfume.

Grant stuck an adhesive dressing over the ointment. 'Well,' he said, 'that should do the trick.' His eyes met and held hers, and quite suddenly Julia felt something for Grant Tyler with a shocking certainty, and she knew that from now on she was going to be in for a bad time over this woman-hater Game Ranger. Her eyes widened slightly as she looked back at him, caught and held by his stare as she had been trapped by the eyes of the snake. Only this was different. She wanted to be caught and held. It was a strange moment – a moment of waking up – for the very first time.

'Thank you,' she said, and her voice was so low that she could barely hear it herself. She watched, fascinated, as Grant raised a hand so that he could place his fingers beneath her chin. She knew that he was going to kiss her and she knew that she wanted him to but that they were both only trying to prolong the instant.

'What started all this off?' he asked, a moment later, his lips still against her mouth. He lifted his other hand and placed it against her hair which was stirring in the breeze coming through the open window. Although his voice was taut it was apparent that he was trying to keep everything under control.

And then he released her. 'I'm sorry, Julia. As I said a moment ago, I – we're both just a little on edge, I think.' He cleared his throat and turned away from her to close the cupboard.

Julia could feel her paleness, like a damp sheet against her cheeks. While this damp sheet grew colder Grant went on, 'I certainly didn't intend this. You could put it down to – well, just another one of my mistakes of the year. I'm going to give you some of these dressings so that you can dress . . .'

'What a nerve you've got,' she cut in. 'To kiss me and to stand there afterwards and to refer to it as the – mistake of the year! Thank you!' Her voice flaked out. There were shadows and hurt in her eyes.

'I'm sorry,' he said quietly. 'I wasn't being fair – I apologize. I won't bother you again.'

She was filled with a wild fury that he should have done this thing to her. 'And I won't bother you again,' she said. 'You can keep your dressings . . .' she threw them back at him, 'and your ointment and your kisses – the mistake of the year!' She made to brush past him, but he stood in her way.

'Julia,' he said, 'that's a tough condition. I'm sorry – for what happened.'

'Let me out of here!' She pushed him away and rushed out into the corridor and took a wrong turning. She found herself in what must have been Grant's bedroom and, confused, she swung round furiously, as though he had been responsible for that too. 'Let me out of this house immediately!'

'Julia,' he said, and she said swiftly, 'Don't you Julia me! Which way do I get out of here?'

'Through here,' he told her. 'To the left.'

CHAPTER ELEVEN

SEVERAL times during the next few days the idea crossed Julia's mind that Grant Tyler might have kissed her because he had fallen in love with her — but she rejected the idea.

He had gone away again, into the bush, and she wished that the bush would swallow him up and that she might never see him again. Sometimes, however, remembering about his lips on her own she could not think of anything else.

The day he arrived back, looking cool and handsome, despite a three-day-old beard, she took herself into the bush and drove aimlessly about in the car under a sun-bleached sky.

The late afternoon sunlight dazzled her and she narrowed her eyes against it. It was not a very good day for driving — hot and feverish, somehow. The bush looked sullen — the way she felt.

About two miles from camp she stopped the car and stared absently at some impala, grazing upwind, without noticing her, the sunlight slanting across their rippling, molten copper bodies.

Julia opened her bag and delved into it and brought out her mirror. When she examined her face she saw, with disgust, that she was pale beneath her tan. Pale, because Grant Tyler was back and because she was unhappy and in love with him and didn't know what to do about it.

Somewhere close by, a ground hornbill decided to call monotonously and very unmusically, but with a strange appeal, for all that. The bird almost seemed to take on a pleasure from the timbre of its own voice. Idly, Julia considered this. Did a hornbill have a voice? she thought. Or what? She sighed hopelessly and started the car again. At least she knew that it was a hornbill. She was learning all the time.

Perhaps, she thought frantically, as she began to drive again, she would get over Grant by getting away from him. Perhaps she ought to write to Samantha. 'Samantha,' she could say in her letter, 'help me, darling, I'm hopelessly in love with a woman-hater. You know that Ranger who came to collect me at Azalea Park? Well, yes, darling, you've guessed the rest. I shall have to get away, of course. Darling, could I come to you?' She knew, with a sickening jolt, that she had outgrown all that kind of flippant jargon.

She wanted no part of the visitors in their cars, happily scanning the bush for game with no idea that the girl in the pale cream car was unhappy. To them she was just a girl driving about in the sun, a camera on the seat beside her, maybe. So she took loop roads to avoid them.

Her thoughts kept on and on. About Kathy, for instance. Kathy in love with Grant and Grant in love with Kathy, it would appear – or at least, well on the way to being in love.

Of Leon. Leon with every gesture slightly larger than life – a sophisticate in art, as he had once referred to himself.

The grass seemed to give off a vapour in the sun and Julia drew a long, famished breath, savouring the feel and the smell of the bush.

When she came to the road by the river which was out of bounds, because of the great floods, a sudden recklessness made her take it, but not without a guilt-stabbed glance into the rear-view mirror. It had been so quiet down here the day she and Leon had driven down in his car, protected – and out of bounds as it was to visitors.

For a moment the car was at a sharp, frightening angle before it went over the rise. The potholes were difficult to miss – all evidence of the terrible floods which had hit the Reserve. She remembered reading about it. Rivers had become swollen out of all proportion to their normal size until the whole countryside gurgled and roared with rushing water. By the time the car had straightened out she was in the small, reed-infested clearing next to the river.

It was almost like a small beach, she thought idly. On an island, somewhere, maybe, and almost as white, in a way, except where reeds had collapsed and were decaying next to the still green water. The water was dark and murky.

Driving as near to the water as she dared, she continued along the strip of sun-baked sand and passed the very spot where she and Leon had parked. From this angle the river looked like a dirty threat. A typical crocodile-infested river – and then she shuddered as she saw the nostrils, all four of them, at the end of the motionless 'logs' – only she knew that they were not logs. They were crocodiles. Her heart contracted with fright, then the fright gave way to a kind of reckless amusement as she thought about the visitors in their cars who would have given anything just to see the four nostrils.

For a while her eyes scanned the river for signs of more crocodiles. That was the kind of mood she was in. She held her breath for as long as she could, so that she could just feel those long, tense moments of absolute stillness all about her. When she released it she thought, with some satisfaction, how brave she was really, to be sitting here on her own.

She refused to think about the rules. After all, she was not getting out of the car.

The silence, which had just begun to be oppressive, was broken by the warning call of some tick birds, which were hidden from sight. She felt a shiver of alarm. The first palpable intimation of danger, and yet, she thought, why should she feel alarmed? Actually, now that she came to think of it the olive-green and brown scene possessed a remote and strange beauty, contrasting with the white sand. All she wanted was *not* to feel alarmed or guilty but just to sit here for a while, so that she could collect herself together after seeing Grant again.

Eventually she started the car, but she kept it running while a thought flashed through her mind. She felt a spasm of fear. Something was wrong, very wrong. She did not quite know how to go about getting the car out of here.

It was strange – she'd parked on mountain slopes before, she'd absolutely jammed herself into a parking space in town, she'd parked on the very edge of the Nagal Dam once, on the top floor of a skyscraper garage in Durban, and on these occasions she had know just what to do. She hadn't even had to appeal to Leon for help – because on all these occasions she had been driving Leon's car. However, this experience did not equip her with the knowledge which was required of her now to get herself out of this lonely spot.

Feeling suddenly cold and clammy, she summed up the

situation. Within a few feet, in front of her, reeds blocked the way. So she could not go forward, quite obviously. She shrugged – well, that was fair enough. It was a pity that she had come so close to the water's edge because now she was in danger of sinking into the soft mud and decayed reeds if she reversed crookedly. So that was out.

In fact, now that she came to think seriously about this, she would need several swings of the wheel before she would be facing in the right direction to take the hill.

At last she made up her mind. *She would have to reverse.* But it was going to take some doing. This was going to be no ordinary reversing. This was going to take skill. She would have to go slowly, keeping her wheels absolutely straight, because of the mud and the water so dangerously close. She would also have to go far enough back to enable her to swing the front wheels to take the steep hill which would take her to safety on to the road above.

Now, of course, she could see why it was out of bounds. 'Well, you live and learn,' she thought impatiently. She was certainly learning everything the hard way. It was not just the *road*, down to this particular spot, which was pot-holed beyond all recognition as such, that was out of bounds – it was the whole set-up down here. The area which had become so reed-bound that it was nothing but a little half-moon strip of river bank. The rest of the bank, on both sides, was just reeds.

Leon had managed, she thought. How, then? She switched off the engine and the silence was like an explosion. Her mouth was dry and her hands were not as steady as she'd like them to be – with all she had to do to get out of here still in front of her.

Leon, of course, was a fanatically marvellous driver. A tense, dedicated kind of driver. Behind those dark glasses he took everything in at a glance. He must have summed up this situation the moment his car had come down the hill. What was it he had done, then? Think, Julia. Think! Suddenly she remembered. He had not come as close to the water as she had herself. He had kept well up. Also he had not come as far along, as she had herself. Still, that could be rectified. She remembered that directly the car had come down the hill Leon had turned the wheel and straightened out immediately – thus avoiding going too close to the water's edge. When they had finished scanning the river for crocodiles he had started the car again and, without having to turn his wheels very much, he had taken the hill. There had been no fear of falling back into the mud and finally being sucked up by the river. His car was not as large as her father's car. It had taken up less space and it was almost a racing job and had the heart of an army tank.

She tried to keep calm, having thought it all out now. She switched on again and put the car into reverse and let out the clutch, then she backed right down, concentrating on keeping those wheels straight until the reeds at the back warned her to stop.

When she turned the car, however, it was with a sick frightened feeling that she saw that she would never be able to take the rise without getting back into reverse and slipping back a little and then forward and then, perhaps, *even again*. Keeping herself under rigid control, she knew that she would have to make these three-point turns, no matter what happened, no matter how long it took. Even if it took all afternoon.

All afternoon? Her green eyes widened with shock as she noticed, for the first time, the waning light. The afternoon was very nearly over. Her eyes flew back to the river. The nostrils were still there.

It was useless, though. She just couldn't make it, and after this nerve-shattering discovery, she switched off and sat staring through the windscreen.

'You'll have to reverse up,' she said aloud, and then suddenly she felt madly light-hearted because, of course, that was exactly what Leon had done in the very first place. There had been no stupid turning and turning in this sick, sad, reed-ridden, crocodile-infested area.

She actually hummed beneath her breath as she took the car forward again, so confident did she feel this time. And then, when it came to that time when she had to give the car everything it had to go up the hill backwards, the wheels just spun round uselessly.

When the hopelessness of her position hit her, it knocked the last bit of strength from her. Worse now, she was facing the river where she could look down through the wide windscreen at the crocodiles which were facing her now, because they had moved slightly. The hill was behind her, which meant that she could not see it unless she peered into the rear-view mirror, and having the hill behind her was a potential threat. Anything might come over it without her seeing it until it was right upon the car. A lion, maybe. There were lions in the Reserve, her father had told her. Most of the Rangers had seen them, however, and from time to time visitors had seen them. The lions were in the Reserve, although they were not frequently seen, and there were rhinos, hyenas, jackals, leopards and baboons – with yellow teeth.

Near panic, her thoughts whirled about uncontrollably, then she tried to get a grip of herself.

Work this out. Work this thing out, a voice was saying considerately inside her. Animals are smart, Julia. They don't come down to drink where they know there are crocodiles. They just know. Jackals only come out in the morning, not the evening. Now who had told her that? She'd read it somewhere, perhaps. She must have, for her to know it. *Know it?* That was priceless, because what did she know about animals and their habits in the first place? Exactly nothing. No wonder Grant Tyler got impatient with her. She was too headstrong. She thought she knew everything.

'Damn it,' she pounded her fist on the wheel. 'You can't just sit here like a helpless Victorian maiden, Julia Munro. Get out – and see what's causing the wheels to spin round like that. Put something under them. Leaves, reeds . . .' her voice trailed away and floated across the river like a disembodied spirit. Perhaps there would be something in the boot of the car. An old sack, maybe – a bit of canvas, some wood.

Brave all at once, she opened the door and stepped out into forbidden territory. There was this uneasy stillness in the air and she tried to ignore it and got down on her knees, so that she could look under the wheels. While she was in this position, she heard a rustling and got to her feet in one swift movement and flattened herself against the door which, like a fool, she had closed.

Her heart was racing so much that she felt she was going to suffocate right there on the spot. It seemed to be beating right inside her mouth, then, when the heartbeats had dropped to nearly normal and she had convinced herself that it was nothing but a false alarm, she got back into the car, not wanting to tempt fate.

For a while she just sat there, revving the car uselessly, while she tried to keep active, because being active kept her calm to a certain extent. Calm enough, at least, not to get out and run screaming through the bush.

Then she switched off, and the silence was terrible. Like a big empty space after an explosion, with her inside it.

Well, better the silence than a lot of wild animal noises. But this, she knew, was just a passing thought – after shock. With or without wild-animal noises, she was terrified. The nostrils had submerged completely, but she knew they were there – waiting.

Behind her, the hill rose sharply and higher up, on the other side of the road, the clumps of trees were indigo against the darkening sky.

A hopelessness settled on her as she realized that the light had faded and the half-light had brought with it an eerie chill that was communicating itself to her. She was aware of the smell of dank vegetation and water. When she thought she saw a movement she had to remind herself that the mind often played tricks. You didn't have to know an awful lot to know that, but inside her dust-coloured slacks and royal-blue shirt she felt cold and frail and frightened right down to her royal-blue rope-soled canvas shoes. Still, to be frightened was only being feminine, after all.

The half-light soon became night, and under the dark sky, she felt very vulnerable and completely isolated. Foolishly, she found herself feeling sorry for her father's car out there, all by itself at the mercy of everything.

For a while, because she knew that she was well on the way to becoming hysterical, she concentrated on listening for the sound of cars, but not a car passed on the road above. Well, that was not surprising. They were not all out breaking rules the way she was. From sunrise to sunset. That was the code around here.

Darkness came. It hadn't come quickly. There had been this half-light for a long time, but when it did come, it seemed frightening and sudden. Up to now there was no moon and her nerves began to run riot. She could feel herself getting all emotional again and she knew that before long she was going to howl.

Was it any use turning on the lights, she thought, or blowing the hooter? Or would that startle the animals out of their wits and send them stampeding all over the place?

Animals, keyed up as they were, as they grappled with death the whole night long, were apt to do anything.

She supposed they'd look for her. They always did. Anywhere – the Alps, Table Mountain, the Drakensberg. Every time some fool lost himself or herself, some other fool would start a search party – risking everything, sometimes, gaining nothing.

The moon started to rise. It rose majestically, higher and higher, and its burnished copper round shape turned to pure white silver. Julia watched the reflections on the water and the dark shadows which rippled silently where the crocodiles were hiding. Somewhere, high up on the road, most probably, a hyena heralded the moon; and it was more than Julia's young nerves could stand and she went to pieces.

When Grant Tyler arrived on the scene she was crying hopelessly, her head on the steering wheel and her hair a tawny, moon-tinged tangle which hid her face.

He was just a dark shape, when she raised her head, and she sucked her breath in noisily ... and then when she realized that it was Grant she just caved in.

'Grant!' she cried hysterically, rolling down the window, 'get into the car! There are crocodiles down there, and hyenas – up there!'

'What the hell are you doing down here?' He opened the door. 'Do you realize that you've had me – had your father half out of his mind with worry?'

'Get in,' she moaned. 'Didn't I tell you that there are crocodiles down there? I've seen them, I tell you!'

'To hell with the crocodiles!' he snapped. 'Move over. Let me get this car out of the mess you've put it into.'

'You can't,' she told him, pushing back her damp hair. 'The wheels just go round and round. I know, because I've tried it. I've tried everything. You can't do a thing. We'll just have to leave it here until the morning.'

'Shut up,' he snapped, not sparing her feelings. 'Just you watch me. You're driving this car home if it's the last thing you do. What the devil took you down here in the first place?' He started the engine. 'You must have seen the

notice up top there – *strictly out of bounds to visitors.*
How did you know about this place, anyway?'

'I came here with Leon.' Her mouth went dry. 'When he
was here with Kathy.'

He swore then, not sparing her feelings again this time.
'What right had he to bring you down here? Was *Kathy*
with you?' He asked this as though *Kathy's* welfare concerned him more than anything else in the world.

'No. It was when Kathy was with you – on the three-day
walking trail. We came here alone, without a guide, but
we didn't get out.' She tried to put things right for Leon.

Grant switched on the lights, flooding the river bank
with yellow light which obliterated the moon shadows and
the sparkle on the river. 'Julia,' he said, beginning to ease
the car forward. His voice was very soft. Dangerously soft.
He took a tired breath. 'I've had enough. I'm damned if
I'm going to be responsible for your safety any longer.'

She held her breath as he stopped and slipped the car into
reverse and then the car shot back. The wheels skidded and
revolved uselessly before they caught and held and Grant
took the car to the top – out of the pit without a name.
Just like that.

The Land Rover was parked a little way off. 'I – when
I came here I was perfectly aware that I was breaking a rule,
but I had a reason,' Julia started to say, but he cut her short.

'Look,' he said, 'I'm too tired to differentiate between
your reasons for coming here and the rules laid down.' He
got out of the car and slammed the door. 'Take her to the
cross-roads,' he said, through the open window. 'I'll be
following behind to see that you don't break any more rules.'
His voice held disgust. 'From there I'll lead, just in case
you find any more reasons for breaking the rules and getting
lost again.'

She had recovered her composure to a certain extent.
'All right,' she spoke with deliberate calmness, trying to
get some of her self-respect back, but she knew that her
voice was shaky.

Then she watched Grant striding away towards the Land
Rover and found that she was trembling so much that she
could hardly keep her legs still. Apart from reaction setting
in, she was deeply hurt. He might have been kinder to her,
she thought bitterly, after all she'd been through. He must

have known what she'd been through.

The lights of the Land Rover flicked across the rear window of her father's car and still she could not find the strength to drive off. Grant hooted, several quick notes, then he hooted again.

The engine was still running, just as he had left it for her, and she left it running while she opened the door and got out into the night.

The dusty road ran white beneath the moon. The bush was filled with an eerie radiance. A wild rage took possession of Julia and, with complete indifference to her safety, she walked along the road towards the Land Rover.

Grant was leaning out. 'What's the matter now?' he asked impatiently. 'Why don't you get going?'

'I'll tell you why I don't get going,' she said, and her breath was coming fast and hard – so hard that it hurt her. 'You're always telling me *what* to do and *why* to do it and *how* to do it and *when* to do it and – I'm sick of it! Now I've got something to say to you and that is – *shut up*! Stop hooting me. I'll get going when I'm ready to get going – and not a minute before. I'll drive that car when I've finished shaking. Right?'

He expelled his breath noisily. 'Well, now that you've had your say get back into that car, before you get hurt. Right? And when you've quite finished shaking, get going. Right?'

'I don't care if I do get hurt. In fact, it wouldn't worry me at all. Frankly, I wish that I'd – I'd get devoured!' She practically shouted the word at him.

'Well, I do care what happens to you, for the simple reason that I happen to be responsible for you,' Grant replied, in the same harsh voice. 'God help me.'

She drove very slowly, while her limbs still performed their uninhibited dance. At the cross-roads she stopped, obeying Grant's orders, although she knew perfectly well which way to go. It was just a case of turning off and keeping straight on.

Grant drew up alongside her. 'Did you have to go so slowly?' he asked. 'You couldn't have driven much slower if you'd tried, could you?'

'I didn't want to break any more rules.' She was amazed that she could be sarcastic, when all she wanted to do was to cry her heart out.

No visitor, viewing the calm exterior of Parks Board Superintendent Stan Munro's thatched-roof bungalow, with its exciting new lamps glowing inside it, could have the remotest idea of the scene which was taking place there.

Roberta was there. Her parents were there. Carl, who had just got in from searching for Julia, was there. Stan Munro had, apparently, also been out looking for his daughter, and *he* was there and everybody was talking at once.

And then there was a silence, a terrible silence while Stan said, with gravity, 'Where in heaven's name have you been, Julia? You've had us all very worried, you know. What happened?'

'I'm sorry,' she said. 'I broke one of your rules – you know the one. I was out of bounds. Two rules, actually – I also broke the from-sunrise-to-sunset rule, of course. If it comes to that – *three*. I broke three. I got out of the car – to look underneath the wheels. I'm sorry.'

'What happened to the car – not that it matters? It's a relief to find you all right.'

'Nothing happened to the car, but I got stuck.' She turned away and Roberta placed her arms about her. 'Oh, look, Julia,' Roberta was saying, 'I can't get near you with the baby and everything. I must be going to have twins. Never mind, Julia darling. Come, let's go through to your room. Let these people simmer down. They've – we've all been very worried about you.'

In Julia's bedroom Roberta said, 'Julia, you should just have seen Grant. When your father told him that you were missing, he – just about went *berserk*.'

'Well, he did go berserk in the end.' Julia burst into tears. 'And to think, Roberta, that I imagined myself in love with him! To think that's why I went to that reed-infested spot, in the first place, to try and sort myself out over him. I hate him! How could I ever have thought myself in love with him?'

She tried to reassemble the pieces of herself, but it was hopeless. She just went on crying. 'I can't help it,' she sobbed. 'Roberta, what do you do when you just can't *bear* something?'

'You just cry it out,' said Roberta.

'Well, I want – very much – to be by myself when I do

it, Roberta, please.'

When Julia went back into the living-room her father was alone, as she had made perfectly sure that he would be. He had poured himself a drink and was standing at the glass doors looking out into the moonlit night. He turned.

'Well, Julia?'

'I'm sorry,' she answered unhappily, and she didn't even care about her face any more. In a way, she hoped it would never come right again – just to show how she'd suffered.

He smiled. 'Cheer up. It's not the end of the world, after all.'

'No, but it's upsetting, nevertheless.'

'I've poured you a little sherry,' he told her, 'and then Samson's waiting to serve dinner. I hope it hasn't become – but it doesn't matter.'

'Thank you.' She took the glass from him, feeling closer to him than she had ever felt. 'Having *Grant Tyler* find me was the worst thing that could have happened to me,' she said. She sipped her drink and looked at him above the rim of the glass with wide, hurt eyes.

'Well, that's for you to sort out,' said Stan Munro. 'Go to him. Say you're sorry.'

'I won't go to him.' Her voice was choked. 'I won't go near him!'

But she did. Not the following day, because Grant was not there, but the day after that – towards sunset.

CHAPTER TWELVE

No one looking at her as she stood on Grant's verandah could have guessed how fast her heart was beating. She could see him through the open doors. He was standing reading something from a sheet of paper.

'Grant,' she said, from the verandah, and then moistened her lips.

His blue eyes travelled from her eyes to her olive-green shirt and matching stovepipes and down to her gold-strapped sandals. It was just a flick of a glance, but it almost had the power to devastate her.

'Yes?' His voice was curt. It would be, she thought bitterly. 'What is it?' His eyes dropped to her sandals. 'Another snake-bite?'

Humiliated, she turned to run, but he was there beside her, gripping her wrist, then he swung her round with some force to face him. She had never been manhandled like this before and she shook back her hair, which had fallen across her face. They looked at each other like life-long enemies and she hated him at this moment.

When his grip tightened she looked down at his fingers. 'Let go of my wrist, if you don't mind!'

'Not until you tell me what you came here for.'

'I came here to explain to you. . . .' her voice faltered and she tried to wrench her arm free. 'But it doesn't matter. . . .'

'It does matter. Very much.' His eyes stared down into hers.

'Nobody could explain anything to you,' her breath was fast. 'I don't know why I came here, what I expected. . .'

'Well, vaguely, then, Julia, just *vaguely* – what did you expect?'

'To be able to apologize, I guess. I'm sorry about – the other night.'

'Well, that's definite enough.' He still did not let go of her wrist.

'I went there because I – was unhappy about something,' she said. 'I had something to sort out.'

'What have you got to sort out, Julia? How to make time

go faster so that you can get out of the Reserve?'

'Oh, you're so stupid!' she exclaimed. 'You're so busy playing it cool that you don't want to see anything good in me. You keep remembering everything of *minor* importance about me.'

'You have absolutely no idea what I want to see in you.'

'Yes, I have. You want to see the worst. You like nothing better than seeing me make a fool of myself – you don't want me to fit in here.' She flung back her hair again. 'Will you let go of my wrist, please? You happen to be hurting me. You're not holding one of your juvenile crocodiles now, in case you've forgotten.'

'I haven't forgotten,' he replied, then her anger and hurt got the better of her and she acted on the good old-fashioned impulse of slapping Grant Tyler hard across his handsome face.

'Thank you,' he said quietly, as he released her wrist.

Julia ran then, across the lawn, past the tamboti tree which stood out in all kinds of weather – the orange sunsets, in the evening, and the moon at night. The weeds were still where she had left them on that last day she had been gardening and she ran towards them, longing to be inside the bungalow, where she could lock herself in her bedroom. And then before she could stop herself she was making for the snake which lay there beside the weeds. As she trod on it she actually saw it strike out at her.

It was so quick and yet, to her, it had almost a slow-motion effect. She froze in a second of disbelief, then she was running again – back towards Grant's bungalow, because she didn't know what else to do. The fear she was feeling seemed to be hollowing out her stomach.

'Grant!' she shouted, as she took the steps to his verandah. 'Grant, you've just got to believe me. *This time I have* been bitten by a snake! You've got to help me, quickly. Cut it open, or something. *Please!*'

Grant took one look at her face and then he was beside her. 'Where?' he demanded, gripping her wrist again. 'Where, Julia?'

'On my ankle. I actually saw it strike out at me. My ankle is smarting. I'm terrified – do something, can't you? Don't just *stand* there!' They were inside the living-room now and the bungalow felt chill.

'Keep still,' Grant snapped. 'Let me look at the damn thing. What was the snake like?'

'Oh, I don't know. Short, fat, flabby – a puff adder, I think, but I don't know the difference. Don't just ask me about it – do something!'

'That's precisely what I intend doing, if only you'd shut up.'

She began to sob dryly. 'Even when I've been bitten by a snake and I could be dying, you still go on like this.'

'Oh, hell, Julia, shut up, can't you?' In one quick movement he picked her up and carried her to the kitchen. She was grateful for the feel of his hard male strength. He put her down on a chair. 'Let me get the serum from the refrigerator,' he said. 'Just keep calm, Julia. It's not the end of the world.'

'Isn't it?' she whimpered. 'It might well be – for me.' She was aware of a tight feeling across her chest and of giddiness. God, could it be happening so quickly?

She could sense Grant's tension and she began to shake when she saw that his hands were shaking.

'You said you'd treated snake bites before,' she said, almost accusingly. 'Have you?'

'I've treated a couple,' he said. He was working quickly.

'You're shaking,' her voice was frightened. Grant was nervous and it was an almost staggering change.

'Well, wouldn't *you* – under the circumstances?' His voice was curt and her eyes widened.

'What circumstances? Is – it hopeless, Grant?'

'Look, Julia,' he said. 'I happen to be in love with you – that's the only *hopeless* thing about this. Because I'm in love with you, I'm trying to be as quick as I can – as calm as I can. It would help matters if you tried to keep calm as well, but remember that under the circumstances, I don't want to bungle this.'

Astonished, her eyes clung to his face, then she watched him as he began to apply a ligature bandage between the bite and her heart. The snake bite was oozing watery blood and the area was swollen.

'Are you going to cut?' Her voice, and what was going on about her, seemed apart from her now.

'No cutting. That's old hat now.' He opened the ampoule, holding it firmly, with the blue spotline facing him. Then he struck the neck sharply with the back of a stainless steel knife.

Julie agitated him, with her eyes, to get a move on. She bit her lips as he inserted the needle of the syringe into the serum and slowly drew it up until the barrel was full.

'Grant,' she said, 'all this seems to be taking such an age. *Hurry!*'

'It has to be done. Keep calm. Fussing won't help.'

Before he injected her he filled her with a terrible despair as he held the syringe needle upwards and pressed the piston rod lightly until a drop of serum oozed from the needle point. 'Oh, Grant,' she wailed, accusingly. 'It will be too late, just now.'

'I have to expel any air,' he told her, 'that might be in the barrel.'

Quickly he disinfected her skin, then injected half of the serum of one bottle between the bite and the ligature and the other half into the muscle higher up her leg.

'How do you feel?' he asked, turning from her to fill the syringe again.

'All right. A little tight-chested. I hope it's my imagination.'

'Just keep calm,' he ordered. 'We're doing all right.' He injected the contents of the other bottle of serum into a major muscle of her upper arm and she noticed that his hands were still shaking, but he did not hurt her. 'The ligature's not – hurting, is it?' he asked.

'No, but the bite is. It's terribly painful – smarting like mad.' She tried not to cry. 'And I'm scared, of course. Will I have to go to hospital?' At the thought she started to cry, but didn't care. 'I feel awful, Grant. I can't even begin to explain how I feel – all tight. . .'

He put his arms lightly around her. 'You're going to be all right,' he told her. 'I'm going to carry you to my room and put you right into my bed, to keep you warm.'

'Don't leave me, Grant!' she wailed, as he carried her.

'I'm going to have to leave you for a few moments. I want to get some black coffee going. I want to send word to your father. I have a feeling that I remember speaking to a doctor here at the camp. Your father will know, for sure, if he's still here. If he is – well, we'll get him to give you a check over. Let's hope he hasn't left.'

'It's all taking so much *time!*'

'Look,' he said, 'each bottle contained one 10-ml.*dose of serum. That's what counts. It's wise, however, it's a *precaution* to be under medical supervision.'

'A precaution against what? Please tell me. I'm so frightened.'

'There could be side actions. I'm not saying there will be – but there could. You were great,' he added. 'Relax now.' He propped her up in his bed and covered her up. 'It was on the cards that you had to be bitten by a snake, Julia. I guess it was always on the cards.' He took her hand. 'I've got to get busy,' he said. 'I'm not going to give you anything for the pain until I find out about the doctor. He'll probably give you a small sedative. It won't be long now. I'll be as quick as I can.'

Biting her lips, she nodded. *'Please!'*

Soon afterwards he brought her black coffee and helped her while she drank it. 'Your father scribbled a note back,' he told her. 'He's gone to look for the doctor who, by the way, is still here. I don't see any reason for you to go to hospital now.'

As Grant had said, everything seemed to be on the cards that she had to be bitten. The doctor was on holiday in the Reserve, for one thing. As it was sunset he was in, for another, and he was here now, with her father.

When he finished with Julia he went through to Grant's living-room and Julia could hear him talking. 'I'd keep her here,' he was saying. 'That should be possible, eh? Just a swop round of bungalows until she's fit enough to be moved. I believe the young woman, Mrs. Bramley, has her mother here at the moment? She stopped me, as a matter of fact, on my way here. This – er – Mrs. Underwood has offered to spend the night here with Julia. I'm just across the way – number six, but I'll keep coming over from time to time. There should be no sensitivity reactions. She's not susceptible to hay fever or asthma, or anything like that. We must just watch those fang punctures for any signs of sepsis. And by the way, keep her quiet. What's more important,' he dropped his voice, 'however, she must not be allowed to become the victim of her own fears.'

By the morning, the throbbing in her ankle was not

* ml.—millilitre

quite so severe. She did not feel quite so tight-chested and wretched. Mrs. Underwood and Roberta had settled her in Grant's bed for the night, and it was strange waking up in it.

Broodingly, Julia touched the sheets. *His* sheets. Mrs. Underwood had decided not to change them – Julia remembered that much. Only the pillowcase had been changed. Emotionally, Julia resented this – until she remembered that Grant had confessed that he was in love with her.

While she thought about this the sun helped itself to a bit more of the room, sliding across such colours as blue, grey, oatmeal – a dash of orange.

When Grant came to see her she had already had a visit from the doctor and been attended to by Roberta's mother.

'How do you feel?' he asked, looking down at her.

'Fine,' she answered. 'Shy.'

'Shy?' His blue eyes searched her face and he sat down on the side of the bed.

'About – being in your bed.'

He grinned, and she noticed that his hair was damp again. 'Actually, I like to see you there, Julia. You look dead right.'

'There's no need to be – nice about this,' she said, and her green eyes mocked him. 'I'm sure I must be breaking another rule. Am I?'

'You are,' he told her, 'but I'm going to overlook it, Julia. There are some things that should be overlooked.' She could tell by his voice that he was also shy. 'By the way, you were great yesterday.' He took her hand and held it between both of his.

'I wasn't great at all,' she answered. 'I went to pieces, and I didn't want to go to pieces – not in front of you. You of all people.'

'Why me of all people? Why do I happen to be – different?' he asked, looking at her in a most disturbing way.

'Well—' she turned her head and looked away from him, 'I suppose I've – I've always wanted to try and prove something to you. But I – never seemed to succeed.'

He released her hand and stood up. 'What was it you were trying to prove, Julia?'

'It – doesn't matter, under the circumstances.'

'No,' he said, 'it does matter.'

She stirred restlessly. 'Grant,' she said, in a small voice, 'you've always associated me with – Philippa. Haven't you? I guess you associate every girl with Philippa – except Kathy, maybe.'

When she looked up at him she saw that he was pale. 'Who told you about – Philippa?'

'I can't reveal my source of information.'

'Please don't. But I have a good idea. It was my mother, wasn't it? Well, Philippa left a scar, I suppose. I hadn't realized that it had healed, though. So that leaves Kathy, and *you* brought Kathy up, Julia. I didn't.'

'I always thought that you and Kathy. . .'

He cut her short. 'Let's examine the facts, Julia. You were assuming things about Kathy. It was easy to feel indulgent towards Kathy when I knew she meant nothing to me and couldn't touch me. Actually, it was *you*, not Kathy, I telephoned to ask to go dancing on that last night in 'Maritzburg. Kathy just happened to be handy when I rang back a second time to find out why you hadn't phoned me. The maid took my number and promised to get you to ring me back. You didn't.'

'I wanted to explain about that,' Julia told him, 'but you never gave me a chance.' Briefly, she explained about Tina's handling of the telephone call.

'In any case,' his eyes met hers, 'you seemed to be having a swell time with Leon. What about Leon, Julia?'

'Now *you* are assuming things about Leon. I explained about Leon. He even kisses Floria Lanfield – he calls her darling.'

Grant sat down on the side of the bed again and she tried to sit up, but his weight on the blankets pinned her where she was. 'Even before Roberta told me last night why you were out of bounds at the river I kept on asking myself what I was going to do about you. Even when I thought I might just – have a chance with you, I deliberately struggled against my love for you. I was afraid of the disorder you might have brought into my life. I was afraid to trust another girl.'

Julia realized that she had been holding her breath. 'If – Roberta told you,' she said, with embarrassment, 'why all the questions – about Leon? You must have known, before you asked them, that I'm not in love with Leon.'

His mouth went up. 'I just wanted to make it authentic – I wanted to hear *you* say it.'

She thought about this for a moment, and then smiled, adoring their intimacy.

'Well, we've sorted them out, one by one – Philippa, Kathy, Leon. That leaves only the – *disorder*. How much more disorder can you take, Grant?'

'Plenty,' he said, and his mouth turned up faintly at one side again. 'Let's face it, I can't live without you, Julia.' He placed his fingers beneath her chin. 'I've got a feeling that we talk too much, darling – and I want to convince you of this.'

'Well,' Julia's lashes went down, as he bent his lips to hers, 'go ahead and – convince me.'

Harlequin
Omnibus
THREE love stories in
ONE beautiful volume

The joys of being in love...
the wonder of romance...
the happiness that true love brings...

And there's still *more* love in

Harlequin Presents...

Yes!

Six more spellbinding
romantic stories every month
by your favorite authors.
Elegant and sophisticated tales of
love and love's conflicts.

Let your imagination be swept away to
exotic places in search of adventure,
intrigue and romance. Get to
know the warm, true-to-life
characters. Share the special
kind of miracle that
love can be.

Don't miss out. Buy now and discover
the world of HARLEQUIN PRESENTS...